BA

BRAVO SIX

WOLFHOUNDS IN THE MIDST

LARRY W. GARLOCK

outskirts
press

Badger Bravo Six
WOLFHOUNDS IN THE MIDST
All Rights Reserved.
Copyright © 2016 Larry W. Garlock
v1.0

Outskirts Press, Inc.
http://www.outskirtspress.com

ISBN: 978-1-4787-7944-5

Outskirts Press and the "OP" logo are trademarks belonging to Outskirts Press, Inc.

PRINTED IN THE UNITED STATES OF AMERICA

PROLOGUE

Captain Larry Garlock reports in this narrative as a past heliborne infantry company commander of the United States Army. His war encompassed America's involvement in the Republic of South Vietnam's terrible struggle with the Communist North Vietnamese Army but most often with the better organized and savagely proficient indigenous Popular Front "Viet Cong" guerrillas.

The upper Mekong Delta northwest of Saigon was strategically important to the innumerable communist insurgents. This mostly swampy area was called the Plain of Reeds and was also the southernmost entrance of the Ho Chi Minh Trail into South Vietnam only forty-five kilometers from Saigon. The local insurgents were experts of small unit warfare and would resort to any tactic in pushing the "American devils" out of the way of North Vietnamese troops and supplies. These local Viet Cong units occasionally assisted large NVA units that made tactical forays into the 25th Division area of operation.

The author served at the same time at the same place. In 1967 Captain Larry Garlock commanded Bravo Company of the First Battalion Second Brigade of the 27th Infantry "Wolfhounds" of the 25th Infantry Division based at Cu Chi in Hau Nghia Province. The events of these chapters are from the embellished memory of the author. He has modified and even improvised to provide a realistic overview of what those soldiers were expected to endure to be successful in their duty. Few would dispute that those American young men had disproved the futility of taking the fight to the storied Viet Cong. The author has changed the identity of the involved persons to protect their privacy. He has also altered the names of tmost organizations and places to avoid misrepresenting their histories and reputations. If any person should surmise any negative impression, it is hoped that he will understand that the author is striving for reader recognition of characterization and storyline. Accordingly, Garlock would be the first to admit that the Hasel Smithe of this book was a more gallant commander than he was.

After forty years of afterthought and viewing many Hollywood movies that provide "conscience camouflage" for older liberals and probably fool the younger generation, Garlock still believes that most of those millions of dissenting Americans who caused our premature withdrawal were either too uninformed or too stupid to realize their mistakes or were actual communist sympathizers- especially those quasi-intellectual Hollywood celebrities. Of course, some young men were simply lying to cover their cowardice. At the end, thousands of brave Americans and millions of Vietnamese were dead, and three more countries were lost to the cancerous evil of this communism. The author certainly means nothing derogatory toward any person who may imagine something unbecoming of himself in the description of any of the characters. In spite of any impressions surmised from this book, the author bears no grudges against any of his colleagues. He considers himself richer for knowing all of his contemporaries there. He realizes that another given officer in the same situation could regard any other person or event with a much different perspective.

The author presents these chapters with a regard for realism that any veteran would surely agree with or remember. He believes that the "Wolfhound" units were militarily special during the Vietnam War and deserve to be honored. The following chapters are meant to especially honor the officers and soldiers of the 27th Infantry Wolfhounds as a rumination of their operations in Vietnam. He also hopes that his lay readers will understand a little more about that terrible chapter in America's never ending struggle to preserve the legacy of liberty earned by Americans and other freedom-loving people of the world.

CHAPTER ONE

RIGHTABOUT AT DUC LAI RAHN

The Vam Co Dong River meandering through the upper Mekong Delta provided excellent transportation and cover for the native Viet Cong guerrilla combat operations. When the U.S. Army infantry attacked those suspected places at the right times, the Viet Cong suffered severely. However, no matter how powerful their war machines and weapons, the American field officers most often lacked the tactical simplicity and slyness of the Viet Cong field commanders for small unit guerrilla warfare. Our subject character of this contrived narrative, Captain Hasel Smithe, had been assigned to "shadow" Captain Marl Whitehead, the reputable CO of Bravo Company of the "Badger Battalion" as an intern to be ready to eventually take over that command. After little more than a week, an errant bullet through Capt. Whitehead's left knee made the transition premature.

Our captain had now gained command of Bravo company with the "Badger" heliborne infantry battalion. Ready or not, he is "Bravo Six". These highly mobile combat units of the strategically designed Patriot Infantry Division "Wolverines" were helicopter- transported directly to attack real or suspected enemy positions anywhere and anytime. The "Wolverines" were responsible for much of War Zone C in the Plain Of Reeds area northwest of the Mekong Delta. After insisting that he receive a combat assignment in Vietnam, Captain Smithe had spent his first two months of duty with the Badger Battalion as the much involved but inglorious S5 public relations officer working with the indigenous population of local hamlets before fortunately becoming an apprentice commander.

Ever since arriving, Capt. Smithe had always worked hard to execute his duties with accomplishment but, at best, only marginally impressed his patronizing and contumacious commander. He even alienated his fellow staff officers who invariably preferred to accommodate and "suck up" to their pseudo-intellectual superiors for the sake of their own efficiency reports. Popularity and personnel ratings be damned, he was single-minded in executing his mission with whatever "right" way that would win the day. Local villagers, anxious for the attention of the resourceful Americans, were instrumental in his accomplishments for PR, albeit on a strategic low level. However, "winning hearts and minds of the populace," although a hopeful broad concept of the overall American mission, was never fully realized.

After three weeks of relatively uneventful routine re-connaissance but successful probing actions, one particu-lar canal near a little hamlet called Duc Lai Rahn became the first major battle of the inexperienced Bravo Six. This typical area of rice patties, sugar cane, and pineapples was about fifteen kilometers south of the sprawling Bam Nam U.S. Army base. The long range planning of the Viet Cong schemers there rivaled that of chess champions.

Charlie Company had landed on the south side of the canal to routinely sweep and search the area. They immediately encountered enough resistance to cause the classroom-trained battalion commander to think that he should quickly deploy another company upstream on the north side. He chose to deploy Bravo Company to support Charlie Company as a base of fire to hold this "probable squad" of guerrillas in place. The novice Bravo Company commander, "Six" should handle this without "screwing-up" too badly. Two helicopter gunships on call would cover any escape downstream.

A competent field grade commander should know that nothing in combat is ever as it appears. One could imagine the Viet Cong's amazement as the Americans naively followed the proposed strategy of their diaboli-cal plan. A squad of Viet Cong would never open fire on a company size unit unless a detailed deceptive plan was about to unfold. With favorable terrain, adequate fire-power, and skilled execution, the Viet Cong could score a great victory by isolating an American company and ravaging it.

An open field lay in "perfect position" for a squadron of helicopter transport "Hueys" to deliver the Bravo troops. Luckily they landed a little too far from the camouflaged assault line of the well-armed massed guerrillas to allow the maximum planned carnage. Most of the "choppers" took at least a few hits while lifting off, but a mortally wounded crew chief and a co-pilot with just superficial bleeding were their only casualties.

The Bravo soldiers had only been able to leap to the ground and flatten themselves in the foot high grass. The crackling guns of the VC on the south and west cranked out an indiscriminate, continuous hail of bullets covering all of the company. Three Bravo soldiers, including one squad leader suffered a hit. He and one other died from loss of blood.

With the fervid encouragement of the platoon leaders, finally the Bravo guns became active enough to cut the percentage of the VC fire superiority. However, about half the original sixty beleaguered soldiers still cowered face down at the wailing of two more fellow soldiers hit. A concerted team action was sorely needed. Letting "good ol' George do it" didn't work in a tight firefight situation. Those with some experience agonized over what the VC would soon do next. Bravo Six would have to do something to effect a change-whatever it was.

One of the terrified soldiers was PFC Shawn Lieberman. He lay quivering with his face in the grass. He tightly closed his eyes and sobbed with childlike groans and whines. He would have done anything to make all this go away. He really didn't ever want to fight. He never even wanted to shoot a gun. They shouldn't want to hurt or kill him, If only something would happen to enable him to go home. However, his home was the milieu of his failures.

Shawn had always been somewhat below average in every way, but his family wasn't. His father was the CEO of a lucrative wholesale food distribution company. His mother was brilliant, beautiful, and very priggish about her syndicated fashion column. Even his tall and physically attractive older brother and sister had been outstanding in scholastics and athletics.

Shawn excelled in nothing other than pointless collections of fad items. He appeared to lack the mental and physical abilities or even the gumption to engage in any reputable activities. Even the housekeeper often complained about his lack of expected decorum and personal habits.

Soon after his high school graduation, the anticipated draft notice interrupted nothing but a nondescript job at his father's company. Nobody in his family sympathized with his lamentations about becoming a soldier. They instead spoke proudly about their "little Shawn" serving his country. They had previously protested within their social circles about U.S. involvement there.

Shawn survived boot camp as a self-styled "dud" which caused him to be arbitrarily assigned to the infantry. Since arriving in Vietnam, his entire squad constantly rebuked him for "dogging" and a few brawls with insensitive tormentors within his platoon revealed that he had no propensity for self-defense and often sobbed in despair. He had no friends and longed for the days to disappear on his premature "short-timer" calendar. While others survived emotionally on the pleasant promises of home, Shawn only continued to survive painfully within hell-laden anxiety and angst.

Now while he cowered in the grass, it happened. A VC bullet ripped open a nearly inch deep gash across both cheeks of his quivering butt which had been arched a little too high to avoid an enemy rifle sight. He let out a squeal that would have impressed any banshee and leaped to his feet to leave that place. Before wildly stumbling ten meters, he fell atop his squad leader. Sgt. Phillips, the squad leader, had been doing the best he could to return fire and to convince his young soldiers to use their weapons. He pummeled Shawn viciously and cursed him for his cowardice.

"Get back over there, you worthless little shit! Get back to your rifle! Where the hell you gonna go?"

Phillips was pulling at his fatigue shirt and punching him. Shawn broke away by suddenly standing, but the overwrought Phillips kicked him in the groin to put him down again.

Shawn rolled and scrambled away hysterically back to his rifle. He never really cared about the communist enemy, but now, crazed with anger and inflamed with stinging pain, he meant to kill his nemesis. At this moment, Sgt. Phillips represented a climax in Shawn's harried bid to deal with the ridiculous demands of society and would die for it.

As he reached for his weapon, another VC bullet tore open his right cheek and ripped off a piece of his ear causing him to spin to the ground. His face flushed hot and his body shivered from an electrical tremor through his spine. Now wild with rage, Shawn screamed in madness and charged amok toward the real enemy for about twenty meters while firing his M-16 all across the brushy cover of probably twenty astounded guerrillas.

In addition, without much doubt, the bullet that ripped Shawn's face also saved his life. If he had returned to Phillips with a weapon pointing at him, that battle-savvy young sergeant would not have hesitated to shoot him. Phillips had been in the U.S. Army for sixteen years and was an infantry squad leader for the past nine. He had seen the best of men but also the worst of "duds" and "fuckin' fruitcakes" as he called them. He often said that he would die for his country but not for some "simple-minded sack of shit". He was satisfied and proud to be a Sergeant E-6 squad leader and didn't want any further advancement. However, he was also a boozer and a brawler and was very good at that too. Like so many other career soldiers, he was often an administrative problem, but had enough combat expertise to be a valuable asset to a Wolverine infantry unit.

It's doubtful that Shawn had hit anybody during his frenzied attack, but most of the stymied guerrillas stopped firing long enough for his fellow soldiers to increase their own firing for a larger percentage of fire advantage. One could correctly surmise that he had saved a few American soldiers from becoming casualties.

Now Bravo Company should have been ready to move. Bravo Six figured that First Platoon could probably move to outflank the enemy's western position. After the radio call from Bravo Six, Lieutenant DeWitt, the "clean-cut" and very conscientious Mormon, braced for a classic "over the top" attack. In only his first week as a platoon leader, he was courageous enough but lacked experience with men frightened to this degree. He shouted the "Follow me" assault order that he heard at the Fort Benning Officer training school and raced about twenty meters toward the enemy before discovering that he was alone. Not even old Sgt. Mueller had moved, and who could blame any of them.

Lt. DeWitt actually fainted from the shock. Miraculously, no bullet had found its mark. He fell flat and lay with his face twitching. More bullets were snapping the earth just a foot from his body. He regained consciousness clearly enough to know that he would have to stay put. He survived the experience but not the embarrassment of having to later rejoin his platoon where several were surprised that he had survived.

Even Bravo Six had thought that Bravo One had been hit and was perhaps lying dead. DeWitt just wasn't ready to act without the sage advice of his battle-experienced platoon sergeant. A battlefield is a tough classroom, but the lessons taught are well learned and never forgotten.

Bravo Six then didn't know what was wrong with First Platoon, and he still had to get his company moving. Because of the proximity, helicopter gunships or artillery couldn't help. He also knew that with another deployed company, aggressive action would cause friendly fire casualties.

The Viet Cong were still in charge. They could inflict a few more casualties, escape in twos and threes to a rally point and then sneak back to make the helicopter evacuation very costly.

The enemy position had to be broken. It was an acute situation for a novice commander like Bravo Six. His always very edgy battalion commander, as usual during any firefight, was running his mouth on the radio to overshadow his own situational indecisiveness. "Damn it, Bravo Six, do something. Get moving!"

Bravo Six then did what causes one to be decorated, killed, wounded or "canned" depending on the outcome. He radioed his platoons to stay put and maintain effective return fire. He also instructed his only experienced officer, Morganello, lieutenant of the second platoon, to be prepared to take charge.

He had now decided to crawl toward the edge of the canal on the east flank. With Sp.4 Forney, his half- reluctant RTO (radiotelephone operator), Bravo Six forced himself into determination. Four riflemen of the third platoon, also rather reluctant, obeyed his signal to follow. He and his five "volunteers" quickly wriggled and rolled the fifty meters to finally slide into the shoulder-deep water under huge ferns and overhanging brush.

While wading downstream about forty meters, the four riflemen were thinking that they knew very little about this new captain and wondered if they might rather be with their beleaguered fellow soldiers. Specialist Fourth Class (Sp.4) Trevor Forney was more concerned about the canal. Being only 5'5" was a problem in water averaging about four and a half feet deep with a spongy bottom, especially with a PRC-10 radio on his back.

Finally, Bravo Six judged by the battle noises that he should stop to check his position. He pulled himself up the bank, peered as much as he dared through the foliage, and marveled at the opportunity. He could see at least three dozen black garbed Viet Cong wearing web gear and bandoleers of ammunition. They were crouched in position only about twenty meters away and were intently aiming and firing at the American invaders that they had suckered into a disadvantage.

At Bravo Six's signal, the others slithered to join him. He used exaggerated facial expressions to keep them quiet and encourage them. They lay wide-eyed and tense as if on a bed of nails as they gazed upon a scene that few in that war would ever see that close.

Bravo Six's ears felt hot, and he could feel the hairs of his neck tingle as he solidly gripped his AR 15 Commando submachine gun in a stiff firing position and nodded for the others to do the same. He had that weird "green" feeling throughout his jaws as he whispered "On three." If he had allowed himself to think, he would have worried about these sopping wet young American boys

actually blasting away at close range to kill the legend-
ary, fearsome Viet Cong who right now outnumbered
them at least four or five times. Given a little time, they
may have individually tried to back off, but on Bravo
Six's determined louder count of "three" they grimaced
and let it all go.

The outflanked and unsuspecting guerrillas probably thought that a whole company had opened up. Six
automatic rifles can empty twenty round magazines
quickly. The rhythm of their barrage continued as they
changed magazines to continue firing until all the fleeing
foe were out of sight.

The VC had panicked and flushed like quail except
for nine that lay twisting in the throes of death. In succession, the rest of the Viet Cong on the north flank broke
cover as they surmised a rout. Five of them suddenly
dropped when they errantly ran into Charlie Company.
A few hid under the canal bank-a favorite hiding place,
but most just kept running.

After the initial burst of fire, Bravo Six told Forney
to radio for the company to move forward. He then cautiously walked his heroic but still scared little detach-
ment into the abandoned enemy position as the rest of
the company came into view. All shouted for friendly
recognition.

Suddenly one of those unexpected encounters of war
rudely tested Bravo Six as a survivor. At no more than
four meters ahead in some thick small ferns a severely
wounded VC guerrilla lay on his back, nearing death but
still clutching his rifle across his chest.

Bravo Six had been looking too far ahead at his approaching company when their eyes met and their rifles moved simultaneously. Without any thought or hesitation, Bravo Six fired a five round burst into the torso of that tall, but thin as usual, grimacing Viet Cong. Then in a few seconds of shock and awe, he gazed at the contorted face of that wiry young guerrilla, now in a death twitch, and saw a communist soldier who probably wouldn't have wanted to die any other way. RTO Forney and one of the other riflemen stared wide-eyed at both the gagging VC and their commander. The guerrilla relaxed and gurgled blood during his last breath. Bravo Six felt a wave of nausea through his jaw, lower guts, and groin. He would never forget any second of that encounter. Forney vocalized his astonishment in a strong North Georgia accent. "Damn...sir... You sure nailed his ass!"

Bravo Six quickly took the Chinese carbine from the gnarled hands and moved on to organize his converging company. That rifle was in battle worn condition and probably had passed through many experienced Viet Cong fighters. Most significantly, one bullet was chambered and ready for use. Either Bravo Six beat him to the shot or this doomed guerrilla just wanted to let destiny happen-probably the former. Captain Smithe was able to take that rifle and bullet home. What a souvenir!

The scurrying Americans briefly searched the other bodies but, as usual, the fleeing guerrillas had grabbed all the other weapons except one U. S. Army M-14 and two AK47 submachine guns. The Second Platoon found a sobbing teenage boy crawling through the brush with two bullets in his back. One was in his shoulder but the other had gone through a lung. He was dressed in the usual VC garb with a small backpack but had no weapon other than three hand grenades. A medic dressed his wounds and called for a "dust off" helicopter but he died on the way to Bam Nam.

Wise old Mueller, Plt. Sgt. of First Platoon, taught a fast lesson on how a dead soldier could still be dangerous. He used a rope to turn over a VC body lying with both hands under his stomach. When a secreted grenade exploded, all who witnessed were further convinced that this old "lifer" had "seen the elephants" of combat. His experience was invaluable to these mostly teenaged American soldiers.

To follow up, Bravo Six reorganized his company and radioed the battalion commander that he was sweeping downstream to assist Charlie Company in searching for hiding Viet Cong and Badger Six "rogered" that he understood. However, before going fifty meters, Bravo Six quickly had to radio the helicopter gunships to cease-fire. Without mention of Bravo's movement, Badger Six had released them to search the same area by aerial surveillance, which usually involves reconnaissance by fire. Miraculously and ironically, one medic standing beside Bravo Six was the only one hit by all those strafing rounds that snapped the earth all through the lead squad. "Friendly fire" stupidly misguided by poor coordination, often was as deadly as the enemy and always loomed as a threat. "We didn't know you were down there" was usually the correct defense. Bravo Six ordered them out of the area, but Badger Six just didn't say anything about it. By avoiding any further comment, Badger Six could hope that his tactical indiscretion would be unexposed.

Charlie Company had "dusted off" its casualties and was sweeping downstream by shooting and dropping grenades into the edge of the canal banks. One grenade blast literally blew a hiding guerrilla out of the water and two others dropped as they bounded from a camouflaged bunker.

Nothing further was found on the sweep, and both the companies were heli-lifted back to the battalion bivouac. Despite the contrasting events of the day, the VC had suffered a severe defeat.

Bravo Six rested late that evening lying on his back and staring at the sky. He contemplated the day's events and, mostly, himself. While he prayed, he also thought of the men that he would have to work with to endure in this command position. He wanted to be successful, but he also wanted self-satisfaction for his ideals and his masculinity. He opted for his conscience at any cost. The dictates of military protocol be damned. Nonetheless, he knew his intellectual limits and was grateful for his good fortune so far.

He also thought about how many VC they had fought that day-probably about sixty. A mere half dozen guerrillas pinned down Charlie Company and suckered in his Bravo Company while the rest waited to spring the trap. An overzealous or inexperienced battalion commander falls for it every time. A small, well-trained, experienced guerrilla band can inflict severe damage to a conventional command unit if the company level officers and sergeants fail to respond wisely and aggressively. Nerve-shattering moments of terror sporadically interrupt the tedious hours of daily mesmerizing boredom... Somehow these communist "Charlies" must have learned about the unethical but effective "good ol 'American sucker punch.". A commander needs a cool head and well-timed violent response to effect fire superiority and cause the enemy to disengage prematurely. We win by taking the fight to them and making them pay for their ill-fated audacity.

That battle at Duc Lai Rahn Canal was a victory only because the Viet Cong lost some confidence. Neither side gained or lost any territory. The next day the same scene could happen at the same place. One could calculate each side's losses in different ways. Individual soldiers mostly win or lose battles with themselves. The battalion commander, "old acid-mouthed Badger Six" as he was often called, got the credit for winning the battle, mostly through his own attestation, and he wasn't even on the ground. To no one's surprise, he never even debriefed his company commanders.

However, Bravo Six received a great acknowledgement in a better way. All the sergeants of Bravo Company signed a recommendation for their captain and the five others of that courageous unit that broke the impasse to receive recognition for their bravery. Consequently, Captain Smithe accepted the Silver Star Medal and all the others received the Bronze Star for valor.

Two weeks of routine, relatively uneventful search missions passed. Bravo Six was a fast emerging company commander. He knew that he had plenty to learn, but every experience helped to set his bearing and sharpen his decisiveness. Many lesser officers always seemed to be starting over every day. The phantom-like nucleus of his company was fast assimilating him as a crucially needed leader that they could call "straight."

By the way, Shawn Leiberman returned to the company after a month of healing. He was now calm, reserved, and impressing everyone with a soldier attitude to compare with the best. On the third day, Leiberman found a quiet moment to apologize to Sgt. Phillips. Soldiers can be extraordinarily humanistic. Sgt. Phillip's response was to tell Shawn about a Bronze Star Medal recommendation for his bravery and a Purple Heart for his wounds. With all forgiven, he also led thanks and congratulations from everyone in his squad. Shawn Leiberman was reborn.

That night Shawn sent his first letter home after two months in Vietnam. He wrote of his experiences and impressions of Vietnam as if he were there for an action-packed extended vacation. Only a few weeks before, he wouldn't have recognized his own words. Of course, his family was emotionally awestruck and the letter became a treasure in the Leiberman family.

CHAPTER TWO

FACE-TO FACE FRIGHT

The monsoon season was new to the Americans. How strange that the temperature was relatively constant while the rain came every day for months and then not at all for months. The indigenous pests of the Mekong Delta, however innocent, seemed to side with the Viet Cong in driving out the "foreign enemy dogs.". Most of the boys were not too happy about seeing rats every evening, snakes every morning, and a myriad of insects all the time.

The battalion had been tactically surveying an approximate ten square kilometer section of Hau Nyghia Province in a "search and destroy" operation along the Vam Co Dong River. After three days of traversing the dangerous rainy season quagmire varying from ankle deep to waist deep, the guerrillas who should have been there were too elusive and employed the terrain itself as an effective ally. Carelessness and fatigue caused two quick drownings. Everyone had the experience of a few leeches that could even draw blood through the heavy canvas on the sides of combat boots. Scorpions and poisonous spiders stung a few of the soldiers. The instant swelling and pain necessitated an evacuation. Vicious hordes of red ants and swarms of large bees would suddenly cause a soldier to yell and thrash about while other soldiers sympathetically came to his aid. At night, the mosquitoes came in clouds and caused everyone to wish for a strong enough breeze to thwart their suicidal bloodsucking attacks. In addition, humorous as usual, someone would fall up to his chest in a smelly "honey-well" (a storage pit for animal and human waste now camouflaged by the flooding).

That is the way it usually was in the infantry. One could suffer endlessly from the discomforts of nature or pine away the boredom by remembering or planning about the "Good ol' USA". Then, not entirely unexpected, the spectrum of human consciousness would be engulfed in the noisy terror of combat. Such strain caused by a war of attrition, as this was usually psychologically debilitating in varying degrees to all but the strongest. With only one month remaining of his one-year tour of duty, all Bravo Company was very sorry to lose Lieutenant Morganello. His nerves finally caused him to break out with a severe case of hives.

A few more days of this operation would be all the battalion could stand. The enemy would have to be found and soundly defeated or the VC would actually have won the "battle". The Plain of Reeds area of the Mekong Delta was never forgiving.

Usually any sizable plot of ground high enough to stay dry during the monsoon rainy season was populated with a small village or farming hamlet. That left vast stretches of mostly miserable terrain very often resembling the American Okefenoke and Everglades. You could imagine them at their worst. Now add the destruction and huge pockmarks of battling and bombing. The consequent seething pollution of war chemicals and general filth severely compromised the natural beauty of the fertile grasslands. Historically, continuous war and insurrection caused no Vietnam native alive in 1967 to have ever known a time of communal peace and prosperity.

Bravo and Charlie companies had trudged together through the steaming, verminous half-jungle and half-swamp for the past three days. They were tiring of a search in vain for the equally verminous Viet Cong who had recently demonstrated their presence in great numbers and had viciously pronounced their murderous intentions to control Hau Nghia Province.

Battalion S3 Operations ordered Bravo Six to spend one more night and day to complete the operation. He knew that the VC were not afraid. Unless accidently found, they would fight on their own terms-sooner or later-and probably win one way or another. Unlike back in the USA, one could not call the Viet Cong "chicken" for not fighting on demand.

The now brushy dikes of a large ancient square rice paddy provided a defensive position for Bravo's overnight bivouac. The everyday rains had saturated the weedy and brushy ground inside the yard-high dikes where Bravo Six established his command post. Even the best spots felt mushy. The platoon and squad leaders would do their best to provide some comfort for their men without compromising the safety and integrity of the position.

The American soldier learned quickly about the versatility of his poncho and towel. In addition to every other use a civilian might imagine, both these items were a big help against the clouds of hungry mosquitoes that were only partially limited by the liquid repellent issued by the U. S. Army. The luxury of a strong breeze wouldn't keep them away this evening.

Bravo Six had another personal problem. His trousers were split open at the rear. Because everyone often moved through waist-deep, or higher, foul water full of little "wiggly things", nobody wore underwear, which would quickly become a raunchy net. That left Bravo Six with a very obvious and embarrassing flaw in his comfort-not to mention his decorum.

It was yet early enough for supply helicopters. Bravo Six radioed battalion headquarters to get him a pair of trousers his size. Normally the supply personnel were very good at honoring such a small request without questions. However, this time, Sp.4 Quigley radioed back that trousers even close that size were not available until morning.

Quigley was an outstanding RTO who knew the "ropes' and really had done what he could. Now he chuckled as he listened to the overwrought Bravo Six explain his further instructions.

"This is Bravo Six. You tell that S-4 (supply officer) that I said to find any captain back there at base who wears my size He is to take his pants, and get them to me ASAP. I will take care of the heat later. Over."

Bravo Six's words were not angry, but he spoke slowly, distinctly, and positively.

This had been an eventful day for the whole brigade. In addition, by now, Bravo Six had enough influence to get away with such a demand, and involved personnel happened to be in a mood to entertain the notion of actually following through with it. Bravo Six really would "rattle someone's cage" but really did not expect to get the pants.

Sp.4 Quigley relayed the exact message to the permanent brigade base at Bam Nam. He had said nothing but "Wilco" (will comply) to Bravo Six but was very emphatic to Spec.5 Geno Spadaro on the supply frequency that something had better be done.

Spadaro then quickly found the brigade supply officer who just happened to be in the next building. S4 Major Reno was not amused but he did have an eye and ear for matters that the commander would want to know and when he should tell him.

As an old hand at military politics would, Col. Langham received the message in good humor and surmised an opportunity to impress the usual gaggle of staff personnel, messengers, and anxious news correspondents, etc., waiting for his arrival at the end of the day. Why he returned in his "scivvies" would eclipse that day's lack of action and would promote him as a commander close to his subordinates.

He responded to Major Reno that he would personally take care of it. He also knew that Reno had the discreet insight to arrange an effective delegation to witness his return.

"Badger Bravo Six, this is Bearcat Six. Over."

RTO Forney subconsciously jumped to his feet when he answered. "This is Bravo Six Alpha. Wait one." He then briskly covered ten meters in about three steps to interrupt Bravo Six's conversation with two sergeants. "Sir! Sir! Bearcat Six is on the horn!" Bravo Six knew what this had to be about and was shocked that his trousers and/or light reprimand was coming from the usually stoic and analytic brigade commander who appeared to be aloof to anything but overall concepts and operational results.

"This is Bravo Six. Over."

"This is Bearcat Six. What is the problem with your pants? Over." Bravo Six could hear background helicopter noises during that transmission. He listened intently to discern the colonel's mood but found it as fleeting as usual.

"This is Bravo Six. Mine are split up the rear. Over." He had thought to say as little as possible.

"This is Bearcat Six. S4 cannot get pants for you before dark. However, I am very close your size. Do you want to borrow mine?"

Bravo Six had to decide in about five seconds if this question was only the sarcastic prelude of a high level verbal reprimand for his pretentious attitude, if this "blue collar" colonel actually understood the degree of discomfort and really did care that much, or if this eccentric colonel was perpetrating a public relation stunt and wanted him to be a "player.". He decided to leave an opening for "whatever."

"Ah. Bearcat Six, I really would not want to risk your safety for something non-essential. I'll be okay. Thanks for the offer. Maybe my pants will be on the last chopper. Over."

"I'll give you mine. I am returning straight to home base. Smoke an LZ. Over.'

"This is Bravo Six. You could just drop them from the air. Over."

"Smoke your LZ. Out."

Aside from bordering on the ridiculous side, if he had not landed, his show of humanitarianism would have been lost at squad level where he wanted it. Now Bravo Six wished that he had never started the whole thing. Too much could go wrong.

"Green smoke out. Approach from the south," Bravo Six directed.

The command "Huey" landed and remained at a fast idle since dust was not a problem and a few seconds would save time for a fast getaway. When the colonel exited with two aides, Bravo Six walked briskly to greet him, but Colonel Langham only motioned for his favorite company commander to accompany him. That personable commander quickly visited several sergeants and some of the "grunts" at their positions, offering a few complimentary remarks. Then, about fifty meters from his chopper, and still without saying anything about it, he removed his trousers and handed them to Bravo Six.

"Sir, I'll never forget this."

"Not too big, are they?" That middle-aged big man had an air of confidence and command even when publicly standing in his underwear.

"They're much too big for me, but the size is just right, sir." Bravo Six surprised himself with that clever response. He also realized that he had involuntarily just gained valuable command capital that was bound to benefit his tenure.

Colonel Langham smiled and told him to take care of himself. Bravo Six watched as the "fortyish" colonel in his white boxer shorts walked with his aide at his side started to the chopper now slowly increasing its rotor speed.

Then started the acme of the episode. A sniper, at a safe enough distance for himself, opened fire at the company area. Because it was an automatic weapon and probably in a tree, most likely nobody would be hit nor would it last more than ten seconds. However, the concerned colonel was caught not quite halfway to his chopper.

Snipers who rarely ever hit anybody and mostly were just out for an egotistic thrill often harassed the hated American soldiers. The Bravo soldiers returned fire when they could identify a location, but mostly only took cover. The snipers almost always immediately left the area, and, if nothing else, had reminded everyone of combat discipline. This time, hardly anyone could keep from staring at their brigade commander to see his reaction.

Sometimes, however, snipers were trying to establish the perimeter of a unit for a subsequent attack of a larger parent unit. However, they usually don't fire at a command helicopter because the subsequent retribution would be overwhelming and probably final.

Langham, middle-aged and overweight, upon hearing that burst of gunfire, had only a second to choose his reaction. He could have flattened himself on the ground causing his helicopter crew to spend a longer time in that very vulnerable position. No, that would have looked self-centered. He could have been almost as safe by sprinting to the chopper. No, that would have been too embarrassing. He had not sprinted in years and would have looked ridiculous even if he did not lose his balance. So the pompous but not superciliously sophisticated brigade commander gritted his teeth, tightened his abdomen and buttocks, and simply walked briskly managing as much dignity as anyone could even while the sniper fired another ineffective burst Several Bravo soldiers returned fire indiscriminately.

A couple anxious hands helped the colonel aboard, and the chopper immediately strained for air speed to escape to the south. What could have been a disaster of discretion resulted in a two-fold victory for the diversity and durability of that proud colonel's dignity.

Now Bravo Six had this high-level visit figured and was glad that he indulged it. He admired this strong commander as an example of modern masculinity and an excellent role model for young officers. It would be hard for a civilian to understand, however.

As Bravo Six changed into the colonel's pants, he laughed with the nearby soldiers as they shouted various teasing comments. Nevertheless, they really were impressed and grateful for the colonel's visit. The older sergeants certainly knew the value of that. Next, two hours later, Bravo Company got a pleasant surprise. An unscheduled supply helicopter landed with a load of beer, soft drinks, potato chips, and fifty-pound blocks of ice. This was not the first time for such treats, but all the men were especially appreciative. They supposed correctly that they could thank Colonel Langham.

The beer and soft drinks in Vietnam were usually in the old style cans that required a "church key" opener, but the brands were familiar to everybody.

Capt. Smithe insisted that every Bravo soldier was always limited to two beers per day while on a field mission. Nobody had any cause to complain, but a little joking circulated about some of the men not being officially old enough. However, nobody figured Bravo Six to be that "chickenshit" (extreme observance of rules even in unnecessary situations) to exclude them. When Bravo Six also taught them how to hand roll the cans on a block of ice to chill them, they praised him as a scientific genius.

At the first platoon area, Sgt. Phillips savored his allotted two cans of Carling's Black Label as if he may never get any more. He closed his eyes while he drank alternately from both cans and humorously groaned and chuckled in pleasure. Sgt. Mueller remarked loudly, "That crazy bastard thinks he's holding two young whores!"

Everybody close by laughed again when Phillips responded. "You ought to know. You're too old to do it any other way."

This homespun entertainment continued as they good-naturally insulted each other a few more times and even feigned a fistfight. Mueller and Phillips were two of the best. Their subordinates had always respected their expertise and eventually learned to be glad for their rough and often tactless but sound "advice" on soldiering.

Bravo Six ordered at least a "slit trench" defensive position for the overnight defense. Every soldier used an entrenching tool (a folding short-handled shovel) to dig a hole long enough and deep enough for his prone body to be below ground level. Thus, this precaution significantly minimized the danger of shrapnel and grazing fire. According to the demands of certain terrain and situations, the squad leaders might instead order the construction of three-man foxholes complete with sand-bagged firing positions.

The Bravo soldiers were ready for sundown and were relaxing in hopes that the rumor about going to Bam Nam base in the morning was correct. They had had no significant contact with the enemy during this entire arduous operation, but they really did not care. A few complained that the ARVN should be the ones trudging through these swamps.

The Army of Vietnam (ARVN) did not have a very good reputation among Americans anywhere in the country. In many ways that was well deserved. However, most of the right-minded ARVN were simple villagers who were smart enough to realize that the Americans only wanted to defeat the enemies of their freedom and then go home. They knew that they could own and tend their small farms and raise their families in peace bet-ter with the albeit corrupt democratic/dictatorship of the Saigon regime than with the communistic govern-ment of Hanoi which would own their land, their bod-ies, and their minds. The Americans here were major supporting characters in this plot about civil conflict but most of them were not sure if they were protagonists or antagonists.

An ARVN military outpost guarding a strategic vil-lage about eight miles to the southeast of Bravo's position obviously had been using the old tactic of pretending not to notice Viet Cong movements. In return, they were never attacked. Sometimes the communist activists were friends, relatives, or cohorts of politically appointed commanders more interested in black market activities.

Obviously fed up, a local rice farmer, probably continually thwarted in his quest to improve the lot of his family, notified MACV medical workers outside the village that a large VC unit was camped in an overgrown pineapple field adjacent to the hard-surfaced main Highway Number One about two hundred meters from the outpost building.

So that is where they were! With only a couple hours of daylight remaining, the message went like wildfire through radio channels manned by excited division level staff officers looking for a morning report bonanza. The Badger Battalion was in the best position to react. Even with the obvious danger of rushing into this attack with incomplete information, the helicopter pilots and all command personnel dropped everything to charge headlong into this VC unit caught at disadvantage.

Badger Six snapped a very brief sharp command to his two best companies. Captain Bartam's Alpha Company was already airborne from the battalion ready reserve position and approaching the objective while Capt. Smithe was frantically mustering his Bravo Company to board ten waiting Hueys manned by impatient, zealous crews almost too anxious for action. The Bravo troops had not only been spread over a large area but were dressed down for relaxation and personal maintenance. Some even had to dress in the choppers. No one had to tell them that the overtones of this feverish urgency signaled an impending firefight and they'd better be "ready to rumble."

Alpha Company had already engaged the enemy but had not cut off the escape of about twenty-five VC. Capt. Bartam had maneuvered his platoons to cover two sides of the five-acre pineapple field. He had set -up the area perfectly for a pivotal assault by Bravo Company. Gerald Bartam's expertise was well known. Everything seemed to go right for him. No contingencies ever seemed to happen or, at least, they never bothered him. He was not only proficient at command but also managed a good rapport with his superiors through creative diplomacy . Bravo Six admired the tactical ability and confidence of his friend, Jerry, who had already commanded six weeks more than he had. They became close friends and both enjoyed joint operations because they always considered the plight of the other. Most commanders, and especially staff officers, thought only of "covering their own butts".

The stage was set and Bravo Company was coming in -ready or not. The helicopters landed on the south side of Highway One. The VC didn't fire, but Bravo Company couldn't either because a large bus stopped on the highway in the line of fire. Apparently, the driver was startled and confused by the sudden landing of ten intimidating battle helicopters and sixty infantrymen jumping out with rifles pointed at him. Bravo Six fired his submachine gun into the air and waved frantically for the driver to get out of the way. The Bravo soldiers then spotted the VC and began firing. The passengers quickly

---

realized that a battle was really happening, but instead of diving to the floor, they strained to be waist high out the windows for a better view just as the equally curious American public would probably do. The driver quickly double-clutched through four gears with the rush of American .30 and .223 caliber bullets barely clearing the rear emergency door. Some passengers were still gawking out the windows on their right as the bus sped away.

With this additional company advancing and firing toward them, the VC broke and ran to find better cover. Then both Alpha and Bravo Companies immediately increased their fire and five VC fell. Two small groups of the guerrillas ran past the ARVN outpost within twenty meters of the walls. A few rounds were fired at the gawking heads of three of the defenders sheepishly peering out the windows. The VC were sure to blame them for their predicament and seek retribution.

If the Americans were around, it was very common for small ARVN units to avoid fighting if possible. They always just explained that they were confused or afraid of civilian casualties or some other convenient excuse.

Alpha Company was sweeping to the north to make contact again. Bravo Company was searching the battle area for weapons, equipment, and especially any VC still hiding.

A small brushy canal fifty yards in front of the ARVN outpost yielded a hiding guerrilla. A few Second Platoon soldiers had been dropping grenades into the edge of the water.

A doomed VC was blown from under the bank and seemed to spring to the surface. The concussion alone was enough to kill him, but two soldiers shot him four times before his body submerged again. Next, two more panicked guerrillas leaped from hiding and were cut down in a hail of gunfire. Suspicious movement was spotted along the opposite bank about twenty meters farther downstream by a tall blond teenager in his first fight as a combat infantryman. The third squad leader and the five soldiers of his lead fire team riddled the bank. A limp body slowly floated toward the middle against a rock. That new soldier had "counted coup" before two weeks in the war. He had "arrived" and wanted to write home.

Bravo's First and Third Platoons searched nine bodies among the pineapple bushes where Alpha Company had previously left them but nothing of interest was found. As those platoons finished the sweep, Bravo Six changed his attention to where his Third Platoon was in reserve and covering the landing zone. He began walking to the rear accompanied only with his radioman. Because he had mustered so quickly, he had taken off with only one RTO, Forney, who had neither a weapon nor even a shirt. Third platoon knew he was coming. The distance was only about eighty yards and everything appeared to be about over. Bravo Six seemed to neglect the risk, being interested in wrapping up a successful mission.

Because the two American platoons had just moved by and were out of sight, three Viet Cong rose from their hiding place and moved about four steps. They suddenly froze in a stepping position. To their left only fifteen feet away was a big "Dawi" (captain) with a submachine gun and his wide-eyed radioman.

Bravo Six had seen them a half-second sooner and had also involuntarily froze in step. Like an electric shock, his nerves stopped his breathing, flushed his face, and compressed his stomach. The three VC rifles were pointed away but his Commando AR15 happened to be aimed at them about waist-high. The three guerrillas were copies of each other. They wore black shirts and pants, a red headband, and an ammunition belt. All three stared at their enemies face-to face with the same fearful anxiety. The radio on the second American made them sure that the big one in front with the weapon was a commander, but he was so far doing nothing but staring back.

Bravo Six was regaining his discernment and was aware that he had only three rounds left in his magazine and three guerrillas to contend with in a win or die situation. He had been firing into the canal edge and knew that he should be reloading but just hadn't yet (inexperience again). With a full magazine he probably would have yelled for them to drop their weapons with his finger ready to fire if they didn't respond. On the other hand, maybe he would have tried to take out all three anyway. The VC were expecting one of these moves but neither happened. The mouth that may have gained three prisoners was mute from shock, and his intuition told him not to start firing with only a few bullets.

The standoff encounter had lasted only five seconds when one guerrilla began to move his rifle toward the big American. It didn't appear to be a move to fire but certainly was meant for something to happen. That was enough to snap Bravo Six into full awareness. He fired once at the middle VC without moving his weapon and dived for the shallow ditch to his right. During the next few seconds, his eyes bulged with fear. He wanted to reload with a full magazine but that would leave him defenseless for a few seconds. Of course with his radio man lying on his legs, reloading would have been difficult anyway. He could only hope that nothing would happen to force him to fire those last two rounds.

He strained for as much view as he dared to protect himself. All the while, the unarmed and unnerved RTO Forney lay on his captain's legs and was yelling, "You shot one of our men!" Bravo Six told him to shut up and call Third Platoon for help. The RTO regained his senses and the radio wasn't necessary. The unflappable Sgt. Laird had heard the shot and the shouting. His platoon arrived on the run. It was over. Sgt. Laird gave Bravo Six a knowing smile. Those fifteen seconds would re-run a thousand times for Bravo Six-probably for his RTO also. One VC lay dead from the shot. The other two left a huge mud swirl in the stream where they fled in panic. The ending was not ideal but acceptable.

Two squads searched the area but the two guerrillas were gone. Not more than ten feet from where Bravo Six had stood, that dead Viet Cong lay flat on his back. That one shot had hit him almost square in the navel and tore a ragged golf ball sized hole through the middle of his back, obviously separating his spine. His rifle was a U.S. Army M-16. The Division S2 would trace the serial number to determine how he got it. Nothing was in his pockets except a piaster bank note issued by the now defunct Bank of Indo China. Maybe the ouster of the French military was somehow sentimental to him. No matter, that note was now going to be a personal souvenir for Bravo Six.

In addition, to his surprise, they also found another dead VC hidden in the hollowed dike beside the ditch about three feet from where Bravo Six had lain. That one had likely been hit during the earlier firefight and pulled into the hiding place by the other three. Other than his clothes, he had nothing but an ammunition belt and a long sock full of rice. He had bled profusely from a gaping wound in the groin that would have made even the most experienced medics wince.

Bravo Company re-grouped and returned to the bivouac area. Badger Six took careful notes of the tactical results, body count, and estimated number and direction of the escapees. He said that he was glad for no friendly casualties, but, as usual, he appeared disinterested and resentful when RTO Forney started to mention that he and Bravo Six had had a frightening experience.

Later that night, Capt. Smithe lay on the ground with his poncho over him and wished that he had three prisoners or "three body count." However, he knew that he came very close to being dead himself or badly wounded.

In retrospect, he was satisfied. He at least had killed one, and was probably a better soldier and commander for the experience. He and his company had done well. He was alive and still in command.

A few days later in Bam Nam, Badger Six asked Bravo Six about the Viet Cong that he had killed. After hearing the brief story, he said that he was glad that it turned out okay. However, he then patronizingly explained that a company commander should not get himself into predicaments like that. The U.S. Army had spent a lot of time and money to train him to guide his platoons to accomplish the mission. His riflemen should do the actual fighting.

Bravo Six said nothing. His company had just put in a tough week and had performed well. That is what he wanted to hear. This admonishment about him personally engaging the enemy in close fighting was only academic. Captain Smithe knew that he could lead well up front and that is what he would continue to do. The American public expects even the football game quarterback to grab a fumble or make a tackle at critical times.

CHAPTER THREE

PHAN NY'S REVENGE

Three days later the battalion was ordered to the
site of an old French garrison only about three kilometers from the Cambodian border. Transient guerrilla units were known to use sanctuaries in this general
area. Several relatively prosperous farming hamlets and
numerous tidal waterways were convenient for enemy
supply and fast transportation.

From the air, the outlines of old walls, ponds, and
other ruined displacements made one imagine the best
days of this small French garrison and also the dread-
ful day it was overrun by thousands of Ho Chi Minh's
protégés and sympathizers. The surrounding area was
mostly grassland cut by small wooded tributaries of the
mighty Van Co Dong River. Some of the streams had
been dredged to facilitate irrigation and small barge traffic. Our battalion's mission was to evaluate the overall

effectiveness of closing the area to the enemy and challenging them to a showdown.

The challenge was tactically and strategically smart. In open terrain a helicopter assault battalion of the modern U.S. Army, with all the available artillery, aircraft cover, and reinforcement available, was definitely twice or three times that French battalion of one generation ago with at least twice as many men. A new horde of General Giap's conscripted attackers would not be much different now. In addition, any local natives, not sure of the pending communist government, would see that the Americans were capable of going anywhere and staying as long as they pleased while demanding nothing but peace from the civilian population.

The Badger Battalion headquarters was established at the old fort grounds guarded by two rifle companies and the mortar weapons platoon of the third alternating company, which reconnoitered the area and visited the villages by day. To their surprise, they were well received. Attached MACV and ARVN teams, that offered free medical treatment, were met with long lines containing almost everyone in the village. Agricultural and household gifts were accepted readily. Bravo Six ordered extra dishpans and soap, the most popular items.

Outside one village, a squad battled with a few "hoodlum" young VC, who did more running than fighting after their combination of booby traps and ambush failed. Bravo Six then talked to the resident elders about how restitution could be made for damages to two houses and a small Buddhist temple. Those three old men gained much "face" as the rest of the villagers watched them "negotiate" a settlement of fifty pieces of galvanized sheet steel roofing. These reparations and gifts were not always possible, but when the supplies were favorable, the supply staff was very accommodating with the company commanders. They also knew that supply materials had better keep moving if future requests were to be readily honored.

By night, American ambush patrols watched all main passage points at irregular intervals. But after eight days, the Division "top brass" were getting concerned that nothing was happening.

However, Bravo Six was impressed with the planning and execution of the operation thus far. He had to admit that his much-maligned battalion commander was working very hard to make a good show and was succeeding, albeit with no enemy to complicate his plans.

Bravo Six was enjoying the villages. It was the first good opportunity for most of these American boys far from home to observe this completely different culture. Everyone seemed to be smiling and bowing as if the war was over.

The simple, thatched houses and the ancient daily routine of these small, thin natives providing the necessities of life for themselves reflected practically nothing familiar to the Americans. The children appeared to have some responsibilities but could laugh and frolic as any others. They would often stand staring in small groups and were especially curious about the black soldiers. To the delight of one black soldier, a small child spit on his hand and rubbed it to see if the color would smear.

Leading families twice invited Bravo Six to dinner. On the first occasion, he was cautiously worried , but his trusted interpreter okayed the risk and he was glad for the cultural opportunity. Sergeant Nguyn Lam Lee was not only very intelligent but also a quite worldly and trusted friend. Bravo Six was confident that Sgt. Lee could interpret the language, the mood of the speaker, and the venue for any danger. With the first family, Bravo Six found the conversation and main rice dish to be surprisingly good. He didn't care for the smell of the nuoc-mam, the salty fish sauce, but it really didn't taste too bad. Sgt. Lee warned him to eat everything he was served but to also leave just a little to avoid insulting the host about portions. He also found that if one has steady nerves and determination, chopsticks are not impossible if one holds them correctly.

Bravo Six then showed them pictures of his home and family and offered a gift of a large ceramic bowl decorated with American flowers and birds in relief. It was the best the pilot delivering mail could find for him. He even thought to add a gallon of sweet blackberry wine and a large box of fig newtons. That was joyfully shared by that family's neighbors. They were genuinely appreciative of such unusual gifts. The bowl would surely become a family heirloom.

The other dinner party, three days later, was at a

nearby hamlet and probably the result of an important family "keeping up with the Joneses". This time the mail pilot provided a pretty polyurethane American rooster napkin holder, and even managed strawberry shortcake with whipped cream. One should not be surprised at what was possible at high level supply. This was a hit for all the neighbor adults and children Also, what a fabulous memory for Bravo Six! Buddhists and Christians were expressing sincere human fellowship in an atmosphere and environment beset with the evil visages of warfare.

On the ninth day of the operation, as Col. Langham was about to issue new orders, a break in the lull came from a very old woman named Phan Ny (Fan-nee). Her name gave Capt. Smithe a chuckle. As she talked with Sgt. Lee, her betel nut stained mouth quivered and her eyes closed often in fear, but her much wrinkled, sallow face reflected the down-to-earth wisdom and sincerity of one who has always had to earn her way but accept only second best. Her hair was tied in the common bun at the nape of her neck, and her clothing was nothing more than the pajama type white work shirt, black pants, and homemade flip-flop shoes. It was a safe bet that she had never owned an ao-dai, the fashionable dress of Vietnamese women.

As she related what she thought was bad news, she was smiling, but Bravo Six knew that a smiling face in Vietnam often had to be interpreted much differently than one would normally assume. She was concerned about a

Viet Cong platoon planning a raid to punish a neighboring village, Hau Ba, for accepting American gifts. She said that it would probably happen that night and by boat, since they planned to hide far down the river.

Bravo Six, of course, immediately reported the information to his battalion commander. Bravo Company had been scheduled to remain in bivouac that night, but Bravo Six successfully requested to be assigned this new mission.

Badger Six would rather have had one of his other three company commanders gain credit for a needed battle victory to appease the "upper brass" who planned this, thus far, fruitless operation. However, since he doubted the validity of this bizarre information, later he would be able to explain how the "fair-haired hero" of the ballyhooed Duc Lai Rahn Battle had now caused everyone to get excited for nothing. He also doubted that this relatively inexperienced captain could handle a difficult night operation that could even be a very nasty trap.

Bravo Six and his platoon leaders planned their strategy well and then briefed the squad sergeants and their fire team leaders together. Only M16 riflemen and M60 machine gunners of the Second and Third Platoons with their leaders were going. The much-experienced Sgt. Mueller with his first platoon could maintain the battalion reserve position back at the bivouac.

Bravo Six further instructed the platoon leaders to camouflage their men, have them wear soft caps, issue extra ammunition, and bring Starlite scopes (electronic devices that enhance night vision), and Claymore mines. Afterward, he spot-checked the men himself at the ready position.

At heavy dusk, they departed. As he led the double-filed platoons, silently traveling about ten meters apart, Bravo Six zigzagged their course. It is normal for a Buddhist to light a handful of straw at certain times as a ritual, but it could also be a VC scout signaling an enemy troop movement. Even though a curfew had been imposed, a small flare-up was reported at the left rear. As previously instructed, Sgt. Kazarski, in the Second Platoon point squad, also lit some straw and fired a few shots to cause fear and confusion among any civilians sympathetic with the Viet Cong.

Because navigating the Vietnam outback was usually the most difficult and dangerous phase of any night operation, the men of both platoons were relieved that they had no trouble finding their positions at the canal. However, knowing that Bravo Six always accompanied them on the most hazardous missions, his presence now caused uneasiness in the ranks.

Bravo Six had assigned Second Platoon to watch the land approach. Sgt. Tiega was without a lieutenant, but he was both experienced and capable. In fact, he probably didn't really need one. Lt. Tucker and Sgt. Laird of the Third Platoon were certainly capable but might have trouble with their less experienced three squad leaders in a tough fight, especially at night at such close range. However, since Bravo Six expected at least part of the enemy to be coming by water, he personally wanted the well-seasoned riflemen and machine gunners of Third Platoon's fire teams.

Bravo Six helped Tucker and Tiega move everyone into position while RTO Forney "broke squelch" with his "hand mike" three times to signal the base camp that the ambush positions were secured. The Battalion RTO acknowledged with two breaks. Bravo Six had assigned his own heavy weapons platoon to support him with 81mm mortar barrages on call. He knew that he could trust craggy old Sgt. Gomez to be accurate and even more important, awake. It was going to be a Bravo Company show, hopefully with the desired denouement.

The triangular ambush position was suddenly very still. In turn, every third man of the fire teams was allowed to close his eyes for a half hour at a time. A few men had brought a poncho to lie on or to thwart the annoying mosquitoes, which had seemingly also been waiting to ambush.

Lt. Tucker and Sgt. Tiega each were with a fire team of their second squad to guard the rear of the position upstream and downstream respectively. Bravo Six was with the stronger first squad at the stream edge. Each man, lying with his weapon in a ready position, had been reminded that only Bravo Six was to spring the ambush. Bravo Six was well aware that simplicity of organization and communication was strategically vital to effective execution and victory.

Four of the men at the water had displaced a Claymore mine. This black book-sized weapon stood upright on small legs stuck into the ground. Each exploded at the squeeze of a remote handheld electric generator and dispelled 750 steel pellets. The Claymore's convex shape caused the pellets to fan into a short- ranged but deadly hail bound to lend confidence to anyone on the concave side.

The soldiers of the first squad pondered the careful planning and efficient execution thus far. Routine night ambushes, more often than not, were sleepy, humdrum "bummers" that rarely "panned out." However, they knew about Bravo Six at the Duc Lai Rahn Canal and his penchant for decisive action. Right now, he lay with them, staring and almost mesmerized by the ebbing tidal flow of a small stream plenty deep enough for the shallow draft of a long sampan. And, along with sharing their captain's "gut feeling,", the misty fog and darkness punctuated by the seemingly anxious quietude helped make it easy for all eleven of them to stay braced for a sudden battle that they had better win.

PFC Charles Mayberry lay with his right hand at the trigger of his M16 rifle and his left hand on the small generator that would detonate the Claymore mine only ten feet in front of him just over the edge of the bank. His closest "combat buddy," Veryl Weeks, had just tapped him twice to spell him "on alert,", but he had already been awake thinking about home in Pennsylvania. He was remembering hunting for whitetail deer at his favorite "crossings" in the brushy, rocky outskirts of his father's alfalfa and cornfields. When "young Charlie,", as his

---

neighbors called him, killed his first deer, a doe, with his .243 Winchester Christmas present, he felt good about providing some meat in a kind of primeval masculine way. Then, just two weeks after his fifteenth birthday, when he then got a buck, Charlie felt that he had finally "arrived.". Everyone was saying that "young Charlie" got a nice "five-point.".

Charlie was now hunting again fourteen thousand miles from home. He had fired his mundane M16 rifle several times during the last six months directly at the enemy, but he was uncertain that he had ever hit any of them. Six months of good combat "soldiering' caused his sergeant to trust him with that Claymore mine. If Bravo Six yells "fire,", he will not hesitate to squeeze the trigger of the generator and then "rapid fire" his rifle to hit as many enemy as possible. Probably most of the American soldiers, had no compunction about killing Viet Cong soldiers. One once remarked that it was like killing rats, groundhogs, or anything else. Right now, discipline was vital. Even a premature detonation, could cause a failed mission and many American casualties.

On the farm, Charlie had been used to the unsavory sights of livestock slaughter. Here, killing had a different meaning and he had already seen human suffering of various sorts and heard the pitiful noises of racking pain. He had seen some frightfully mutilated soldiers on both sides that he thought would be better off dead. From what he learned about these Viet Cong, they appeared to be subhuman and predatory. He is hunting again, and young Charlie is going to get a "Charlie" (VC soldier)-maybe tonight.

Nearby, and just as expectant, PFC Aaron "Jazzman" Carter lay with his finger at the trigger of an M60 machinegun that he had adopted as the herald of his character. Upon his arrival, he was asked to learn that weapon because he looked strong and tough enough to handle it. After a month as a gunner's assistant, He shook hands with "big bad" Jerome Wiley of Washington, D.C., who very seriously told him to take care of his "ol' lady". Jerome had personalized his M60 with the same spiritual sentiment as is the motorcycle of those men who use a sexually symbolic material object to proclaim a quasi-masculinity. He had said earlier that he was glad a "blood' was getting his weapon. His charismatic voice, usually spewing vulgar criticisms, had then sounded rather compassionate.

Big, bad Jerome with that distinctive tiny goatee and still wearing sunglasses and a black "doo rag" on his head, then tentatively waved a final good-bye from the mail helicopter on his last day as if he might not be quite ready to leave. An icon of Bravo Company, who had admirably done his job through all that Vietnam could offer, Jerome had completed his duty and was going home.

Now, Aaron, currently reputed to be the best gunner in the battalion, had been carrying that M60 machinegun for the last four months. He loved the confidence the others had in him to effectively fire burst after burst of glowing red tracer bullets to guide friendly fire as well as intimidate the enemy. His squad had nicknamed him "Jazzman" because they thought it odd that he could enjoy jazz music for endless hours from his tape player and ear bug. Aaron would also often think of his "turf' buddies back in his Chicago "hood". Although they actually knew very little about any other place, they were never concerned about living in a ghetto. Aaron practically grew up on the street with friends who always seemed to have a little less than a comfortable life. By contumaciously clinging together they cherished a unity and felt tough and wise enough to handle the outside world. Aaron had enlisted to please his mother who hoped that the Army could give him some discipline and direction.

Here in Vietnam, he laughed, argued, and worked well with multi-racial American friends and, again, depended on them. Now, much like Big Jerome, he was on a downcount of about six weeks and would invariably say, at least once every day, that he was "too short for this shit". All joking aside, he really was anxious to go back to his mother and the old gang. Aaron was not worrying about his mother's questions, but he knew that his gang would want to know if he had actually killed a VC. In all the shooting he had done during numerous firefights, he had surely hit at least one "Gook" as he liked to call them. However, just like Big Jerome before him, he really wasn't certain.

Aaron had listened closely when the captain said that possibly a boatload of Viet Cong would be coming. Even with the danger of this extremely close range, he really hoped that they would show. He wanted to be complete. It was his old gang sitting behind him watching their hero.

Bravo Six kept his eyes fixed on the hazy upstream edge of the canal water. It was close to midnight now, and if anything were to happen, it would have to be soon. He lay in hope that these young American boys beside him, that he hardly knew, would have the nerve to kill at such close range. He wanted to lead the shooting himself to give the men confidence. He was also glad for the dim light of a three-quarter moon in a clear starry sky that could remind one of home. Just a few days ago, he had overheard someone mention the "Big Dipper,", but it was not discernible this night.

Beside Bravo Six's right hand were ten shotgun shells in a line. His twelve gauge "pump gun" was already loaded with five shells, each containing nine 00 buckshot. It would make a sound easily recognized by his own men. In addition, at this five to ten meter range, the cone shaped shot pattern would be as effective as using it for hunting small game back home.

He was mostly worrying about old Phan Ny's tip maybe being a diversion or even a trap. If it were a trap, Sgt. Tiega's platoon would be hit very hard before they could be effectively relieved. He also hoped that a Viet Cong unit would not come walking along the stream on either side or from either direction. This setup would not get more than two or three, and might cause enough confusion resulting in several "friendly fire" casualties.

Then it happened. Like an apparition, the bow of a boat suddenly appeared under the dark overhanging limb that Bravo Six had been staring at so intensely. It was a long, low sampan crowded with people and guided by a man wearing a conical bamboo hat. He stoically stood at the stern and steered with a long pole. The incoming tide was enough to slowly propel them. As he stared hard to see a weapon, Bravo Six's heart pounded so hard that he thought that they would surely hear it. As the boat approached the "crunch point" of his ambush, he had about ten seconds to give a command that could solidify his reputation as an effective fighting commander, or cause him to lose everything for massacring unarmed civilians or even an ARVN unit.

Without proper execution, he could also become a buffoon for screwing up a great tactical opportunity if they really were Viet Cong. Badger Six would play that opportunity to the hilt at every level of command. Wearing bamboo conical hats and dark clothing, at least twenty of them sat so tightly together that no weapons could be seen during the first five seconds. Bravo Six held a deep breath with his mouth wide open and strained for his decision as his pulse throbbed in his neck and ears. Any second one of his men could shoot anyway and cause uncontrolled firing before he could yell "Civilians!".

About two seconds later, with the boat almost squarely in front of him, his burning eyes spotted what must be rifles moving to an aggressive position. Several persons in the boat were turning their heads toward shore and beginning to rise. A percentage of the surprise was gone but Bravo Six could now clearly see weapons.

Seven seconds after the ill-fated boat's ghostly appearance, Bravo Six's loud command of "Fire! Fire! Fire!" and the heavy concussion of his shotgun blast ripped the silence and caused an ear cracking thunderous burst of hundreds of Claymore steel pellets and bullets. The boat and all it contained were simultaneously riddled, as all nineteen of the ambushers fired at will at whatever they could see and even at what they could not see.

During those first few murderous moments, the boat listed to its right and dumped the thrashing panic-stricken crowd of guerrillas into the shallow water. Bravo Six rose to one knee and continued to fire round after round to give his men assurance.

Along with the wild slapping and splashing sounds of the water, pitiful human voices were both screaming and moaning. One anguished "Troi Oi!" (Oh, God!) was all that could be distinguished. The barrage continued for almost thirty-five seconds while only a few of the terrified guerrillas attempted to return any fire. Intermittent struggling dark figures could be seen in the water and at the far bank. Then, even the remaining wailing of the desperate and dying ceased.

Now Bravo Six had to stop the onslaught and begin the phases of the aftermath. "Cease fire! Cease fire! His sharp commands were echoed by several of the others. "Reload!"

The silence rushed in as fast as the noise had begun,

and nothing could be seen but motionless bodies and the capsized boat aground at the far bank. Only the metallic clicking sounds of friendly weapons being reloaded could be heard.

Bravo Six felt that familiar wave of nausea through his lower gut and groin. His mouth was twisted as he gazed in an intense stupor and bit the side of his lip. What he had done was horrid, but all he wanted a "clean" victory if that is what this really was. He ordered the squad leader to send three men to stand in the water downstream to watch for anyone crawling away. Those three made sure everyone knew about their movement and new location.

"Massaro! You still have your Claymore?" He was supposed to keep his in reserve.

"Yeah, I do." Massaro had been in Bravo Company for only three weeks but he always remembered to never say "sir" or salute, or even say "sergeant" outside of the main base at Bam Nam. One never knew when a sniper was looking for the best target.

"Good, keep it ready. Throw a grenade at the far bank. It might make someone move."

The darkness impaired the young soldier's judgment on distance, causing him to throw a little short into the water. The underwater coughing sound succeeded only in causing enough concussion to make sure of a few already ghastly bodies. His squad leader spoke calmly with a light reprimand.

"Massaro, those dudes are dead meat. He wants you to get one on the bank. C'mon, man."

This time he did. It probably went a little too far, but the blast would reveal any hiding VC. The others of the squad kidded him about his throw. They also started to talk to each other, which was good for their composure.

Bravo Six had more to do. "Second squad!" he shouted, "Stay put and watch for the Second Platoon." He then pointed to Forney who knew to radio Sgt. Tiega.

"Bravo Two, this is Bravo Six Alpha. Over."

"This is Bravo Two. We're on the way. Are you O.K.? Over."

"We got 'em all. It's over. C'mon in, slow and loud. Yell at us. Out." Forney said the right things but could not hide his stress. He also really did want the aftermath to turn out right. Moreover, he was just as glad as Bravo Six that these definitely were Viet Cong.

At the same time, Bravo Six called the battalion headquarters. "Badger Six, this is Bravo Six."

Bravo Six forced himself to be calm and businesslike. "We ambushed a boatload of Viet Cong. At least a dozen body count. No friendly casualties. Request to remain for final body count. Over."

Always the nasty skeptic, Badger Six snapped in an accusing voice, "I hope you have some weapons with those bodies. Over."

Bravo Six's confident tone never wavered. "I saw weapons, and they did return fire. We will make a thorough search at daylight. Over."

"See that you do and don't leave until I get there. Out." His tone and inflections smacked of hope that he would find at least a little evidence to minimize the victory.

Some excited chattering between those familiar with each other indicated that Second Platoon had arrived. After giving them a little time to grasp what had occurred, Bravo Six ordered Sgt. Tiega to form a defensive position about a hundred yards upstream. Too many men in one place during darkness, especially after an exciting engagement, could cause a friendly-fire accident. Besides, another VC unit could have been attracted by the battle noise. Bravo Six also ordered all the men of the ambush unit to maintain their positions and resume a silent watch.

Two and a half hours passed before the creeping light of dawn brought the carnage even closer. Nothing could be heard to indicate any wounded guerrilla was trying to sneak away. The American ambushers, as they stared through the breaking light and foggy mist hanging over the defiled stream, wondered about what they had done. A few even thought about how well it had been executed. Even in that very dim moonlight, most were sure that they had hit a few of the panicky, wildly splashing guerrillas. All had at least emptied two magazines even if they had only fired wildly into the water and at the opposite bank. None felt remorse for the deaths of these scoundrels.

Not all the Americans were awake. Two soldiers, already hardened to this grisly game, and usually caring about nothing except their own welfare, even now, slept for about two hours.

The light, leisurely and nonchalantly, was replacing the darkness. Nature, as always, was oblivious to the problems and plight of humanity. The dead guerrillas increasingly seemed closer, and more obviously lifeless beyond doubt. Finally, the dark was dawn. The telltale bodies, partly submerged and undulating with the ebbing tide lay in bizarre contortions as if they had fallen from great height. It was evident that the ambushers had killed their own number- maybe more.

Bravo Six decided to switch the first squad ambushers with the third squad guarding the rear. Because this scene was gruesome, even for this war, any soldier already unnerved by the intensity of the action should not be staring too long at what he had helped to do.

He then also stayed on the scene to help Sgt. Tiega direct his second squad in pulling the bodies from the water, positioning them, and collecting the weapons, ammunition and various personal items. Sgt. Jefferson, with an RTO and two riflemen, searched the opposite stream area to provide security.

Sixteen men and two women were laid side by side on their backs. So far, no one seemed to care about covering those ghastly faces. Twenty-one "Chi-Com carbine" rifles and two pistols indicated that possibly a few had escaped. All the bodies were intact but some were shot beyond count.

A young teenaged girl found by Sgt. Tiega caused a small commotion about twenty meters from the boat. She had been bleeding badly from numerous Claymore pellets in her legs and right arm. Now discovered, she cried and babbled loudly as she tried to remove her clothes in a desperate attempt to prolong her life a little longer at any cost.

Her American capturers only stared in pity at her weak efforts. Tiega called in the medic and Sgt. Lee, the interpreter. Lee told her to trust the medic and that a helicopter would be taking her to a hospital. She continued to cry and was glad for anything other than a final bullet.

A few days later Bravo Six was informed that she had survived her wounds and had told a hospital interpreter at the Bam Nam M.A.S.H. that she never had a weapon other than a backpack and the bag of grenades on her belt. She was helping her boyfriend after running away from her aunt in Phu Cong near the Viet Cong stronghold area called the "Iron Triangle" just below Ben Cat.

She explained that this recently formed guerrilla unit of sixteen men and two other women was ordered to burn one of the small hamlets that had befriended the Americans. They were to hide the next day and then travel downriver to destroy a small but important canal bridge and the ARVN outpost guarding it. Their leader, Hau Dinh Cam, a well-known and experienced rebel from northern Tay Ninh Province, had explained that the people would then believe that the Americans and the puppet government of Saigon were "paper tigers" and could not protect them.

Col. Langham and Badger Six along with a photographer arrived by helicopter at 0800 hours. What a thrill it was for Bravo Six to throw a green smoke grenade to mark a secure place for their landing. He briefed them on the action as they walked with him through the display of bodies and weaponry. Bravo Six was bubbling inside but talked with an air of routine business and praise for his men. Some sauntered about and even struck heroic poses for the bustling photographer.

Brigade Commander Col. Langham loudly exclaimed that Bravo Company had virtually eliminated probably the strongest VC threat in at least a fifty square kilometer area. However, he barely listened as Bravo Six tried to acknowledge the foresight of his own Badger Six who stood tight-lipped and secretly disgruntled. Col. Langham already knew the disposition of his officers.

The exuberant colonel also told Bravo Six that he wished he had been with him. He saw in his face that he could believe that. He also said that Bravo Company would be the highlight of the morning briefing at Division Headquarters.

The "upper brass" was already familiar with the guts and gall of Badger Bravo Six. They would smile at the mention of his name and imagine how his commander, Badger Six, himself, was probably wishing that the Pentagon General's son, who commanded Charlie Company, had been involved somehow. That would have been a boon for his own career. He was very aware that good political connections help with promotions, especially in the military.

One snickering major at the subsequent division

morning staff briefing reminded the others that this was the Bravo Six who just a week before could not find three hiding VC that had been seen by MACV personnel after an aborted early afternoon ambush near Trang Bang. Badger Six, in a helicopter above, had been loudly berating Bravo Six and had finally scornfully said that maybe somebody should show him how to conduct a search. The operations staff had been monitoring that frequency since nothing else was going on. Their eyes widened and they smiled at each other when they next heard Bravo Six dare to invite his own commander to try it himself by saying "smoke out" in an impertinent tone. The telltale bubbling yellow challenge of that smoke grenade had ended the radio conversation.

The impetuous Badger Six landed to save his ego. He tried hard with much bellowing and impatient insistence to force a fruitful search. However, through his inexperience on the ground with tired, unenthusiastic troops late in the afternoon, he succeeded only in causing dangerous confusion. Exasperation had caused him to misalign the platoons for an on-line almost shoulder-to-shoulder search. Bravo Six had been silently watching nearby. When Badger Six ordered a "march and fire" to rout the hiding guerrillas, Bravo Six quickly counter-ordered and explained to his indignant commander that the second platoon would be firing at the first platoon about sixty meters away in heavy brush. That classroom trained colonel had never learned that combat troops had to be led as well as ordered.

Abashed, Badger Six conceded as he briskly walked to his helicopter. His embarrassment was complete when, after attempting to jump over a small pool of stagnant water, he had to be pulled from the sloppy mire oozing up past his knees. That was a month ago, but nobody ever forgets the lighter moments of war.

In a command ceremony at Bam Nam, Bravo Six was awarded the U.S. Army Commendation Medal for his total success with the Ha Bau ambush. He had also recommended his unit leaders. They, in turn, listed their own men. All received at least a certificate of achievement.

Charles Mayberry, that farm boy from Pennsylvania, had probably been the first by a hundredth of a second to discharge his Claymore mine that night. He then continued to fire with his M-16 rifle at the scrambling enemy as they vainly struggled to escape. Five months later, he made it home to his relieved family. Although undaunted by his war experience, the indelible memory of the Ha Bau ambush would flash in his consciousness every deer season.

Aaron Carter, the machine gunner from Chicago, had fired over two hundred rounds and was satisfied that he could tell his "hood" how his M-60 had hastened the death of several "gooks" However, as he then stared at the glazed eyes and gaping mouths and riddled bodies, he thought of how well they, too, must have known each other as they ate, slept, and fought together. Aaron returned home and wore a camouflage fatigue shirt for four years afterward. After his mother died, he found that money was easier in drug trafficking. He and three of his new "friends" died from a car bomb.

The area around Ha Bau was left better than the Americans had found it. There were many other examples of success in the Pacification Program. This is not to say that either of the two wars was going very well. Even with all the military success that could be claimed by the American forces in actual battles, whether large or small, the communists continued to be flexible and resourceful enough to be capable of a full-scale assault on any military installation or city anywhere in the country by quickly consolidating their scattered units from all over the provinces.

The other war to "win the hearts and minds" of the South Vietnamese populace continued to be beset with corruption at every level from local provincial governments to the Saigon docks.

It should also be noted that many field grade American officers were making stupid decisions concerning civilian property. Those flimsy, thatched houses were more important than assumed by the shallow-brained "experts" who often ordered them burned because a few shots had been fired from that vicinity. Moreover, it was true that some moral atrocities were committed by American soldiers in some areas. However, those same men would probably have committed the same crimes in the United States if left to their own volition there without the fear of effective authority.

One ugly or nonsensical incident often erased the

hard work of many dedicated men and women in assuring the villagers that they could be free and safe at the same time. However, Bravo Six was not the type to "pick up his marbles and go home" when things did not go right. In addition, he was always close enough to his men for them to know that "his house only had a front door". Who was the enemy? What did he look like and what does he do? Honest men had to fight on several fronts.

Thank God that many more were like Bravo Six. Despite the ongoing problems he had with his commander, Bravo Six would be the first to commend this haughty man for his sympathy with innocent civilians. Anytime possible, he warned them of danger and paid them for their personal losses. Moreover, even though he had problems with condescension and compassion, he would at least listen to the requests of "rank and file" soldiers within his command and often honored their requests.

Bravo Six also knew that the lowest ranking soldiers could "make or break" any unit commander. Their laziness, lying, listlessness, notwithstanding, they are forced to play an unpopular game. The rules are not fair and the spectators are always booing. The team that quit first would lose because the score did not matter anyway. Consequently, Bravo Six figured that, if for no other reason, his soldiers would fight with him if they knew that he would fight for them. His sergeants were able to filter out and handle almost all his "in house" problems.

However, when any man was referred to Bravo Six, he made time for a one-on-one discussion and then consulted his senior platoon and squad leaders before making a decision. Even if the problem required upper staff assistance, Bravo Six instructed his Bam Nam base sergeant to "hand carry" it through the necessary channels of communication.

A case in point was PFC Dorsey Torchunka, who took a single action Chinese revolver from a dead guerrilla at the Duc Lai Rahn Canal Battle. It was in excellent condition and personalized with inlaid initials and four notches in the teak grips. Of course, "Tork" wanted to take that exceptional prize back home. However, he had good reason to believe that it would become "lost" during the intelligence processing and military police permit procedures. Bravo Six knew that his supply sergeant, Glenn Dourf, was familiar with such matters. He asked him to do everything necessary and personally secure that pistol. Sgt. Dourf liked to "run around" anyway and was happy to comply with enthusiasm. Bravo Six didn't care that he had to spend two days in Saigon for "processing".

PFC Torchunka could hardly have been rated an asset to his squad before getting that pistol. However, he was greatly impressed with the considerate attention afforded by his superiors whom he thought too busy to grant such a favor. He did not think they would even care about the personal request of a wretched rifleman. From then on, he fell into the fold and tried hard to "soldier."

Bravo Six knew that enthusiasm could be just as contagious as lethargy. Any organization usually assumes the personality of its leader. He must stay "straight" to survive the unexpected and uncompromising trials of combat command. He further surmised that the best way to command was to think of himself as the unit's brain and Bravo Company as his "body". He further knew that he had also been outperforming his capabilities and that he had better keep himself in perspective to continue with success.

CHAPTER FOUR

SILENCE FOR VICTORY

The Badger Battalion was sweeping a remote six-kilometer sparsely wooded stretch of the east bank of the Vam Co Dong River only a few kilometers from the Cambodian border. The area had no active hamlets but was strewn with many family group rice farms mostly abandoned for the last decade or so. Uncultivated but plentiful pineapple bushes, coconut palms, banana trees, and bamboo grew everywhere. The scattered two and three room thatched houses were intact but barren. A few large concrete walled houses had ceramic tiled roofs and had probably been very comfortable and beautiful.

The Viet Cong guard units must have scurried from their camouflaged camps just ahead of the American helicopter troop landings. The two Badger assault companies immediately began reporting warm rice on banana leaves around still burning fires, a few chopsticks, live rats in cages (Yes, they ate them.), small fish in traps, and various articles indicating guerrilla soldiers instead of civilians.

Because the Viet Cong had expected this area to be searched someday, also found were booby traps and a sack full of antipersonnel mines. Punji pits were camouflaged postholes in the ground about knee deep. They contained sharpened bamboo splints smeared with manure to infect a wound. A leg entering the hole pushed down the sharpened splints that then prevented the leg from pulling out without injury. An experienced soldier did not try to pull out his leg, but instead waited for assistance.

Black fishing line was stretched between trees to cause careless soldiers to trip the pin of hidden hand grenades. Even a wooden plank over a small stream was partially sawed through in hopes of causing a dim-witted soldier to be impaled on the hidden bamboo spikes beneath the surface of the weed-ridden water.

The Americans, through past experiences, were familiar with these nasty devices, but fresh replacements had to be advised and continually reminded. Sometimes during these searches, a lazy, selfish, or even spiteful soldier would neglect to warn others of a danger. One Bravo Company soldier in Third Platoon suffered a nasty bruise from a friendly rifle "butt stroke." The veteran soldier walking behind saw him step over a trip line and then just walk on. Nobody blamed the irate young rifleman who twice before had trouble with that same man.

Bravo Six moved his sixty-two field troops farther southeast to search a small complex of abandoned houses and rice paddies along a heavily brushed tidal canal. He walked with the new lieutenant of the First Platoon while the other two platoons skirted the flanks.

Two soldiers of the Second Platoon waved to Bravo Six and motioned for him to come quickly and quietly. Lying asleep on the floor of a very small one-room house were two Viet Cong soldiers in full battle dress and regalia. They both wore filthy black pajama uniforms, a paisley blue neckerchief and headband, tire-treaded sandals, and even two leather bandoleers of ammunition. Their much-valued Communist AK-47 submachine guns rested against the far wall along with a long black cloth tube filled with cooked rice and tied to be worn like a horse collar.

With a half dozen empty cans of Carling's Black Label "bomb-de-bomb" at their feet, Bravo Six smiled as he figured that these two had partied most of the night. It was anyone's guess how they got American beer. From the Saigon "black market" to the underhanded command level supply personnel, there was no shortage of thieving Americans who would sell anything to the enemy. The alcohol probably had not mixed well with the mild narcotic in their betel nut chaws. They had spat the red juice on the floor and noticeably vomited just outside the door. Both were very dark and stouter than a typical Vietnamese, probably due to a Montagnard or maybe Cambodian blood tie. Bravo Six was thinking that he was glad to have this advantage over these swarthy specimens of probably superior experience and ferocity.

Not chancing if one or both would try a break, even with five rifles pointing at them, Bravo Six grabbed the long coarse black hair of one and woke him by jabbing his face with his Colt 45 pistol. His bodyguard, Rahskle, about the same size as the guerrillas but probably stronger and just as fierce, held his Bowie knife ready as he kicked the other sharply enough to bruise a rib or two. That guerrilla awoke suddenly in vile anger but quickly changed expression to reflect both fear and hatred as he glared wide-eyed at the big knife now gouging his throat. His eyes moved to scowl at the cold green eyes of that forbidding white foreign face that he knew meant business.

Sgt. Mueller , the grizzled old veteran of WWII and Korea, gagged them, tied their hands behind their backs and fettered their feet to allow walking but not running. He always knew what to do and was probably the best field expedient soldier in the brigade. Sgt. Lee told the prisoners not to be afraid, and that they were going by helicopter to a prison camp. One spoke a few words to him in a sinister tone, and both glared at him with the piercing eyes of unconscionable killers. The comparatively slight Sgt. Lee then turned his head in obvious concern and walked away. These two threatening guerrillas probably had punishing headaches and queasy stomachs from a hangover to accent the embarrassing circumstance of their capture, but they could still frighten the best of fighting men at any given time. The other Bravo Company soldiers could not keep their eyes off them.

Rahskle was to escort them to Bam Nam. While boarding the helicopter, one suddenly balked and threw himself to the ground. He started kicking and biting and managed to rub his gag loose. Rahskle quickly looked to Bravo Six who nodded his approval. He then started stomping at the groin of the writhing VC until he finally had to turn on his side. Knowing this VC might prefer death to prison, he next tied his feet to his hands and looped the rope around his neck to cause a strain on his back. He would be uncomfortable for a while but certainly wouldn't cause any more trouble.

Of course, this sudden resistance was a diversion. The other must have signaled that he could get his hands loose because he lunged at the same time to knock down a nearby rifleman. He had probably planned to seize a weapon but couldn't succeed before several more soldiers leaped atop him. It looked like a fumble in a football game. Rahskle punched him in the kidney and trussed him the same as the other. RTO Forney radioed ahead that all involved personnel should be warned about these two.

About a month later, Bravo Six was informed that both were infamous throughout Hau Nghia, Tay Ninh, and Long An Provinces for their ruthless criminal activities and were feared even by their cohorts. After only two weeks in prison, one had died of wounds suffered while killing another prisoner in a fight. The other, while leading an escape, helped to kill two guards and severely wound another. However, he was found the next morning shot in the back about a mile from the prison. Without a war, these two would have been scoundrels and murderers instead of Viet Cong political activists.

Bravo Company was continuing to search the other houses and outbuildings. Everyone suddenly cringed at the distinctive explosion of an anti-personnel mine mixed with the pitiful wail of the unfortunate First Platoon soldier who happened to step on it. He was looking in horror at his leg lying almost severed from his left knee. Only a few seconds later another explosion close the same spot resulted from a medic and the new lieutenant carelessly rushing to help. Both suffered severe shrapnel wounds in the groin and legs. Bravo Six quickly informed Badger Six and ordered his company to "freeze" in place and to look for mines around their feet.

The Battalion RTO found the tell tale three little prongs of a stolen or black-marketed American antipersonnel mine camouflaged under a leaf. More were reported by all three platoons. Even Bravo Six discovered one only inches away from his last boot imprint in the dark loam. He ordered a path to be cleared for the platoons to move in single file in common footsteps to a safe rally point about two hundred yards south to the river. Charlie Company could cover this vulnerable movement. Bravo Six could only wince in emotional pain as two more explosions took the legs of a young sergeant and killed a new machine gunner who had transferred the day before from Alpha Company. The same explosion partially disemboweled his tall teenaged ammo bearer from Philadelphia who often bragged that he feared nothing but rats.

Bravo Company was later ordered to coordinate a mutually supportive defensive position with Charlie Company for the night. Rahskle returned with the supply helicopter, and everyone reflected on the day's events. Again, the men traded off the least favorite items from their C-ration boxes and some heated the main course can with a flaming ball of C-4 plastic explosive. Every soldier knew that he ate better than his enemy did, but could C-rations taste different on some days?

Badger Six conducted a surprise command briefing for all the battalion commanders at his position with Alpha Company. The Badger Battalion had been ordered to hold its position and would be reinforced by another battalion the next afternoon.

The command intelligence staff had reported a likely NVA movement in this general area. The Vam Co Dong River was only about two kilometers from the Cambodian border and could be easily crossed at night anywhere in this vicinity. The 25th Infantry Division Headquarters, aircraft buildings, and other facilities of the sprawling Cu Chi Base Camp would be a viable target for a foot mobile enemy regiment.

At the onset of dusk, even before the briefing ended, concerted automatic rifle fire from two different sniping positions raked the perimeter of both Bravo and Charlie Companies. Well-placed bursts from obviously expert gunmen came from different vantage points and continued to stymie any attempt of the platoons to effect counterfire.

Many soldiers caught out of position were forced to lie motionless on the almost bare ground of the old rice paddy. Those at the one to two foot high mounded dirt of the dikes were not anxious to raise their heads high enough to sight their weapons. Three men of Charlie Company and one of Bravo Company lay wounded.

At the outset, Bravo Six along with RTO Forney left the meeting and sprinted the nearly three hundred meters back to his company command position. As he ran, he saw streams of fiery tracer bullets strafing the mostly anonymous large group of Bravo Company men who represented nearly family responsibility for him. He dashed the last twenty meters to his command group through a hail of bullets meant to kill whoever was important enough to be carrying a map and running beside a soldier with a radio on his back. He dived to the ground unscathed and rolled to avoid being pinpointed. At least one tracer had burned through the air about two feet in front of his face. Another burst of about ten rounds kicked up the dirt near him. This time he saw a blinking muzzle flash in a tree at about one hundred and fifty meters. He crawled to Rahskle who had been carrying his AR-15 Commando submachine gun and was now holding it out to him.

Bravo Six squirmed to steady his favorite weapon that was always kept loaded with three thirty-round magazines taped together. The other sniper was still at work while Bravo Six waited for the next muzzle flash from his target. It didn't take long. He then split the air with a staccato thunder that spewed a stream of thirty .223 caliber bullets at the targeted tree. Even as he changed magazines, his left hand stayed locked in a solid grip around the front barrel metal jacket.

Rahskle loved the high tension of these terrifying moments and loved to watch his commander person-ally take the initiative to influence an urgent situation. He had now also located the target with his miniature binoculars, sent by his favorite uncle upon request, and yelled with a sadistic joy to see a dark form fall through the branches.

"You got 'im! He fell! You got that son-of-a-bitch!" He pounded Bravo Six's back as he leaped in an emotional fit and then quickly apologized for combat indiscretion.

The immediate sharp admonishment from Bravo Six was abrupt but unnecessary. The other sniper seemed to sense the kill and broke his cover to flee causing an erup-tion of fire from a few harried but vindictive American defenders.

Rahskle went with two others to find the body. That sniper had chosen a tree easy to climb and descend. He probably had just turned his back as Bravo Six's hail of bullets stymied him. One wound on the side of his right thigh never had much time to bleed. Two more holes were almost square between his shoulder blades surely splintering his spine and instantly killing him. The sec-ond squad leader of the First Platoon reported the body to Bravo Six and gave him the Communist AK-47 sub-machine gun and ammunition found nearby. A stained family photo was the only other item found.

This relatively rare behavior of snipers in this particular area combined with the intelligence warnings plus the discoveries and day's events made Bravo Six certain that he had better check his platoon positions and advise the novice Charlie Company Commander of his suspicion that a large enemy unit really was nearby. However, as usual, Captain Ruppert thanked him with a casual and arrogant distain.

Everything on Bravo Six's own defense perimeter looked good to him. However, the nature of the terrain and the overall battalion defense plan required his company to cover too great an area. His platoons were stretched too far to allow for an effective reserve. For emergency assistance, Bravo Six made up a "ready squad" of four newly arrived soldiers, Rahskle, and a lanky red-haired dolt from Second Platoon who was fist-fighting over whose poncho, fashioned into a tent, was just punctured by the sniper fire.

Right or wrong, Bravo Six knew that these boys all had different personal anxieties and attitudes about being in combat and often worried over family problems and other conundrums back home. He always tried to talk a few minutes to them as a father or a big brother or a sympathetic friend instead of impatiently growling his authority. He took time to tell this distraught boy that a sore nose, a poncho with two holes, and a bruised ego were small things that would soon pass. Right now, he was living one of the greatest adventures of his life and needed to keep everything in the right perspective. An honorable reputation as a combat soldier would cause discerning men and women to envy and revere him for the rest of his life. He also stressed that, most important-ly, he was needed right now by the whole company as an experienced fighting man to help deter the real enemy. Bravo Six looked at him squarely as he spoke and that boy stared back in humble approbation.

Rahskle would also help him understand some of that. He, himself, had gone from closely supervised disciplinary probation to a trusted command group bodyguard . Bravo Six had given him a chance to avoid a courts-martial for dereliction of duty and half-killing anyone who complained about his defiant behavior. He also got a promotion in rank which floored him emo-tionally. Was he now a corporal or a visionary five star general? Bravo Six, and especially his seasoned platoon sergeants, were making decisions to affect both the tacti-cal and psychological needs of this combat company that rivaled the best of any of the U.S. Army. Necessity often brings out the best of men, sometimes even beyond their abilities. Caring and desire are two important factors that cause good men to succeed.

So on after dark, all were warned that a large, prob-able NVA unit was indeed in the area, earlier than anyone had expected. Bravo Six figured that the snip-ers could have been seeking the extent of the American perimeters while also trying to demoralize the defenders. Overrunning at least one company of this battalion field unit of the U.S. Army might be more tactically feasible as a lucrative target of opportunity. Bam Nam Base was not going anywhere; it could be hit another time.

An NVA infantry task force would probably be coming tonight with the definite intention of executing a classic Sino style "wave attack". Black as this night was, the attackers had a great disadvantage of terrain disorientation. In general, an almost exclusive rice diet caused the vast majority of Vietnamese to suffer significant night blindness. Local Viet Cong guides could help but might misjudge the exact American perimeters. A chaotic victory would likely be costly.

Bravo Six reminded every firing team to be silent, no matter what, unless directly assaulted. It had worked for the Viet Cong on other occasions as a weapon of confusion and incertitude against massed young soldiers far from home. The NVA conscripts were usually somewhat uncertain of their propagandized personal commitments to communist ideology, and generally harbored underlying fears of these strange foreigners of superior size and firepower.

Bravo Six commanded, "Don't shoot 'til you see the whites of their eyes!" That sounded very American and memorable. After all, it worked for General Prescott at Bunker Hill. When Bravo Six personally said things like that as he moved from position to position, the boys would invariably smile with assurance. He also asked them to pray for the company. This also underlined the seriousness of the situation and broke their smiles.

Bravo Six and all his experienced sergeants knew that if they could beguile the enemy into "screwing up" their attack, it would be a victory of little expense. However, if the communists succeeded as planned, Bravo Company could be virtually annihilated, along with many of the rest of the battalion. The NVA liked to attack with a ratio of at least four or five to one. Even the approximately ten thousand French defenders of Dien Bien Phu underestimated the ability of the NVA to move masses of troops and munitions over impossible terrain to achieve that ratio.

Even though the attack ratio could be many times greater against Bravo this night, discipline and concealment were valuable weapons. Probably no infantry company in Vietnam had a better combination of platoon sergeants than what Bravo Six had. First Platoon had Sgt. Mueller. He was red headed, middle-aged, and experienced at everything. He was the best friend of Sgt. Tiega of Second Platoon who had fought against Batista in Cuba. Fidel Castro had promised freedom from corrupt dictatorship.

However, Tiega left Cuba in 1960 when he angrily realized the camouflaged evil plans that Castro had later unveiled. At the same time that he was now vehemently determined to hurt this same evil in Vietnam at least as much as he had helped it in Cuba, he was also personable enough to be the most popular sergeant in the battalion.

His platoon could likely function as a separate tactical unit. These two were complemented by Sgt. Laird of Third Platoon who appeared to live by the U.S. Army manuals. He was the "mother hen" of the company and never slept unless he could account for all his men. They did not mind his continual scrutiny because they knew that he really cared. In his platoon, socks were as important as weapons.

All three sergeants were really too knowledgeable and too proficient to need a second lieutenant to lead them. Most of those inexperienced young officers really weren't savvy enough. Many were immature, headstrong, and even downright dangerous. They usually did not last long anyway. Almost all either overexposed themselves to the enemy or were transferred to an administrative position. Some got sick and even broke down emotionally. That is not to say that none were successful. A smattering of young lieutenants quickly adapted and became beneficial to their units. Bravo Company didn't get many of those.

Bravo Six had always tried to advise his new lieutenants about seriously establishing good rapport and heeding the counsel of their sergeants, but under the circumstances, it was difficult to be patient with their mistakes. Right now, he had none to worry him.

Every Bravo soldier was informed and ready. Although all were at least a little scared, they knew their job and felt needed. Now with darkness, the vigil would begin with two of every three men at each firing position awake and personally musing. Even those taking a turn to nap were in position and subconsciously alert. All had weapons in their hands and ammunition, along with a few hand grenades ready near their faces. Despite an underlying mistrust in their toughness, these soldiers had no problem with shooting at the enemy when presented with an assured target.

Bravo Six had constantly reminded his men that discipline, patience, and confidence could be more valuable than superior firepower. The highly mobile Viet Cong units depended on those same principles, but the hordes of NVA conscripts usually were not so much sure of themselves. Just the same as the Americans, most of them only wanted to go home. Bravo Six, as he had many times before, prayed for the company.

Bravo Six lay satisfied that his company was ready as an interdependent combat body. These were the times that caused him to excel in leadership. His defensive perimeter was so tightly organized that his men might just as well have been wired to a keyboard at his command position. In addition, while he intuitively knew that the enemy was near, Bravo Six wondered if he subconsciously wished that the NVA would come. Maybe he should worry about his own zeal instead of how much he feared the enemy. Was he starting to lust for "kill" more than victory? Was personal confidence weakening him as the commander his men needed?

Bravo Six had napped for a half-hour when a shot startled him. It was followed by ten seconds of silence.

Two close shots then came from about a hundred meters to the right of the first. Then the silence he hoped for seemed to engulf the whole area with the uncanny intrigue of the precursory "calm before the storm." This probing tactic of the enemy was meant to cause nervous inexperienced soldiers to fire aimlessly into the night. It was often contagious along the line causing near-panicked soldiers to then fire at any little noises or imagined movements. Such response only exposed the friendly positions, wasted ammunition, and unnecessarily caused the guile of the enemy to be overestimated. So far, the Bravo soldiers were keeping a cool silence.

Next, the familiar sound of mortars from a couple hundred meters to the north caused everyone to flatten even a little lower. Probably two dozen 82mm mortar (our 81mm rockets could be used in their mortars but we couldn't use their rockets) tubes heavily coughed three rockets apiece. The swarm of deadly ordinance was silently traveling an arched trajectory calculated to point detonate throughout the Bravo Company position. If effective, only a moderate percentage of the American defenders would be killed or wounded. However, almost all would surely be psychologically "softened" for the synchronized onslaught of grim determined riflemen poised with fixed bayonets.

The rumbling thunder of the enormous barrage then obtrusively and destructively disturbed the natural nocturnal serenity of the entire swampy river basin. If guarding gods were present, they caused every rocket to land errantly beyond and east of the defensives of Bravo and Charlie companies. The NVA communist commanders probably did not then know that the intended effect of the barrage was categorically nil, because immediately, in traditional oriental style, the shrill bamboo whistles of the communist intermediate leaders signaled the attack and caused an eruption of thousands of rounds of tracer bullets and a stampede of yelling assailants. By the hundreds they charged on line, three and four deep, across the north end of the sodden paddy adjacent (!) to the one occupied by the amazed Americans!

Bravo's young defenders were content in their successful seclusion. They viewed the frightening display of warfare and as one would upon sneaking into an outdoor drive-in theater. These displaced North Vietnamese conscripts were possibly killing each other! If the situation changed, the Americans would fight as well as they could, but certainly preferred this peculiar defensive as long as it lasted.

So great was their silent resolve that three errant NVA soldiers unknowingly ran through the positions of Third Platoon. Whether gone astray, fleeing in cowardice, or whatever, they ran to the reserve position and stopped. Sgt. Saltelli, the third squad leader of Third Platoon, came running after them. He spoke low and gruffly to the unknown figures that he supposed were "friendlies" out of position. "Hey! What the hell you guys doin'?"

Already in fear and confusion, those foreign words cut through their hopes of avoiding their American enemies or even rejoining their comrades. One fired two shots at the voice as all three turned and bounded into a sprint toward their entry point. Sgt. Saltelli and Sgt. Tulicci beside him, both seasoned in combat reactions, immediately fired a burst from their M-16s at the backs of the fleeing enemy. One fell hard and another hesitated only a second before racing after the third through the darkness toward the now waning sounds of the attacking NVA force. Once again, they ran safely through the American perimeter, but this time they saw the secretive Bravo defenders and strained hard to accelerate and escape their predicament.

No more shots were fired at the two panicked young communists who would live awhile longer with their rare experience. Rare also was the amazement of the three Bravo soldiers at that position when seeing errant riflemen run by them from the front, then back from their rear and fleeing into the darkness. It is no wonder that they didn't fire and only looked to each other. One whispered, "Who the hell was that?"

Their fire team leader, in a barely audible but distinctly different tone, told them to "Shut the hell up!" A small unit of the now fizzled NVA attack must have wandered into Charlie Company positions farther south. Sporadic and erratic defensive firing erupted from a few positions. Those nervous Americans had probably received instructions from their commander to fire at the first sight of the enemy to gain fire superiority. Proudly thinking they had just repelled a direct result, they would never realize how inadequate their defense would have been had that NVA horde hit them directly. Their second generation "army brat" commander had survived his blind ignorance once more.

The rest of the night was quiet as the enemy obviously decided that the attack could not be salvaged. The next morning Badger Six commended Capt. Rupport of Charlie Company for his "tight" defense that was alert enough to thwart the assault before it could gain any momentum. He only half-believed and half-listened to Bravo Six as he explained his "ludicrous version" of the misguided mass attack. The only "body count" of the night lay at Bravo Company, but that was explained as "proof" that the Bravo defenses were ill planned and casually commanded. Little did that colonel realize that even he would not have survived to see the light of day had his obstinate Bravo Six not preferred intuition to textbook tactics.

After another day of sweeping the area and finding nothing more of the enemy, the flights of Hueys carried the battalion to its Bam Nam base camp to await another mission.

If Bam Nam had really been the primary target that night, it certainly had been spared a lot of damage. Sgt. Tulicci won a coin toss with Saltelli and would take home the bolt-action Chi Com carbine of that unlucky NVA soldier that one of them had shot.

During the next few days, Bravo Six reviewed the usual administrative paperwork with his executive officer,

First Lt. Sulzberg and the B Company First Sergeant. These two maintained the base camp functions and rarely ever left that area. Bravo Six walked through a few perfunctory inspections of the mess hall, supply room, and the barracks. In addition, as usual with the others, he relaxed with a few beers in the makeshift officers club and enjoyed camaraderie distinctive to men, and women in combat.

Bravo Six also would occasionally have a few drinks with the sergeants and other enlisted men at their club. His superior officers were not only disgruntled with this impropriety, but were also envious that he was likewise accepted there as a colleague. Contrary to their presumptions, he never discussed the logic of any of their combat decisions, but he did enjoy the banter to unravel the denouement of the recent operations. Bravo Six liked that for the enlisted men. When a battle was over, it was nothing more than an exciting memory. With the officers, afterthoughts of battles were fraught with resentments and lingering umbrage. The shared laughs here were genuine because they knew that Bravo Six would both fight the enemy with them and fight anyone else for them. They also said that he was "straight" with them. Bravo Six always "leveled" with the soldiers when they came to him. They also knew that his worst character weakness was to overreact when a subordinate lied to him.

Several nights Bravo Six lay in bed contemplating himself as a U.S. Army officer. He figured that he probably was not intelligent enough to be the best tactician nor cunning or crafty enough to succeed in the political cliques, but he knew that only a few were as good as he was as a front line infantry company commander. Whatever else might be said about him, especially in the lower ranks, no one would ever say that he could not or would not lead men to fight. Conscientiously, he knew that he was doing his job better that what the criticism of his superiors indicated. They actually did not want him to be successful because he was the antithesis of their preferred disposition and temperament. He often fell asleep in faith that truth was stronger than the varying incompetence and character weaknesses that subconsciously caused some of his superiors to fabricate the premises of their judgments.

Whatever, he was not going to compromise, or even argue. He would fight anyone or anything but not himself. The winner will take all, and the devil be damned. He thought he may as well go for it. What the hell, so far he was happy.

Bravo Six had been in Vietnam now for seven months. He had regularly corresponded with his parents and had tried hard not to worry them. All he ever asked for was sweetened Kool-Aid, cookies, and family photos. His mother sent plenty.

However, the letters from his wife were getting fewer and farther apart. He was apprehensive of what he was sensing between the lines, but he was increasingly caring less. Probably his own letters had also been sending silent messages. In a whirlwind of passion and innocent adoration, they had married only three months before he left.

Then one day he received a small package from her. It contained his engagement ring, wedding ring, and a brief "Dear John" explanation. Wow! How often does a soldier get a "Dear John" from a wife? He thought it odd that he didn't care. Maybe Captain Hasel Smithe was not the same man. Maybe he was just damned lucky to be rid of her. Right now he had no room in his heart for a self-interested, pathetic woman who obviously was coupling with an opportunist slacker. Someday she could be replaced with someone of stronger character. Again he prayed and asked for a blessing of protection for his American colleagues. However, he was still mystified about the personal blessings he had been afforded.

CHAPTER FIVE
SAVE ALPHA SIX

It had thus far been a quiet morning. With no major operation at hand, the Badger Battalion was conducting its own "search and destroy" missions in "free fire" zones. The companies would land at suspected enemy positions. Usually nobody was there, but at least one could determine what was recently there or had once been there.

All the Wolverines must have been having a quiet day. Wolverine Six, the radio call sign of the commanding general, respected by almost everyone as a good man to have at the top, was in this sector just monitoring things and purposely letting the troops "notice" him in the area.

Bravo Company was resting and having a C-ration lunch on the small runway of an old Japanese airfield. The ten "Huey" helicopters assigned to him were also "shut down". Some of the crew members were performing maintenance checks and others were simply meditating about thoughts that only they or the young infantry soldiers sitting around them could understand. From the Hollywood movies and other misconstrued sources of information, one probably would imagine that these men were always bickering and "running at the mouth" with all sorts of complaints and opinions spiced with the worst obscenities one could muster. However, soldiers who have actually seen the worst of combat know that moments of quiet peace and relaxed conversation with mostly good-natured jesting, were appreciated and cherished. The newer guys were very quiet and not harassed as much as one might assume. Often everyone talked about hometowns and sports. Newspapers from home were passed around, and goodies from moms' "care packages" were shared.

Suddenly, the lull was rent with telltale distant popping and cracking sounds. Bravo Six had been relaxing with his friend Reggie Trainor of Plano, Texas. He was the Delta Six of the Mustang Battalion fourth infantry company. Delta Six was as flamboyant and daring as one could possibly manage without getting "canned" or hurt physically in some horrible way. These two somehow matched perfectly for a close relationship, which was psychologically important for both. Not surprisingly, he wasn't even supposed to be there then.

RTO Forney came running for Bravo Six to monitor the firefight that was imperiling Alpha Six's company. He and Delta Six were both close to that tall, hawk-faced captain from Idaho who was probably the most intelligent officer in the brigade. He was not as colorful as some or loud as others, but he didn't need to be. His insight and foresight made him tactically a leader second to none. And, he was "alright." Back in Bam Nam, he and Bravo Six along with Delta Six could enjoy a beer together and talk about those "deep-down" things. Although not particularly handsome, these three were nonetheless an impressive trio of strong, virile American fighting men in the prime of health and vigor. An artist would be hard-pressed to do justice to such a reflective and germane image, although a contemporary one would probably not have such an interest. At the present, Bravo Six, Delta Six, and their RTOs were glancing at each other with expressions of fright and disgust. They knew that they were hearing words and phrases with voice inflections that camouflaged an unacceptable tactical blunder. The RTOs were of little status but monitored all the business of the battalion officers. Even though personally unknown to them, they were in anguish about the harried soldiers of Alpha Company.

Alpha's distressed RTO was telling Badger Six that Alpha Six needed a "dust-off" along with about a dozen others. The rest of the conversation about the battle involved other radio calls that left much to be surmised by an inexperienced ear. Charlie Company, already previously deployed about a thousand meters away, was obviously being engaged by a sniper squad at a strategically displaced minefield as a diversion.

Again, the VC had ingeniously prepared chosen terrain as a trap. Double agent information probably brought them running from several small camps to execute this clever stratagem devised possibly a few months before. Luck played on their side with Delta Company attached to a small MACV outpost near an old Japanese airfield which was nearly overrun only days before that left only Bravo Company as ready reserve. The Viet Cong could also have known that.

Alpha Company had played the victim unit to land for the rescue of Charlie Company just where the VC had hoped. The Alpha heliborne assault team of sixty men immediately took tremendous automatic weapon fire from six well-hidden fortified bunkers and rifle fire from it seemed everywhere. One helicopter took a rocket hit while turning to escape to the rear. It burned on the ground but the crew jumped to safety. However, the heat and exploding ammunition at the rear of the LZ caused the Alpha soldiers to actually be surrounded.

Because none of them were able to do anything but hug the ground since landing, no amount of concerted return fire was doing any good. The platoon and squad leaders really could not be sure where to fire or even try to move. Alpha Six was shot through the abdomen and lay dying. The heavy enemy fire continued and Alpha Company was out of control. Only confused yelling and cries from the wounded seemed to be an identifiable response to the deadly racket of B-40 rockets and AK-47 fire.

Badger Six so far had done nothing but calmly monopolize the radio with purposeless situation reporting. He was trying to "cover his butt" but was not fooling everyone. Two gunships were hovering in the area and anxious as usual but could not get any direction on where to strafe. Badger Six also knew that to commit Bravo Company would alert Wolverine Six to his blunder and possibly cause another enemy unit to be activated. With mounting casualties, all units committed and unable to move, and no definable targets for artillery or aircraft support fire, he would have no recourse but to ask for help. Wolverine Six, the renowned three star division commander, was in the area and would not be fooled about how this self-proclaimed tactical intellectual lost control of three infantry companies. But insomuch as he was often criticized for "showboating," all knew that Badger Six would bring the fight to the enemy when others would find excuses to avoid risky stratagems.

Badger Six knew that the VC did not like to be exposed for long-especially during daylight. They would be disengaging soon and the whole encounter could be "spinned over" no matter what the casualties by then might be about half of Alpha Company. Often the careers of field grade officers trumped the lives of common soldiers in this war as in all others. Also, as in all wars, this often happened with the blessings of brigade and division level promotion seekers.

All the fragmented radio banter caused Bravo Six's intuition to stir his emotions to an anxious anger. He never was much of an "organization man." This was not the first time he was involved with the "butt-covering" lying maneuvers of incompetent but aspiring career officers. Right now, one of the best men he had ever known was seriously wounded, along with many other soldiers who desperately needed evacuation. Most likely, many more were going to be hit and possibly killed before all was over. If he didn't do something soon he wouldn't be any better than those high ranking pretenders that he abhorred.

Bravo Six also knew that a probable company-size communist attack unit was doing a good job of overwhelming American boys who had traveled about fourteen thousand miles to defend world freedom. They would likely never understand this day's action, but they certainly did not deserve to be a part of the stupidity, lies, and cowardice. Decent freedom-loving Americans were not paying taxes and sons for this.

Bravo Six had already ordered his "stand-by" helicopters to warm up for take- off. He also ordered his platoons to prepare for possible heavy action. Then he did what he knew would surely bring a swift sharp reprimand from the already disconcerted Badger Six. He radioed that he was ready to go and wanted an order to lift-off. As expected, the rebuke was instantaneous and smacked of desperation.

"Bravo Six, get off the air and stay off until I call you." This least favorite company commander of his was the most likely person to foil his self-serving stratagem. He feared that Wolverine Six had monitored that transmission.

Bravo Six would have to be careful. Nonetheless, he was well known for his dogged persistence in following his own mind. His flagrant idealism had survived so far only by his knack for "fighting through". When one wins, the tactics are tough for antipathetic colleagues to criticize. Delta Six and RTO Forney now looked at each other and smiled wryly. This was their guy! This was their hero of impunity! Delta Six then uttered some words of encouragement that were tailored for his ostentatious friend. "'Get 'er done, Buddy!"

What Bravo Six did next sent a tremor through the concrete protocol of the entire chain of command. A company commander is forbidden to call directly outside his own unit command. Knowing that the brigade commander was now out of the area, Bravo Six actually jumped two echelons to the next level to appeal for assistance from a three-star general. "Wolverine Six, this is Badger Bravo Six. Over."

During any firefight, it is common for staff officers at all levels, who usually saw no significant action, to monitor anything interesting on a radio scanner. Now they would be calling for their friends to listen. For better or worse, that upstart Badger Bravo Six would undoubtedly be the main topic at the next morning debriefing.

Bravo Six had broken into the Wolverine frequency! Even so, his voice was clear, his words were inflected and well-defined, and his tone was adamant. Quickly and sharply a division staff officer had started to ask what he wanted when Cyclone Six himself then interrupted and spoke directly to Bravo Six. Nobody had a voice like his unless he was a good father, a battle-experienced soldier and a great general who had earned all those promotions with "hands on" success instead of through politics, as most of the other career aspirants.

"This is Wolverine Six. Go ahead, Mustang Bravo Six." He already was familiar with this tall, sharp-featured brash young captain and remembered that he had once told all his line officers to be first sure that they were right and then go ahead at all costs. He also said that his door was always open to them (Of course, don't they all say that?). He went on to say that courage and battlefield experience were not uncommon but only a successful rebel got everyone's full attention. In an extreme theater of conflict, this three star general would offer the stage to anyone with the best show.

"This is Bravo Six. Badger Alpha Six is engaged with a large force and urgently needs help. I can't get an order. I'm ready to go. Take me in."

"Bravo Six, I know where he is. Listen to me and think only with your brain. Are you sure about this?"

Bravo Six responded without allowing himself to think. "Take me in on line and use the enemy front courtyard for the LZ! Get more gunships! Let's go! Don't wait!"

The old general looked from the door of his helicopter at the ten idling "Hueys" and spotted Bravo Six standing with his RTO. That brazen young captain was glaring back at him with eyes that beamed like lasers. What great general could refuse this spiritual moment? He spoke into his radio handset in an omnipotent voice as if he had just laid a paternal hand on the shoulder of himself in a yesteryear. Heart terrifying stories make good movies, but combat also requires altruistic drama. His voice was clear and certain. "O. K. You're on. Get going."

Bravo Six whirled his arm around his head and leaped aboard his command ship. There had been no time for an operation order, but all of Bravo Company knew the mission as if delivered personally by the Roman god, Mars. Moreover, everyone monitoring that radio frequency knew that this captain-of-the-hour was a knight-errant who was gambling that a big enough enemy unit was there and that he could rout them without sustaining too many casualties. The ten assault helicopters could be shot to pieces while landing or lifting off again if the VC were not overwhelmed with the surprise, shock, and firepower that Bravo Six hoped he could muster from his company that had never yet let him down. What about the pilots themselves? Would they be gutsy enough to follow through? Bravo Six leaned into the cockpit and tapped the co-pilot on the helmet. That wide-eyed stocky towhead removed his helmet and leaned back to listen-something he rarely needed to do.

Bravo Six spoke loudly and distinctly. "Do you know that we are rescuing a pinned-down company and frontal attacking a probable large enemy force?" The answer was a sharp nod of his head. "Get all firepower ready to use going in."

What Bravo Six feared the most was for nothing to happen. If only a few VC were engaged, he would suffer the full fury of Badger Six. The general would be sorely disappointed and disillusioned. Bravo Six would be disgraced and probably relieved of his command (fired!). Nobody could help him and nobody would remember anything else about him. Nevertheless, his heart and bowels had joined his intuition to lead him into the realm of the Berserkers. His brain had tried desperately to speak of social fears and physical dangers, but he had already unleashed that innate factor which sometimes causes certain pertinacious humans to "go for all the marbles" when others think that they had surely "lost their marbles."

Bravo Six now discovered that he had one more than the usual five others in his command group. Besides his two RTOs, the artillery liaison lieutenant with his RTO, and Sgt. Lee, his interpreter, was the redoubtable Delta Six, Capt. Reggie Trainor. Besides being one of the most impetuous fighting men he had ever heard of, Roger was also very "savvy" at grassroots level and certainly too much of a man to just watch his big friend leave to take on both sides of the war. He was not supposed to be on that old airstrip visiting Bravo Six, and he certainly was not supposed to be going on a combat mission with another company and with this mission. In reality, he was abandoning his own company at the airstrip on a whim. He knew that he would probably share in the disgrace, but he hoped to help Bravo Six by helping himself. He too shared the primordial urge to "go fer it" and taste the forbidden fruits of quixotic gallantry.

While enroute in the air, nothing was said between these two. They shared a big smile and Bravo Six momentarily grasped Roger's shoulder as an obliged man would. The Romantics of the Eighteenth Century would have understood. A person experiences such a relationship only once or twice in his life or maybe not at all. These two were again snubbing their noses at danger, disgrace, and disenfranchisement. Roger often said, "You gotta go fer it to git it." On another helicopter, plenty was being said. Specialist Fourth Class Shawn Leiberman (Remember him from Duc Lai Rahn?) was now a fire team leader and about to land again in a hot LZ. Five riflemen were depending on him for immediate leadership. All knew they were jumping into a big firefight and were tense with anticipation and fear. One nervous soldier rose to a kneeling position to adjust his equipment and lost his balance when the helicopter lurched to the left. He fell between the seats in the cockpit area and immediately scrambled to recover his position. Granted the pilots were also filled with anxiety, but the co-pilot backhanded that soldier twice while yelling for him to "Get the hell back there!" and also called him a "stupid son of a bitch."

It was good that the other pilot had control of the aircraft because Leiberman leaped overtop that soldier and smacked the co-pilot's helmet with the base of his right hand. He grasped the shirt of that astonished captain and screamed into his face, "You touch one of my men again and I'll kill you!" Anyone would have believed him.

Lieberman angrily moved back to his usual position on the deck. The other pilot had looked curiously for a few seconds but maintained his concentration on flight control. The co-pilot, flushed with shock and astonishment, looked back momentarily at his assailant, only about two-thirds his size. With more bluster than nerve he was frozen in sullen diffidence. Leiberman's scarred face was glaring at him with the raging eyes of one possessed with many devils. The other soldiers also looked at their fire team leader and forgot their fears. The enemy be damned. Whatever this man does, they will do also.

Wolverine Six had managed complete support for Bravo Six's conjectural adventure that day. He mustered eight helicopter gunships and two F-105 fighter-bombers. The artillery was plotting interdiction barrages. Radio transmissions were noticeably brief. When a commanding general takes charge, the airborne traffic suddenly loses its "banter and bull" and nobody was asking questions or offering advice. Even the other heliborne battalion of the Wolverine Second Brigade was on ready alert. This general was a "general's general.". His promotions were recompence of victories. Invariably the others were promoted with the advantages of good politics.

Once in a command meeting, Wolverine Six stated that only his company level officers and veteran sergeants could know the "inside" of a battle and should be taken into account. Because he was now listening, everyone was listening. That made it "boom or bust" for him on a lower and different scale. Several months ago in the "Iron

Triangle" north of Phu Cong, an obstinate battalion commander had most of a division attached to him during a
furious battle and had the fortitude to rudely constrain
his ambitious peers and even firmly repress a couple
of his interloping superiors who selfishly gave him as
much trouble as the enemy. They wanted to be somehow
involved only as a ruse to share in any medals awarded. That engagement resulted in a draw at best and cost
a great deal of casualties but could easily have been a
tragic defeat. Now, a commanding general was doing
the opposite by reaching into the guts of his huge army
to trust that his powerful remedy was actually needed
for a disorder diagnosed by a neophyte of battlefield
generalship.

The ten assault Hueys were close on line and approaching the rear of the beleaguered Alpha Company.
They had just crossed the Vam Co Dong River where
several panicked Viet Cong were swimming for safety. The unmistakable drone of an airborne attack force
was too familiar to those experienced insurgents who
had previously been lucky enough to escape the overwhelming firepower of the Americans. Of course, Capt.
Reggie Trainor couldn't resist emptying a magazine of
.223 rounds at the struggling little swimming figures.
This immediately brought a pleading reprimand from
the crew chief who feared an errant round striking one
of the flexible but brittle propeller blades. Delta Six already knew that was coming but didn't care. The Viet
Cong were there at a disadvantage and here he was

with a submachine gun. All else be damned. He just had to be the madcap Delta Six.

The chopper engines pounded in unison with the hearts of their armed and mesmerized passengers. That din was soon joined by the concerted staccato racket of the two M60 machineguns on the sides of all ten UH-1B helicopters raking the ground area just in front of the fragmented Alpha position where the Bravo rescuers would leap into action. Some of the desperate Alpha soldiers twisted their heads to marvel and cheer at those great battle machines as they swooped by just about ten meters above their heads.

Nobody would deny the sheer gallantry nor question the surprise and shock of that heliborne light infantry company rescuing a colleague unit by landing in the face of an entrenched enemy of unknown strength. So far, Wolverine Six and the Huey pilots had complied with the audacious requests of Bravo Six. They would finish this extreme agenda with all the gusto essential to their invaluable roles.

Hardy any soldier would have previously voted to do so but practically all leaped to the knee-high grass with their weapons blazing. A few even bellowed contagious war whoops that would have rivaled those of General Pickett's men at Gettysburg. For the attack to succeed, the fervor of the ancient Norse Berserkers would be needed to follow through. The deafening thunder of the helicopter engines now straining to leave was accented by the intermingled crackling of American rifles and machineguns suddenly successfully challenging the fire superiority of the astounded Viet Cong. Although several had taken a few hits, only one helicopter was unable to lift off. The door gunners leaped to safety but the pilots were dead and the engine was burning. The fire quickly grew to engulf the whole chopper sending billowing smoke to the enemy positions. The VC were blinded as if ordered by divine providence.

Nobody had to worry about enough players for the game. Now it was obvious that Alpha Company had unwittingly attacked a Viet Cong unit at least equal in size and well fortified. No doubt the disorganized and distressed Alpha platoons would soon have been run through and decimated had Bravo's deployment not foiled the crafty scheme of the enemy strategists. A small open field about three hundred meters north of the enemy's left rear appeared to be the best LZ to land a support unit if an impromptu decision was made by a harried and inept field commander such as Mustang Six. That would not have helped. Alpha would have been scattered by the forced assault and riddled with extensive casualties. The VC would have gathered weapons and kept moving southwest to disappear in the dense trees and foliage and on to a sanctuary in nearby Cambodia.

That scenario happened too often and however reviewed, the denouement never really changed much anywhere in War Zone C. However, on this day, the renowned Viet Cong masters of deception were completely unnerved by this daring and savage attack by a unit of the most modern conventional infantry the world had yet known.

No less than seventy-five seasoned communist guerrillas had confidently come close to again embarrassing the "foreign dogs" of the Saigon puppet regime. Now, those who could, broke and ran in panic. Some temporarily disappeared out of sight and range but others were dropping from the massive swarm of bullets covering the area from the weeds to the tree line. Some were also trapped in the four concrete bunkers already practically surrounded by anxious young American soldiers who had gained fire superiority and momentum and were not going to let up easily. The intense hail of bullets aimed at the small firing apertures neutralized the bunkers, but nobody could move on until the VC inside were destroyed. Platoon leaders struggled to organize and control their squads, and squad leaders screamed to fire team leaders to keep the firing continuous and move in for the kill. If the momentum and fire superiority were lost, more VC would escape and Bravo Company would suffer needless casualties.

No Bravo soldiers fought more effectively than those of Shawn Leiberman's fire team. They never hesitated to dash forward, in turn, for two or three seconds at their leader's commands and never quit firing. Then, as if the enemy VC were nothing but annoying insects on their arms, they unceremoniously quashed the lives of three hapless Viet Cong in a bunker with rifle fire and grenade blasts. No training manual could have instructed the professionalism of these modern warriors guided by such an experienced leader.

One by one all the bunkers were taken. The doomed VC inside were helpless to do anything but intermittently stick a rifle muzzle through the small apertures and fire a few errant shots. Otherwise, they could only hope for a miracle that was not coming. These masters of deception and purveyors of death and destruction were going to die this day and no doubt they knew it. Bravo Six had no thought of even considering any forbearance. With the speed of the attack, the violence of action, and the mind-set of the attackers, even any guerrilla desiring to surrender would have had a very slim chance. Finally, grenade launchers were fired directly into the bunkers to disable anyone inside and hand grenades finished the job. What a great battle scene for a movie, but Hollywood would probably make it "politically correct" to satisfy the liberals and "girlie-men".

During the battle, Delta Six, to nobody's surprise who knew him, had made a mad dash and leaped to flatten himself atop one of the bunkers. Because the covering fire was forced to stop, an enemy rifle barrel immediately emerged. Capt. Trainor grasped the muzzle with his left hand and jammed a hand grenade through the aperture with his right. The searing pain from the blistering heat of the barrel was not enough to deter his action. That's the kind of stuff that steals the show, but Delta Six was just having some fun.

Then, like the joker he was, he dared to stand for a

few seconds and bow as if acknowledging applause! That brought an outrageous incident. A zealous VC, surely out of ammunition, rose behind him and whacked him on the head with his rifle. Then, as the VC ran directly to the rear, Trainor was in everyone's line of sight allowing that gutsy guerilla to escape to the woods. That was proof of the grit of these Viet Cong, but aside from mild vertigo everywhere inside his helmet, Delta Six actually cherished that donnybrook. He often said, "This war is just a big circus, and we're the clowns." He also often credited the Viet Cong with having "the balls of a brass monkey".

During those same moments, Bravo Six had to run to First Platoon's position. With Sergeant Mueller back at Bam Nam base, he had been worried about them. The bunker there was holding out too well. After a frantic search, he found that the new lieutenant had been shot in the right thigh, and his RTO had broken his radio handset (microphone).

After yelling at the nearby squad leader to cover him and make sure the machine gun kept firing, Bravo Six charged with most of the third squad. They advanced to twenty meters of the bunker before having two men hit. But it had made a difference when their Company CO came running with his two RTOs and yelling "Get Up! Let's get 'em! C'mon! C'mon!"

With Bravo Six running and firing his AR15 submachine gun at the bunker, the fear ridden soldiers leaped to join him with the squad leader also yelling and glad for the help. Then as a grenadier shoved his weapon into the firing aperture, a VC made a break out the back, almost knocking down a surprised American. He only got about ten meters before being cut down by Bravo Six and another rifleman. Three other VC inside were violently dispatched by two hand grenade blasts.

Now with a lull in the action, Bravo Six radioed the Second and Third Platoons to get ready to continue the assault. Bravo Six would stay with the leaderless First Platoon. His company had seven gunshot soldiers but all would live.

This was a chance to "dust off" the Bravo and Alpha casualties. He sent Delta Six to bring the remainder of Alpha Company and integrate them with the Bravo platoons. With another firefight possible, the squad sergeants were glad to reinforce their fire teams and supply them..

Since landing, only about ten minutes had lapsed, but with a myriad of action. Now Bravo Six had a chance to report, but he didn't need to. Wolverine Six had been circling the area at a thousand meters high and already knew anything that Bravo Six wanted to say. That's why he was a great general. He was only having trouble restraining his exuberance for a complete victory. He knew that probably half the remaining Viet Cong were hiding in the heavily wooded brush only about two hundred meters ahead of Bravo Company. He then gave Bravo Six an order to advance.

Now, with over a hundred men, Bravo Six ordered

his reinforced platoons to spread wide and begin slowly but steadily advancing and firing. Wolverine Six had told him that artillery barrages were cutting off the only escape route west to Cambodia. Eight hovering UH-1A gunships were hungrily waiting for the forty or so trapped VC to either swim the river east or break across the hell of the open field north.

Five of the guerrillas suddenly did try the river but never made it halfway. The rest, with no other way to escape the immutable advance of Bravo Six, desperately broke north across that field in a mad dash to the woods about three hundred meters away. What a sight! Those eager gunship pilots, already previously suspected of being overzealous, and now fevered with competitive bloodlust, attacked like maddened hornets. With blazing rapid-fire machine guns, all six gunships crisscrossed each other several times to cut down the panic-stricken black uniformed guerrillas. Two gun ships should have been watching the flanks, but who would volunteer to miss this picnic?

When Bravo Six arrived with his assault force, all the battle noises had suddenly stopped. After securing the area, he counted eighteen dead and eight wounded Viet Cong. All but three had AK47 submachine guns that could not be kept as souvenirs, but other than two American M16 rifles recovered, one lucky soldier did find a valued "Chi Com" carbine. The bodies were searched for paraphernalia that might be important. These poor bastards had almost nothing other than weapons save

---

for a couple ounces of marijuana, a couple photos and a few piasters. As always, the "weed" was destroyed.

Four of the wounded VC died of their wounds but the others were evacuated to the Bam Nam M.A.S.H. An especially hateful one would not stop crawling even when Sgt. Lee advised him that the medic would help him. When three soldiers tried to restrain him, he stabbed the arm of one with a small knife. One of the Alpha soldiers resolutely stepped over to the snarling Viet Cong and suddenly shot him in the head. He walked calmly away, and then sat down alone.

Bravo Six saw the incident and walked over to sit with that overwrought young boy who had seen and experienced too much that day. He probably was not more than nineteen years old, but had the look of a combat veteran who had seen too many months of too many battles, and now today had probably lost a couple more friends.

Bravo Six knew that this frame of mind was unpredictable and dangerous. He took his rifle from him and spoke softly. "You probably shouldn't have done that, but just try to relax a little. We're going back to base now. Try to get some rest and don't worry about this. I'm on your side. Feel free to come to talk to me but don't discuss it with others. See the chaplain, if you want."

That young soldier never looked at Bravo Six. He kept his head down to hide his discomposure. When Bravo Six saw a tear drop from the distraught soldier's nose, he felt a wave of empathy in his stomach. He wanted to hold that trembling boy in his arms, and would have, had he reached out first, but instead he put an easy hand on his shoulder and said, "Take care of yourself; we need you."

The two Bravo RTOs had watched and waited for their commander who had made time for a distressed soldier that some other commander may have ignored or even put under arrest. Bravo Six then sent his body-guard, Rahskle, to find that soldier's squad leader, to give him the rifle and to ask him to allow that soldier to collect himself. Rahskle told the squad leader that a Viet Cong had been killed and that was the end of it.

Bravo Six radioed to report but heard no more from Wolverine Six. The disgruntled Badger Six was now back on the air and even dared to return to the area. He was executing an evacuation to get all his companies back to Bam Nam base camp. This area was too close to the Cambodian border, and the companies would have too little time to be supplied and establish an effective perimeter defense. At least he was right about that, but then again he could never be accused of neglecting the welfare of his soldiers.

The battalion spent five days at Bam Nam. On the third day, Badger Six, looking a bit deflated, walked into Bravo Six's hooch unannounced and without knocking. He rarely said much to any of his company officers other than in his office or during operations. This condescending visit was, of course, to salvage what he could from his faux pas that was turned into the best victory the Wolverines had had for several months.

Bravo Six snapped to attention and then settled into the relaxed conversation that his abashed commander seemed to want. Badger Six led off with telling him that the intelligence report indicated that they had battled the Go Dau Ha Company. At least half were dead and many wounded had been taken to Cambodia. Bravo Six asked how much difference he thought it would make in the local area. The well-groomed and ever arrogant colonel spoke as if he had been involved just as he should have been, and Bravo Six allowed him to go on without any word or even an expression of disgust. He answered by saying that the VC would have to somehow gain face and every hamlet in the area would receive the news with mixed emotions. Some would mourn and some would fear consequences, but probably most would just be glad that the fighting was no more than within hearing distance that time.

Bravo Six agreed with him on that and then "broke the ice" to allow this contrived visit to turn into a "fence mender". Speaking calmly and respectfully, he only came close to apologizing. "Sir, I wish things had gone more smoothly out there. Smashing the enemy was great, but I'm not proud of what I did to you. I should have given you more time instead of interfering so abruptly."

Now the self-important colonel could have taken this cue to make amends and gain a strong ally, or he could have proven himself an ass by acknowledging this unpretentious prompt as an admission of guilt.

He stared for a few seconds and then spoke in a

near apologetic whisper but kept his head high in dignity. "Smithe, that time you were right and I was wrong. There's always two or three ways to get a job done, but you are winning without being a team player. I was trying to set up a safe withdrawal because it appeared that a victory would be too costly in casualties. Your way became right because you won. Otherwise, you could even have been court-martialed. In the face of combat, I have never seen anybody more brash. You are a fighting company commander. Nevertheless, our unit cannot go on like this. So far, we have all been lucky. And, you are not bulletproof. One of these days, we are going to have a command disaster, or even worse. For everyone's sake, we need more cooperation and communication. What do you think?"

Bravo Six listened intently to what sounded like carefully prepared words. He didn't like this man and he disagreed with him most of the time. He really had been covering his butt out there in that last battle, but otherwise he did run a good battalion. Bravo Six knew that despite all, it was not good politics to create a vendetta against himself. He also liked to heed the advice of a socially wise uncle who had advised him to not "shit on his ladder" or "burn any bridges" while dealing with his contemporaries.

"Yes sir, you're right. I was caught up emotionally, and I was very lucky in several ways. I hope I didn't cause you too much trouble."

"You're good, captain, but I have to run the show. You're in for a Medal of Honor."

Although glad for a truce with one of his immediate problems he couldn't help remembering a big concern. "Sir, please do what you can for Jerry (Alpha Six). He really was the best we had and was also my friend."

He said that he would and then left as abruptly as he came.

That evening in the mess hall two of the battalion staff majors together snidely told Bravo Six that he was damned lucky on that last operation and that one just does not do that to a fellow officer. They also said that he would probably be decorated but should have been relieved of command or even court-martialed. Their tone was calm but smacked of contempt, obviously out of blind loyalty to their humbled commander who must later rate them as supporting staff officers. Saying nothing, Bravo Six used his piercing eyes and wry smile to express his disdain for them.

Bravo Six did get another Silver Star Medal, a routine downgrade from the Medal of Honor that was probably never intended anyway. Seven others were simultaneously cited for their courage. Alpha Six was awarded a Bronze Star for valor, and he deserved it. Good victories usually cause a rash of acclamations and commendations. During the special troop formation for the occasion, that general, who was willing to stoop and take a chance, pinned a second Silver Star on the chest of the young fighting captain who originally only wanted to rescue his fellow company commander and friend. Bravo Six would never forget that momentary glance and nod of gratitude coming from a much heralded U.S. Army General who had the foresight to trust a hell bent greenhorn captain with more courage than sagacity. Delta Six wasn't recognized for his actions because he officially "wasn't there.".

Col. Langham was also present and happily assisted with all the presentations. As he shook Bravo Six's hand, he told him that he was proud of him, but also in a muffled tone, he warned him to be careful and watch his back. Bravo Six already knew that being the "fair-haired boy" of a colonel and a three star general could cause dangerous dissension.

True as that was, only the immediate superiors of Bravo Six were much of a problem. The muscular flaxen-haired Bravo Six still enjoyed popularity among the common soldiers and continued to enjoy a cold beer with the sergeants as well as the other company level officers. It was also great when a few helicopter pilots would seek him out for a few hours of lively camaraderie. Just as Reggie Trainor, Hasel Smithe continued to admit that "I gotta be me!"

After three days, Captain Jerry Bartam, Alpha Six, was allowed visitors. Badger Six had notified Bravo Six, which showed some surprising class on his part. A nurse told Bravo Six that a bullet had gone through his stomach and severely damaged a kidney. Jerry appeared to be in good spirits and joked that at first he feared that he would die and then later feared that he wouldn't because of the pain and sickness.

He wanted Bravo Six to relate the whole story. They talked and laughed about every detail as none other than they could. This banter was between two friends of extraordinary professional circumstance who wanted and needed more of their relationship than fate was allowing. Jerry also asked him to write to his wife to tell her the whole truth because she would figure that he was sparing unpleasantness in his letter. Bravo Six did, and he felt good to be trusted with a mission of such magnitude in sensitivity and discernment.

A week later, Badger Six sent Bravo Six by helicopter from a village bivouac to see Jerry again. That should have cued him about what he would see. His face was thin and drawn. His color was bad and his eyes weren't really looking at anything. When Bravo Six mentioned the letter to his wife, he got no response. Once he looked at Bravo Six and desperately but weakly grasped his hand. Then he faded out again to just slowly move his head and feet. Often, as if talking in his sleep, he would mutter a few indiscernible words.

Bravo Six felt helpless. Right now Jerry needed much more that a friend, but that's all he could be. Fighting the Viet Cong had been tough enough. Now Jerry was being attacked by a deadly invisible enemy on a forbidding battleground. Infection was slowly and surely overcoming his resistance and anything the field doctors could do to help. As he often did during these most depressing times in his life, he prayed for his friend.

Only about four minutes had passed, but Bravo Six

didn't need anybody to tell him that this man, whom he had known for only six momentous months, and with whom he had shared such memorable times was not long for this world. This young captain who had been such a brilliant infantry company commander, and who unselfishly shared his expertise with him during the difficult early times was now unceremoniously losing this final battle.

Bravo Six had to go. He had to clear his throat before he asked the nurse to take good care of Jerry. She surely was aware that he couldn't say anymore anyway. His eyes glistened with the threat of tears, his mouth was drawn into a smile of despair, and his throat was choked with the grip of grief. Now he would write again to Jerry's wife. With his hand fighting an emotional palsy and his mind struggling with acceptable words, he penned a letter that probably wasn't pretty but was a true reflection of his deviled disposition. He really hadn't heard Jerry say for him to send that letter, but he knew that he wanted it done. If Bravo Six would ever speak to Jerry's wife, he probably wouldn't talk any better that he wrote.

The Army probably did a good job in these matters, but he supposed that Jerry would rather have it told by a friend who would relate it candidly. Someday he would visit his friend's grave. Maybe he would even meet his wife and baby.

About a week later, SP4 Shawn Leiberman was promoted to an "Acting Jack" squad sergeant so he could wear the three stripes until that official promotion could be arranged. With the help of the unit adjutant, Shawn officially received that E5 promotion. One month later, after being recommended by Sergeant Mueller (strongly coerced by his fire team), Leiberman was awarded the Bronze Star medal for his combat leadership. The public relations specialist sent a picture of the colonel pinning that medal on him to his hometown newspaper. Everyone who ever knew him was flabbergasted. His family was aglow with pride. They read the story about the reasons for his commendation and realized that the boy had become a man's man. He had now matured. Never mind talent or brains or athletic agility. He was a man of mettle that distinguished him without comparison. "Little Shawn" was Sergeant Shawn and everybody knew it.

In addition, that co-pilot had "tested the air" by talking with a few other pilots at the bar about his considerations for action against that "smart ass" SP4 (Shawn) who had threatened to kill him. When Captain Niger Addison, a renowned gunship pilot and popular poignant personality, learned that the SP4 was in his friend's Badger Bravo Company, he could not resist getting involved. He offered to accompany that indignant and usually insufferable captain to confront Bravo Six face-to-face about his disrespectful fire team leader. That pilot was self-centered, arrogant, and obnoxious, but he was not stupid. He saw through that guise of friendly assistance and decided to drop the matter. Addison knew that Bravo Six would have damned near carried out Leiberman's threat and also would have been cheered by the other pilots.

Delta Six had rejoined his company without any problem and no one the wiser. That injury to his head would have been perfect for a Purple Heart Medal, but it would have caused him trouble since he was not supposed to be there. He would not have accepted it anyway. He always said that he only accepted medals for what he did to the enemy, not the opposite. Just the experience of that day was reward enough for him. He cherished his friendship with Bravo Six and wanted to continue an extreme steadfastness with all the ensuing high-spirited hazards. Reggie Trainor's masculinity was full-blooded. He did his fighting with his own definition of courage. Only a swashbuckler of that definition would understand. As Bravo Six prayed that night before falling asleep, he express appreciation and accepted the bad as God's will.

CHAPTER SIX

THE ENEMY VILLAGES

Everywhere for miles, the southern Hau Nghia Province area near the "Parrot Beak" of the Cambodian border reflected the usual Mekong Delta scene. Small villages and hamlets, among squared rice paddies and ancient brushy canals, were accented beautifully with clumps of coconut palms, patches of pineapple bushes, small groves of banana trees, and thick masses of bamboo. The Badger Battalion had been ordered to make a routine sweep of a suspected area to satisfy intelligence reports of residential Viet Cong. However, much more was discovered than expected, and no sweep was necessary.

As Charlie Company, riding with the "Hornets" unit of combat transport helicopters, approached the small village of Ap Ba Thut, several men with rifles ran from thatched houses. Sporadic firing came from several directions as the surprised guerrillas tried to buy time for escape. Troop movement for all three active companies of the battalion increasingly became very restricted because of civilian activity, but the gunship helicopters were delightfully busy chasing and strafing the almost impossibly dodging VC targets fleeing the area.

At the end of the day, five probable kills were reported but nothing was confirmed. One unarmed man was captured as he fled on a bicycle. Several were seen running back into hamlets to hide but then could not be found. Again, the mission was sound, but the planning and execution were flawed. The superficial Mustang Six and his "suck-up" S3 operations major assumed more than they actually communicated to the participants. They usually didn't know exactly what should be communicated anyway.

At this point, the author must note that Bravo Six's opinions of Mustang Six and his S3 often resulted from his personal dislike of them both. These stated opinions were not necessarily shared by all the company commanders. Bravo Six was usually suspicious and critical of many officers of a higher command. That is not to say that he was entirely alone in his opinions.

The three companies were each bivouacked at separate small villages because the terrain offered little cover for large numbers of men. The battalion strategy was to surround and search likely hiding places during the day and set up ambush patrols at night. The first night proved that these guerrillas were well organized, well armed, numerous, and indomitable. All three companies and their patrols reported harassing sniper fire. The enemy seemed determined to be in charge and systematically unnerve the usually confident Americans.

On the second day, Alpha and Charlie Companies each sent a light platoon on a night ambush patrol. Bravo Company was to support them with mortars on call. At 0200 hours, intense firing could be heard from the direction of the Alpha patrol. Bravo Six was awakened by his RTO and they listened together. The shooting continued, but the platoon leader did not answer several calls from the new Alpha Six, who had been struggling with internal command difficulties ever since his arrival. The anxious Alpha Six then nervously informed Badger Six that he was mustering a rescue force from his other two platoons.

Then a pitifully desperate radio call came that immediately started Alpha Six on his way. He had to hurriedly move his reluctant rescue troops over a dark two-kilometer distance at a fast march if he was to save any of the apparently decimated patrol. Badger Six knew that this would be a major "flap". Since Alpha Six was already on the way, he would just let it "play out" to keep himself out of any possible blame.

Because of his inexperience, Captain Fontaine probably would not have found the ambush site, but luckily, this time all he had to do was head toward the shooting. Although he was experienced enough to know that he would likely encounter awaiting sniper fire, the distraught captain did know that he had to get there "ASAP" if any of his ambush patrol were to be saved. The Viet Cong always killed as many Americans as possible to fuel the fires of discontent in the U.S.A.

That radio call came from the shaking voice of a soldier obviously unfamiliar with radio procedure. "Hello. Anybody hear me?" He repeated it several times and sobbed as he pleaded for help. At first, nobody could answer him because he didn't know to release the call button on the hand microphone. Finally he must have accidentally discovered the procedure because he answered for Bravo Six who had been continuously calling him. Bravo Six then instructed him to squeeze the button to talk and then release to listen. The soldier explained that they were being shot to pieces. He said almost everyone was hit, and his leg was bleeding badly. Alpha Six interrupted and said to hold on because he was on the way to him. He urged him to tell the others to keep firing anyway they could. Then he told him Bravo Six would be firing mortar rockets at the enemy.

Bravo Six was glad that the new captain said those things. Then he asked that soldier if he thought that they were in the right ambush position. He answered that he didn't know and nobody had said anything. Bravo Six said that he would to fire one rocket.

Bravo Six had taken charge for the time being. He was supposed to provide fire support anyway, but Badger Six knew what the situation must be and would rather let his company commanders make the moves and consequently take the heat later. As always, Bravo Six would rather get into trouble for something he did, rather for something he didn't do.

Bravo Six ran to Sgt. Gomez, the weapons platoon sergeant, and ordered him to fire one round two hundred meters north of the plotted ambush position. He knew that Gomez would have already been monitoring the radio, but he would rather talk personally to him now. In less than fifteen seconds, the mortar sight was adjusted. Gomez signaled, Bravo Six nodded, and with the familiar heavy explosive "thump" a rocket bounded from one of the two 81mm mortar tubes previously positioned to support the patrol. Along with the others around the gun, Bravo Six nervously stared at the darkness in the direction of the patrol. He knew, of course, that the rocket could very well land on the patrol itself if they had been out of position. That would cause him to be blamed for worsening the situation and please everybody in the battalion above his rank. Even if Bravo Six had been ordered not to fire because that soldier really didn't know his position and couldn't adjust fire anyway, Bravo Six knew that he had to take the chance to save a few of them. The sounds of the sniper fire harassing Alpha Six to slow him would enable the VC leader to estimate how much time he had left. They really could plan these things quite well, and Bravo Six knew better than to underestimate them.

Then the abrupt "whromp" of the distant explosion broke the suspense and the crackling rifle fire stopped.

The shaking voice quickly reported good news. "That's good." He spoke as if it was the best present he had ever received. "Can you do more?"

Bravo Six was also relieved. "You bet. Here comes some more." He nodded to Sgt. Gomez who smiled and signaled the mortar team that already had four rockets ready. Gomez was at his best in a pressure situation. His leadership stressed preparation and coordination which gave his men confidence. They were ready for success at all times.

They executed the "fire for effect" with the gusto and precision of any well-trained professionals who relished the opportunity to ply their skills when competence was crucial and decisive.

The gamble had worked. The VC attackers were obviously leaving and may have even suffered casualties. That harried soldier radioed that all was quiet but he was still bleeding. He also sounded weaker. Bravo Six told him to press something against the wound and stay on the radio until Alpha Six arrived.

Badger Six had been needlessly reminding Alpha Six to keep moving. Although the rescue force was tiring, at least the sniper fire had stopped. Fortunately, the rescuers had not been effectively fired upon. However, they arrived to find what they feared. Of the original eighteen Alpha ambushers, seven were dead including the platoon leader, a second lieutenant in only his third week. Eight more were seriously wounded. The platoon sergeant and four others later survived their superficial wounds, but none ever returned to that unit.

Daylight revealed that the patrol's deportment had been an invitation for disaster. Their position had been close enough to the targeted map coordinates, but they had practically no cover. They could have moved and reported the change, but it probably wouldn't have mattered. Without proper discipline, the young soldiers, some not yet out of their teens, had become very lax. They obviously didn't expect to be attacked, nor did they appear to care about ambushing the enemy. Badger Six did not report later that many of them had taken air mattresses, civilian transistor radios, and snacks. It was tough enough to explain how his ambush patrol got ambushed and almost annihilated. Not surprisingly, he also never mentioned Bravo Company's mortar support. The soldier on the radio had bled to death. Bravo Six, Sgt. Gomez, and his mortar team were certain to have visited him at the M.A.S.H., but war usually doesn't afford selected endings.

That afternoon the whole battalion made sweeping searches of the ambush area but found nothing except more evidence that the villagers themselves had been in collusion with the enemy. The Buddhist ritual involving the burning of rice straw was an excuse to mark the night movement of the Americans and allow time for combatants to hide.

One of Badger Six's few good ideas (if it was his idea) was to requisition five-foot long steel rods ("reebar") used for reinforcing concrete. The soldiers could jab them into the ground to locate enemy hiding places, supply caches, and tunnels. The Viet Cong were adept, skillful, and resourceful. Right beside the houses, steel barrels were found buried open end up with the lid camouflaged with vegetation. No VC were captured but one died in his barrel when the Alpha Company soldier who discovered him preferred to drop in a hand grenade instead. The explosion that tore apart the guerrilla also slightly injured the foot and shoulder of the vengeful American as he held down the hinged lid. Nobody rebuked him, nor would it have been a good time to do so. He could easily have lost restraint from shooting nearby villagers. It could even have further escalated into him shooting Americans and then himself. It's happened before and has always happened during the exigencies of wartime.

Short tunnels were also found leading from some houses to clumps of vegetation outside. Tunnel "rats" (specialty soldiers trained in the tunnels under Bam Nam base) found munitions and explosives in several of them. During the searches, all the villagers were aloof to Sgt. Lee, the interpreter. The local population of this group of hamlets was obviously sympathetic with the Viet Cong guerrillas which probably included many of their family members Sergeant Lee was staying close to Bravo Six as he always did when he was apprehensive about his safety. He really didn't want to talk to anyone. This wasn't the first time that he suffered an enigma of alienation among his own people.

Night clashes continued at the battalion bivouac.

Even the three man listening posts were drawn to within thirty meters after two were hit the next night, causing three casualties. Now, no one had to be told to stay alert. Everybody started to report anything observed without much thought about the significance of the information.

The villagers were obviously passing information to the enemy. After dark, company command posts and even the battalion headquarters appeared to be the primary target of light mortar rockets (40mm), rifle grenades, and bursts of automatic rifle fire. These guerrillas were intelligent, well trained, well led, and very gutsy. The constant harassment at irregular intervals was causing a few casualties every night. They also were succeeding in causing lack of sleep and waning confidence for even the most experienced soldiers. Of course, that was also an significant weapon and an effective tactic.

Bravo Company, although deployed in the most remote position, had not been receiving the heaviest or most frequent attacks. Nevertheless, Bravo Six moved his company into a hamlet of about fifteen houses and set up his defensive perimeter surrounding them. No civilians were allowed to leave or enter, especially children who usually stole munitions and reported about the American positions.

In addition, on the advice of his supply sergeant, who commuted daily from Bam Nam base, Bravo Six sent for PFC Lasinski, one of the company cooks who had never been on a field mission. In his spare time, John Lasinski had made an impressive hobby of practicing with a .50 Cal. Machine gun. Much bigger and heavier than the

.30 Cal. M60 machine gun carried by field troops, this ominous weapon fired bullets bigger than anything the enemy had, at a maximum rate of 800 rounds a minute. Although normally too cumbersome for a mobile field unit, now, in a bivouac situation, this terrifying WWII weapon was very effective since it could shoot at one thousand meters through mounds of dirt, small trees, houses or just about any other cover the VC snipers had available.

PFC Lasinski had never said much anyway, and when the renowned Bravo Six requested to speak to him directly on the radio, he responded only by saying "O.K., Sir." four times during the almost one-sided conversation. John Lasinski was the youngest son of a hard-working autoworker in Detroit, Michigan. After basic training at Fort Benning, Georgia, he had come home on a thirty-day furlough to tell his close-knit family that he was going to Vietnam. He felt good about his bold announcement because his father, whom he admired for his impressive strength and character, had volunteered to serve in Europe during WWII. He had been awarded a Bronze Star Medal for heroism against the German Nazis.

The Lasinski family and many of their friends and neighbors had a farewell party for John that could have been mistaken for one of those rip-roaring "hunky" wedding receptions. Then when he was saying good-bye, everybody took a turn hugging him and smiling and crying at the same time. However, what John remembered most endearingly was his aged grandparents who both hugged him together and then hugged each other afterward. He'll never forget how he could feel them shaking as they groaned and spoke together softly in their native Slovak language. The memories and knowledge they had of the hardships of war and the occupation aftermath in Eastern Europe gave them an insight and a fear that only John's father could come close to understanding.

Later, when John found that he was going to be a cook in Vietnam instead of an infantryman, he remembered his father's advice to not volunteer and not complain. He said to do whatever you are told and do it well. If this be his destiny, so be it. At least he knew that his family would be a little relieved when they got his first letter.

Nevertheless, here he sat beside a massive machine gun almost as big as some of the youngest Viet Cong guerrillas who probably already knew about it. Bravo Six placed him with the First Platoon on the southeast side of the company perimeter where good cover for snipers lay close and only two distant houses would be in the line of fire. Platoon Sgt. Mueller of First Platoon took Lasinski on a tour of his broad area of responsibility to help him judge the range and nature of the probable targets. In addition, Sgt. Lee went along to advise the inhabitants of those two houses, about five hundred meters away, that they should not sleep there.

When Bravo Six informed Badger Six of the .50 caliber machinegun, he reminded Bravo Six that the VC would probably think of something to show the local populace that they didn't fear this ominous weapon. The resulting propaganda would give them credibility. Bravo Six agreed and assured him that the displacement and effectiveness were well planned. Proof of the enemy's curiosity was a constant parade of women and children walking by to "gawk" at the huge machine gun. The children pointed and laughed but they were certain to somehow leak everything they observed to their fathers, uncles, and older brothers. Children were usually the best source of intelligence the Viet Cong had. American soldiers normally liked to befriend and trust them but Bravo Six always warned that they be kept at a distance.

Bravo Six had another concern that worried him even more. If the VC managed to get that weapon, they could hide it and then wreak havoc on the bivouac on a night of their choosing-or even another American unit. The VC would quickly learn to use it and would be resourceful enough to procure the ammunition. Moreover, even at 1000-1500 feet altitude, passing helicopter traffic would be in great danger. He certainly didn't have to be told that any such catastrophic blunder of his own volition would cost him his command.

Nevertheless, Bravo Six reasoned that the advantages were more probable. John Lasinski could make even brief, long-range sniping very dangerous to the VC anywhere in the First Platoon area of responsibility. In addition, an alternate position could be established at the other platoon areas to help them. Four men could move it quickly over the short distance through the middle of the company perimeter. Moreover, if the VC should try to rush the perimeter to take the gun, proper disposition would cost them extensive casualties and negative propaganda.

Bravo Six had been suspicious of a woman whose hut was nearby the big gun. He instructed the soldiers that if she tried to sneak away to let her go. She would report all and help set up the diabolic plan of Bravo Six.

He then warned Lasinski that he would have to be awake on "ready alert" during the hours of darkness. The four-man Alpha fire team of the First Platoon's second squad would assist him and provide local security during daylight hours. After dark, unbeknown to the villagers, the bodyguard, Rahskle, and two other riflemen of his choosing could quickly run from the company command post to provide support.

Additionally, Bravo Six instructed Platoon Sgt. Mueller to set out trip flares. He also ordered Weapons Platoon Sgt. Gomez to plot a mortar barrage fifty meters in front of Lasinski. In effect, that Browning .50 caliber weapon was as much bait for an enemy attack as it was a sniper deterrent. That is what Bravo Six really had in mind. If the enemy was spoiling for a fight, so was he. He wanted to get it on.

He also advised Sgt. Mueller to have a man always checking the First Platoon area with a Starlite Scope, the hand-held device that allowed one to see better in the dark. The Viet Cong, if they really wanted that strategic weapon, would probably come in large force by crawling as close as possible to that position and then suddenly rushing it. With well-planned sniper fire to cover their escape, they could succeed. Of course this tactic could horribly backfire if they were spotted too soon.

The VC may be lulling them into false security and drowsiness before they executed their plan. They knew that the Americans were tired and would probably doze and some would even try to nap. Bravo Six knew that Rahskle would check Lasinski and the others but still he worried. His intuition ran wild with expectations of a pending attack.

At 0130 hours, Bravo Six told RTO Forney to come with him on a routine check of the perimeter. So Rahskle would not be insulted, he started his patrol in the Second Platoon area. Upon his arrival at the First Platoon area, he looked at the small house about fifty meters to the northwest of Lasinski's position. His suspected that it was probably empty. Immediately he sent for Sgt. Lee to check for the woman and her three small children who should be inside since they had not been seen leaving. The night was black with no moon. They could easily have slipped away unnoticed.

When Sgt. Lee went inside and found nobody, he called as planned to Bravo Six who started to the platoon sergeant to warn him. At the same time, the soldier with the Starlite scope saw movement and started to his squad leader to wake him. On the way, he was also going to alert Lasinski who sat drinking cold coffee and staring into the night. He didn't quite make it and neither did Bravo Six.

Practically in unison, about twenty enemy rifles started firing from only forty meters away. At the same time, four hand grenades exploded in the First Platoon area that must have been thrown from houses in that vicinity. The soldier with the Starlite Scope, the squad leader, and one other soldier were killed. Two others were wounded.

Bravo Six yelled "barrage" at RTO Forney and started to dash to Lasinski's position when Rahskle, at first not recognizing him, grabbed his arm and then excitingly told him to come with him. So far, the surprise and ferocity of the attack had allowed only two First Platoon soldiers to return fire. For some reason Rahskle now had only one soldier with him. Just before they reached Lasinski, and after the first fifteen seconds of the attack, the big Browning machinegun finally started banging away even louder than anybody expected it would be. Shock and awe often stymied some soldiers, but now even the most hesitant of the Bravo defenders were spurred into action.

John Lasinski had been sitting with his elbows resting on his knees. One of the first enemy bullets tore an inch gash through his right thigh and ripped open his side fracturing his ribs. The shock and impact that knocked him on his back saved him from several other bullets that passed over him and his sleeping assistant, now wide-eyed but unharmed. John lay in shock, gasping with pain and shaking with the agony of one fearing death. His assistant laid an arm over John's chest to comfort him and hold him still.

John Lasinski had been down about five seconds when he grabbed the shirt of his terror-stricken assistant and yelled repeatedly "Help me up!" That frightened soldier obligingly pushed him to a sitting position but then kept himself flat on the ground. Bleeding profusely and writhing from involuntary spasms in his leg, still John was able to pull the cocking lever, grasp the firing handles, and blast away with a snarling resolve to thwart even the angel of death.

Bravo Six, Rahskle, and the other soldier hit the ground beside Lasinski and started shooting. However, if the big machinegun hadn't already begun firing, the now charging Viet Cong would probably have been overwhelming. The advancing guerillas, probably sensing victory, were now undoubtedly possessed with a high degree of debilitating fear.

Suddenly facing the "business end" of the big weapon, only about thirty meters away, those heretofore confidently charging guerrillas now realized that the machinegun and most of the soldiers around it, who were supposed to be silent, were erupting into an earsplitting, blazing defense. Less than half of the infantry soldiers of WW2 and Korea were said to return fire in close battle. True or not, the maelstrom nature of the Vietnam War usually caused the common soldier to be especially impulsive about using his weapons. Sgt. Lee had set fire to the abandoned house and then scurried off to the east as pre-planned. The blaze of the dry grass roof was illuminating the battle area, and the mortar barrage was blowing apart the safety of the dark woods behind the enemy. Only a few of them were able to flee into the night.

Only one guerrilla, already wounded but crazed with a hateful mania to kill Americans, continued running to the Bravo defenders. He wildly stumbled into Rahskle (definitely a bad move!) with the intent of stabbing him with the long spike bayonet of his Chinese rifle. Rahskle, as strong with ferocity as a normal soldier might be weak with fear, violently flung the guerrilla to the ground with the skill of a seasoned fighter. Fast losing strength and probably already dying, the VC lost control of his rifle as he crashed to the ground and couldn't prevent Rahskle from grabbing it. In the last few moments of his violent life, he probably realized that this seemingly devil-faced foreigner, who stood tall as he beat him with that rifle, was certainly the wrong American to take with him as a gift into the Buddhist heavenly realm of brave dead warriors.

After smashing that guerrilla four times on the head with the rifle butt and using all the strength he could muster again and roaring like a lion, Rahskle drove the spike bayonet through the guerrilla's chest and a few inches into the ground. Then with the calm composure and satisfaction of a killer content with his work, he watched the fractured head slowly blowing bloody bubbles as the body twitched in post-mortem tremors with the Chi Com carbine firmly standing straight up from the torso. Rahskle afforded a wry smile.

Bravo Six had glanced repeatedly at the struggle behind him as he finished his third ammunition magazine. When Rahskle hit the ground again beside him, they never spoke or even looked at each other. Bravo Six wasn't surprised to see his handpicked bodyguard kill with such wrath.

Then as suddenly as it had started, all the shooting stopped. The burning thatched roof only flickered light now as the embers fell inside the mud-walled house. RTO Forney could be heard radioing to Badger Six that it was over, they had won, and that he would get a casualty report.

Bravo Six comforted John Lasinski as he now lay on his back weak from loss of blood. The medics ran about to render aid to all the wounded and assess their needs. Sgt. Mueller, sounding shaken but still able to function, quickly shifted the second squad to re-secure his disrupted defense line. Bravo Six ordered Sgt. Gomez to fire four mortar rounds at the probable area of the enemy escape route. Sgt. Mueller then re-supplied and checked every position. Bravo Six then radioed Badger Six that he needed an urgent "dust-off" for three gunshot wounded (WIA). Two others had superficial shrapnel wounds requiring only a dressing. He was also sorry to report four killed in action (KIA). They were covered with ponchos as was usual. Rahskle's dead VC was cast together with the four dead guerrillas lying just in front of the defense perimeter.

At daybreak, Bravo Six was anxious to survey the battle area. He discovered thirteen more bodies including the mother of the small children who lived in the burned house. None of the children were found which afforded a good chance that they were probably safe somewhere.

The mother had probably acted as a guide, which explained why the trip flares had not activated. Several blood trails indicated a few more dead or badly wounded. More than a few small body pieces were also found, along with a dollar bill-sized section of scalp that were no doubt the work of John Lasinski's hail of .50 caliber bullets.

Badger Six arrived with his command group to get a full report. He was satisfied that the enemy had suffered more than Bravo had. He was also sure that the VC's main goal was to get that machinegun. To "dirty" Bravo Six's obvious victory over this local Viet Cong contingent and to indirectly express a lack of confidence in Bravo Six's judgment in deploying that gun and the ability to keep it out of enemy hands, he ordered the gun sent back to Bam Nam base. Bravo Six argued that the immediate removal of the gun would be used as a propaganda victory by the Viet Cong, but Major Domsavich interrupted to say that the gun should never have been brought out there in the first place and had caused enough problems already. Of course Badger Six nodded his approval at the usually facetious supportive lip service of his equally inept S3 operations officer.

Subduing his burning anger with a long deep breath, Bravo Six turned away to order the gun sent back. He may have sent it back anyway since it had successfully caused the local guerrillas to foolishly concentrate themselves and suffer such a debilitating loss of manpower. Bravo Six just didn't like anybody telling him that he had to do it. For a few moments he watched the local villagers now carting away the bodies for burial since they were undoubtedly their own relatives.

Later that afternoon Bravo Six had trip flares set in front of every position of the entire company. He was sure that the enemy wasn't finished yet. Let them come, he thought. This last attack was a real "wake-up call" for any of Bravo Company who may have been lulled into carelessness.

Limited harassing attacks continued at all the company positions. Even after a few more civilian casualties and much property damage throughout the battalion area, still none of the village inhabitants had left. At Charlie Company, one old man and two women were killed. Two more women and a small child were wounded as they slept during one enemy attack of raking automatic weapon fire. The medic treated the wounded and evacuated them to Bam Nam base the next morning, along with a wounded squad leader who had a habit of sleeping with one knee raised. Of course all the blame was on the Americans. The villagers mused that, "If they weren't there, this wouldn't be happening."

Six days passed with very little success from a variety of search tactics. Every hour after dark brought some type of direct or indirect fire somewhere at the battalion positions. The machine guns and mortars were the most effective deterrent. The antipersonnel loads for the 90mm recoilless rifle, consisting of hundreds of tiny steel darts (flachettes), were effective but slow in response. On the positive side, everyone was getting better at taking cover and returning fire. Mounting casualties were surely also suffered by the Viet Cong. They were probably receiving instructions from their district officers and were possibly reinforced from outside units.

After a total of ten days, the VC were still in charge and the neighboring villagers were going about their daily business-aloof as ever. They were no doubt providers of food and valuable information to their guerrilla relatives and friends. Hand-painted signs on trees translated to "Nothing for nothing" as an insult to the Saigon government. Even the water buffalo being led through the area seemed to snort and feint threatening advances even more than usual at the unwelcome Americans.

Then a move! The companies were suddenly ordered to strike camp and twenty "Hueys" successively flew everyone to Bam Nam base. Everyone would have a couple days to clean up, get a little rest and recreation ("R&R"), and recycle their soldiering attitude.

However, the Americans hadn't actually lost and they weren't quitting. Several days later, Col. Langham briefed his two Wolfhound battalion commanders and their company officers that at 1330 hours they would fly en masse with two attached ARVN companies to surround the four square kilometer area containing those little problem hamlets. The intelligence reports estimated fifty to seventy-five well-armed and well-supplied hard core resident Viet Cong, and everyone believed it.

The kick-off at 1330 hours would have impressed anybody. The upper brass had been busy with coordination, which caused the set-up landing to go exceptionally well. The village residents learned quickly about what had happened. A subsequent leaflet drop urged all inhabitants to come to the ARVN processing station and all Viet Cong to surrender under the Cheu Hoi (repatriation) plan. The leaflets were also very explicit that the area would be bombed that night. After that last eruption of violence and bloodshed, Bravo Six guessed that many of these locals would believe the warnings.

Supposedly, now the Viet Cong were trapped inside and the Americans would be in control. At least it was hoped that at least a few VC were inside and the residents would seriously believe the leaflets. Like always, this could be a tactical triumph, a boondoggle if no results justified it, or even a tactical catastrophe if only civilians were the casualties.

Probably half the residents went through the processing station but no young men. That night, 105 mm. Howitzers pounded the area with a long barrage that was intended to convince the rest to leave. More residents came with a few wounded but again no young men.

The ARVN officers said that practically no useful information was obtained about local guerrillas or weapons.

The American companies had reported no action. More leaflets were dropped, and after dark the artillery opened up again with no civilian reaction. Then at 0400 hours a B52 bomb strike ripped apart an area a mile long and a half-mile wide. It was odd to hear the bombs falling without any sound of the giant airplanes. No other person in any other part of the world had ever heard the subsequent terrifying explosions. The small villages were now gone. The huge bombs had deeply churned the earth, turned it into a slimy black muck, and left very little sign of prior civilization. Any buildings, weapon caches, tunnels and hiding places were undone-including all living things. The lingering odor of pungent chemicals, sour earth, and putrefaction created a pall of death throughout.

More leaflets dropped and more villagers, lucky enough to have been on the outskirts of that last attack, came to the checkpoints. This time five uniformed Viet Cong waving leaflets came to an Alpha Company position. They said that they didn't want another night of bombs. Their leaders had told them that the Americans would torture and kill them but they would be safe in the tunnels. Now they didn't know if any of the rest were alive, and, no matter what, they just wanted out.

The ARVN interrogation team was able to glean enough information from them to satisfy everyone's suspicions and suppositions. The area had been in complete control of two full strength platoons of Viet Cong regulars reinforced with about twenty-five local "Popular Force" militia of sympathetic men and women. These VC were affiliated with units in the Iron Triangle south of Ben Cat and had planned to use their local help to overrun an American position had they stayed longer. With good planning and a little luck, there's no doubt that it could have happened.

In the past, the VC had been successful in disrupting any attempt by the Saigon government to affect local jurisdiction. ARVN troops had been chased several times from the area with heavy casualties. They also said that a few villagers had to be shot, but some did support their cause and assisted them. However true, the ARVN was noted for usually reporting what someone wanted to hear and was advantageous to them.

The Mustang Battalion was assigned to search the bombed area. No live guerrillas were found in the area, but Charlie Company did find two exposed tunnels each containing large rooms. Along with a few weapons and uniforms, they found two American PRC-10 radios, some handmade maps, and a Vietnamese to American translation manual. Everything was damaged severely. Eleven bodies of young men and women were strewn about in such bad condition that the count was difficult.

The small village previously used by Bravo Company was gone. Bravo Six and his soldiers felt sympathy for these simple farmers but empathy couldn't be expected. They wondered if any of the children had escaped and someday would understand what happened and why.

In another exposed tunnel, the body of a black American PFC was found with his hands and feet bound and wearing only camouflage pants His captors had bashed in his skull probably a couple days ago. Later he was identified as a soldier missing from a transportation unit in Saigon. He and his captors may have stopped here en route to a prison camp in Cambodia.

One soldier in Alpha Company sank so deep in the blackened mud that he couldn't pull himself free nor could anybody help him. A rope pulled from the side caused him too much pain. To break the suction, a helicopter lowered a harness resembling a child's swing that he was able to sit in while being lifted straight up. That was something to laugh about amid this morbid mess made of God's good earth and creatures. That was the advantage of being an American. A Viet Cong would probably have been abandoned because they couldn't have helped him anyway.

Considering the evidence found and that the prisoners had stated that all the Viet Cong were entrapped, the unit morning report conclusion emphasized that this enemy stronghold was finished. The surviving inhabitants would have to somehow begin a new subsistence and live with their hearts and minds touched by the trauma of warfare. A MACV political action team offered them transportation and assistance, but only a few with children accepted. Some probably had nowhere to go anyway, other than a refugee camp which they distrusted.

Bravo Six felt that these villagers had to be pitied

for their provincial naivete which had led them to believe that Ho Chi Minh would not be lying to them as he did to those who had believed in land reform in the North. However, he was sure that the rice paddies of the Delta were much more important to "Uncle Ho" than the welfare of the resident human beings who would not even be allowed the dignity of their religion. Bravo Six remembered reading the words of Mao Tse Tung who said, "The guerrilla must swim like a fish in the water. The guerrilla is the fish; the people are the water." The villagers readily provided food and shelter. Mostly they were helping relatives, but sometimes the guerrillas were strangers who would take vicious advantage of the helpless locals.

Mao was right, and the upper echelon of the Viet Cong leadership were wise enough to heed that advice. However, equally wise American leaders like Col. Langham knew that "fish out of water" were doomed. Positive strategy like that used in this operation could have won the war if not for the squint-eyed anti-war activist prevaricators back home and the compromising politicians who submitted to their jabberwocky. Even in times of war, too many of our political leaders cared only about re-election no matter what the cost, human or otherwise.

Of course, Bravo Six didn't forget John Lasinski. Because his wounds required several months of healing, his Vietnam service was over. Clothes would hide the disfiguring scars, but the Purple Heart and Bronze Star medals would make his homecoming even more emotional and glorious. In consideration, it couldn't have ended better for him.

It was also appropriate for Rahskle to again be decorated for his valor. Bravo Six always wondered what he would do without him. Rahskle had cut his hand while killing that VC and was recommended to receive the Purple Heart Medal along with the other wounded and dead. He told Bravo Six that the enemy really didn't wound him and that the Purple Heart Medal would be cheapened. However, he said that he would feel okay with another Bronze Star. Bravo Six shook his hand at that presentation and told him that he wished there was a medal for combat virtue.

CHAPTER SEVEN

ENEMY SURGE
AT CAN THO

Massive NVA movements were necessitating reinforcement of the probable targeted areas. The
Wolverine Brigade's two heliborne combat infantry battalions were detached to the big river area close to the city
of Can Tho, only about twenty kilometers from Saigon.
Possibly two NVA Divisions were reported to be somewhere in the area moving toward a probable attempt to
cut-off or immobilize the capital and its huge Ben Hoa
and Tan Son Nhut airfields. It had been attempted before at the ancient capital of Hue causing great losses on
both sides. With overwhelming force and surprise, the
NVA were capable of defeating any installation or city,
but they lacked the necessary artillery and air support to
hold anything in place.

The Wolverine Task Force Brigade was airlifted

by giant CH47 Chinook helicopters that could carry as many troops as could sit tightly together in rows on the metal cargo deck with a strap across their thighs. It was uncomfortable but relatively safer and certainly faster. A truck convoy just couldn't compare. All of the Bravo Company task force went in one Chinook.

The Badger Battalion landed on an old Japanese airstrip near the huge brackish Mekong River. The company commanders were issued maps of the area and were told to keep their units on "Ready Alert.". During the next few hours, Bravo Six watched the small command OH13 helicopters coming and going. Any communiqué from Badger Six would have been befuddling anyway, but no one had to tell Bravo Six that medium to large Viet Cong units were not the cause of all this hectic activity. He also suspected that when he was finally ordered into action, he probably was not going to get much information or even a chance to respond properly. Bravo Six's fear of fighting the enemy never seemed to be as great as the fear of not leading his unit effectively.

Finally something happened and it was what he feared. A staff major he had never seen before suddenly appeared to order him into action. The polished brass, sunglasses, thin cigar, and brash manner of this hawk-faced pretender were added to the usual slight insult of being ignored by his own battalion commander and staff when other senior officers and staff were around. Bravo Six politely interrupted him and requested confirmation that he was authorized to issue an operation order to him. Although he was within his rights, he knew it was probably unnecessary and would irritate his own senior officers but that would be nothing new. This pesky major would not go away but Bravo Six was letting him know that he would not be intimidated. However, the command level officers would nod approval, and he would have gained time to summon his platoon leaders to hear the orders. They appreciated inclusion in these matters, and Bravo Six always gained a measure of satisfaction from publicly stinging the snobby, "hot-dogging" field grade assistants of the chain of command. Moreover, it always seemed to pay dividends of clout in the long run.

Because he knew everybody would be monitoring for something to chuckle about, the deceitful Major Domsavich saw his chance to radio the confirmation with a deviously controlled tone and a slight attitude of condescension. Easily discerning this state of affairs of the "fair-haired" Bravo Six, the irascible Col. Langham broke in to order that his favored company commander be transported to the deck of the naval ship being used as the operations war room headquarters. Bravo Six looked up to him as a military father. Likewise, Col. Langham always talked to him as he would a key business associate whether in private or in company. The distain Bravo Six had for Maj. Domsavich didn't seem to be shared by any other officers. However, a clash of personalities such as this was not rare in any similar venue. During the relaxation of a few beers, Bravo Six would probably admit that his perceptions and opinions about Major Domsavich were a result of "just not liking him".

Col. Langham knew that Bravo Six was to be used as an important pivot point in the overall plan to stop the advance of the NVA. He further knew that the survival of Bravo Six as well as his company was very much in question. Any worthy field grade officer would have said that an experienced young company commander did not deserve to be cold-shouldered and disrespected by those intermediate senior officers who could only pretend to have commensurate tactical prowess and deference. Bravo Six was conveyed by a command HU1B to the naval ship heliport and greeted by the task force command group. Although all this fanfare was impressive and certainly touched him with discomfiture, he also worried about what they would be asking of him. Were they being nice before they threw him to the dogs as a diversion? He hoped that they were respecting an enthusiastic captain who could successfully act as the crucial protagonist in their plotted strategic plan. Of course, he also worried that he was bringing calamity to his company through his own past conduct of wanting to be the one for any job.

Yes, Bravo Company was ordered to be the strategic blocking unit at one of the most likely night movement routes of the huge NVA task force last spotted in that zone. His position would be along the river about five kilometers upstream from the Mustang Battalion base of operations. A tall, imposing major assured him that sufficient fire support was already plotted to assist him. Bravo Six knew that the plotting of fire support was not as important as the coordination of it. But without it, the appearance of an NVA horde would be "curtain time' for his whole company. He was not shy about asking detailed questions about communication and what he could expect. The answers were comfortably assuring.

Bravo Six included his mortar platoon as riflemen, which gave him eighty instead of the usual sixty in his assault force. When he asked about transporting his eighty, the major brusquely told him that five more Hueys were on the way and tartly added, "Captain, you have more to worry about tonight than logistics. We know what you have and we will take care of our end."

Bravo Six was thinking that only five men instead of the usual six would be in most of the helicopters, but the extra helicopter firepower would be helpful if they encountered a "hot LZ". He was also thinking about how much these "pencil pushing high brass" would know about effectively supporting him.

As fast as he had departed, he was returned to his company. Because he was aware of what had just transpired, that indignant major snapped a steady salute, tightened his lips, and glared at this upstart captain. Bravo Six's steady blue eyes were fixed with dissonant arrogance as he spoke clearly and positively. "My brigade commander told us that saluting in combat areas makes us sniper targets." The abashed major knew that he would lose that one, too, so he just left. As his own helicopter lifted off, he glanced at the Bravo command group and thought about his encounter with this chosen player who would actually "carry the ball.", but would not forget soon about his own discomfiture.

Sergeants Mueller, Tiega, and Laird enjoyed some chuckles and biting comments about the tension during the abashed major's visit. Nothing really surprised them about their big commander. They knew that Bravo Six, when offended, could be quite obstinate toward his superiors, but he also didn't mind condescending at times to have a little fun with the soldiers in the ranks. They trusted him to level with them. They liked that. He was "straight" and would never ask them to do what he wouldn't do himself. If a mission was perilous, he went along. The Bravo soldiers often joked about whether or not their CO was accompanying them on patrols and such.

Bravo Six designed the perimeter for the blocking mission, and the platoon sergeants organized a boarding plan for the fifteen choppers that were now reported to be incoming.

What also arrived was the command reconnaissance platoon. They were to reinforce Bravo Company and that better explained the extra five helicopters. The major at the command center was not clear about this specific platoon in his operation order. The loading plan had to be reorganized, but everyone was glad to have the battalion "Recon" platoon. They had a good fighting reputation and top-quality men, especially Platoon Sgt. Browner. He was tall, wiry, cool under pressure, and very resourceful. His unkempt shock of blond hair was recognized by all that frequented any places of action or camaraderie.

Very few helicopter assault landings were attempted after dark. This was the first for Bravo Company, as well as any Badger company or even for these pilots. This factor of the unknown also caused a greater than normal degree of apprehension within the ranks. The anxiety and darkness caused everyone to check his weapon and ammunition more carefully and listen better to instructions. A few, maybe more, probably had some bad feelings about the environment and unusual preparations, but all were going and would survive mentally through a fraternal dependence understood only by those who have shared such experiences. These young Wolverine soldiers were an integral part of a skillful fighting machine. When given meaningful tasks with effective leadership, even the "duds" and "green" riflemen could be figured into the intrinsic value of the whole.

The lift-off order came at 21:16 hours. Fifteen UH1D combat transport helicopters armed with two side door M60 machine guns apiece, loaded with the Bravo task force of a hundred and five soldiers, and escorted by three gunships, simultaneously rose into the night. Even the most experienced soldiers in the vicinity marveled at this conglomeration of powered-laden resonance, and the awesome sight of an unusually large group of those big insect-like war machines lifting off in a tight formation and charging into the night. All those who knew the mission of this sophisticated, high-tech assault force were gravely daunted by the potential malevolent destiny awaiting it. Badger Six answered a question about who was commanding that armada. Then he paused and affectionately added, "As an officer, he is a barbarian. But, as a fighting commander, he is a Colossus." However, he would never have said that directly to him.

The resounding drone of that swarm of powerful metal monsters complemented the ominous darkness covering the troubled tropical earth below. The pilots and door gunners readied their nerves for their mission of successfully getting Bravo Company to its blocking position or possibly even scrambling out if a few thousand unobliging North Vietnamese regulars had already reached that vicinity. NVA presence would mean that the task force of Bravo Six would be whisked from the area and the ready support fire would immediately bring bloody havoc on the befuddled enemy that would no longer be able to avoid disclosure.

The sound of changing engine rpm's signaled Bravo Six that they must surely be approaching the LZ. Then suddenly he knew that he was being transported by pilots who knew their business and meant to deliver his troops without recourse. Powerful head beams searched the vicinity and door gunners on every chopper raked the ground with tracer fire as the battle group made a long approach at about two hundred meters altitude. No enemy unit within several hundred meters of that LZ could have escaped notice.

Then, just skimming the ground, the choppers

stopped in unison and the feisty Bravo infantryman leaped clear. As Bravo Six rose to jump he waved to his own pilots with his thumb and forefinger joined to indicate a good job. This group could very well be just as good as his regularly assigned chopper units called the "Hornets" and "Little Bears" back at Bam Nam base. Their mission well done, these airlift specialists could retire for the night.

With five platoons and the river as a natural barrier, Bravo Six planned a very strong and flexible defense. His three rifle platoons formed a U-shaped perimeter about fifty meters to a side alongside the river. The recon platoon deployed ready reserve clusters about five meters behind the First and Second Platoons. They could quickly move forward to fortify any ineffective fire team position. Sgt. Mueller's First Platoon was probably the best disciplined and was guarding the likely avenue of approach from the west. that afforded cover. The converted mortar Platoon was to provide local security for the company command position at the river's edge, have one squad ready to assist Third Platoon, and provide a cover fire for a general escape to the river.

If overrun, all survivors were to re-group about a quarter mile downstream. What they would do after that didn't need to be discussed just then. In addition, each platoon deployed a three man listening post about fifty meters outside the perimeter. Fifteen minutes after landing, the platoon leaders had their positions secured.

Now---they waited. Every soldier was quiet and alert. No one had to be reminded about talking, smoking, flashlights, coughing, etc. The three man firing positions allowed one man to catch a few winks, but nobody actually slept. They knew how to be good combat soldiers, but usually needed to be scared to demonstrate it. An appreciated feeling of fraternity pervaded an otherwise diverse group of young Americans. Only during times of relative self-confidence could one afford petty thoughts of prejudice about a certain person lying in such close proximity.

Every soldier was appreciating every soundless minute, but all were also wishing the time away. Three other companies from other battalions were doing the same thing at other strategic locations. If the enemy was moving, something would happen somewhere. By constant jogging, a large NVA unit could travel twenty kilometers in one night to surprise the defenses of a significant city or military post. In any large combat encounter, their losses were high, but victorious attrition didn't seem to bother them. Some whole units never returned to their homeland.

Fifteen minutes after midnight, the western listening post hurried back to the defense perimeter. Breathlessly they reported that someone had obviously stumbled into their trip line with rattle cans attached (stones in C-ration cans). They also reported human voices. Sgt. Tiega had been wise to tell them about not firing their weapons.

Bravo Six alerted his platoons and code-signaled a

radio report to Badger Six. He, in turn, alerted the Air Force of the target area. Three F105 fighter-bombers mustered for action. Their strafing and bombing capabilities were devastating anywhere and could easily break up any heavy combat action on the ground. The pilots themselves always hoped for a chance to inflict massive corporeal damage to a large NVA unit. That is when their sophisticated multi-million dollar flying machines could prove their worth beyond any difference of opinion. These fighter pilots were usually respected in every quarter- especially at an officer's club, where the respect among all brass involved in combat support was mutual.

Ten minutes passed. Every man of the Badger Bravo Company was poised for action. Each soldier strained his eyes and ears and checked his extra ammunition and magazines. Even in an extreme venue such as this, most American men have to be told and even encouraged to perform their personal responsibilities. However, on this night, no encouragement or coaxing was needed. These Bravo soldiers were experienced enough that they could surmise the gravity of this situation.

The NVA leaders had to make a decision. By now, they were also aware that a tactical obstacle was just ahead. It could be an American unit of incomparable firepower, or maybe that string and the sound of men running meant nothing more than maybe a few local VC had been aroused. They did not want to abort their mission without a good enough reason. The point commander led a small probing attack to clear the way or discern the problem. The NVA commanders were well aware of the potential artillery and air support available to their adversaries anywhere in South Vietnam, but tonight, a small probing attack would probably not bring any immediate response. Furthermore, also strategically important, one shouldn't dispel any notion that enemy sympathizers had infiltrated even at the highest American command level and had already transmitted strategic information to the enemy.

Maybe they did not know the exact location of the blocking units, but the NVA commanders were probably aware that such a tactical deployment was in place somewhere in this vicinity. The response to a small unit attack would determine the advisability of continuing in force. The NVA were never in a hurry if conditions were not positive. They could afford patience, and they knew that the Americans were politically impatient. Returning home was not as important to the Vietnamese.

They came stepping steadily but stealthily. About fifty of them, wearing dark uniforms and the traditional pith helmets, moved in small groups through the tall ferns and other dense river foliage about ten meters apart and carried with them the same foreboding anxiety of their waiting American adversaries. The right flank fire team of Sgt. Tiega's platoon saw them first and cut down several at close range. The rest of the defense line, in rapid succession, began to fire short bursts at ominous darting figures and sometimes at just any direction that might need a few bullets. Very few of the enemy fired their own weapons. They dropped to their hands and knees and awaited orders.

In less than thirty seconds, the NVA advance leader realized that the fire intensity of this unit was too great for him to easily force out of his way. A few short blasts from a bamboo whistle signaled a withdrawal. Sgt. Tiega's fervent soldiers stopped firing as quickly as they had started.

The wiredrawn nerves of the grimacing Second Platoon defenders barely allowed for fast but clumsy reloading. Some quaked and some hunched their shoulders as they all braced for another-maybe much greater-assault.

Bravo Six reported the attack as it began. It was his only chance. The upper command echelons had had nothing but this to indicate the NVA location. Be it real or not, they impetuously decided to go for it.

Both sides were concerned about a checkmate. The NVA commanders now had only a couple options left. To go through or around this stubborn, yet undetermined, unit would probably cause forfeiture of the element of surprise and possibly risk disaster. The limited tactical intelligence system of the North Vietnamese left serious gaps of doubt about how much was known about these movements and how much resistance was waiting for them. This night was no different. The indigenous Viet Cong could only help so much and the vast military resources of Saigon weren't very far away.

To hastily return home empty-handed with a supposed good reason might cause this general to "lose face" through the peripheral doubt of his colleagues and superiors. Any amount of explaining would be seen as weakness and incompetence. Their infrastructure was tough. Excuses only satisfied the person who made them. Within minutes of the encounter, the North Vietnamese general had decided to withdraw northwest to an alternative objective, but a well-placed American five hundred pound bomb suddenly moved them forward without decorum. The flight leader immediately radioed Bravo Six directly for target approval. Bravo Six requested more but wanted it closer to the river. Three more times the earth shook and small chunks of mud even fell on a few Bravo soldiers.

When Bravo Six heard bamboo whistles and panic-stricken voices, he asked for a strafing run. The flight leader was elated, but expressed fear of hitting friendlies. Bravo Six responded, "Wait one." He ran over to the Second Platoon line, tore the red lens off his flashlight, aimed it to the sky, and began switching it on and off.

"You see my flashing light?"

"Roger on the flashing light!"

"Strafe about a hundred meters west of that light, and I'll buy you a beer, good buddy!" The sudden furious rushing roar of the F105 Thunderchief fighter jet only about fifty meters over Bravo Six's head spewed thousands of 20mm rounds indiscriminately through mud, foliage, and the flesh of more than a few luckless communist conscripts far from home. Again, the sounds of the harried, escaping enemy made all in the Badger Bravo Company sure that they were on the right side.

Bravo Six's exhilaration was as poignant as that of the pilots. "C'mon! Do it! he demanded. "They're asking for more out there."

He didn't have to ask twice. These pilots were excited about this action. Rarely did they get such an opportunity to ply their skills in actual close combat support with such ferocity.

Bravo Six started his light flashing and again the screeching thunder came. This time two fighters buzzed Bravo Company again to blazon the darkness with streams of red tracers. Warm 20mm bullet casings lightly tapped the ground and the prostrate bodies of some of the spellbound Badger soldiers. One hit Bravo Six, which reminded him of a Korean War veteran musing that a shell casing hitting him was a bullet for the "gooks'. For all them the sound was as soothing as rain on a metal roof during a moment of relaxation. For the enemy, it was a killer hailstorm- - brief, but deadly, indiscriminate and unforgiving. Although surely extensive, the enemy casualties would be unknown even to the NVA general. With practically unlimited human resources, the communists "justified results… no matter what the means.".

Then it was over. The unnerved NVA attackers were in fast retreat while carrying their dead and wounded. They were amazingly resilient, and chasing them would be futile. No matter the situation, they could be as fleeting as wolves in the night.

"This is Bravo Six. You guys are good. I loved it! Have a cold one on me."

"Anytime! Anytime!" the pilot responded. We'll take you up on that. Take care down there."

Bravo Six again reported to Badger Six who was especially happy about no casualties. Because he knew that other "brass" would be listening, Bravo Six also thanked him for the effective response. A little "promo" usually had a way of trickling down in benefits, even from Badger Six.

Suddenly there was nothing but silence, as if it had all been just some exciting downtown movie. . Victories can be complicated. The real soldiers were these young men with small-bore weapons on contrived front lines. As usual, they knew that they had been successful, but they could only suppose the nature of the battle and why it was fought. One might be surprised at the absence of cheering, handshaking, or revelry of any kind. This battle was more for survival than victory. Only a few mumbling comments and varied sounds of relief preceded the checks and cautions of the squad leaders. The NVA could be anywhere or ready to try anything. Even though this fascist general was decisively thwarted in his endeavor to maneuver aggressively against the ARVN and presumably superior Americans, the North Vietnamese Politburo did not send any one-dimensional commanders.

Their chain of command probably was not disrupted enough to cause any panicky movements of fragmented units. Without significant casualties, this scheming general might even continue his present mission.

The rest of the night was quiet. Most Bravo soldiers meditated about their fears, and some of the battle-hardened veterans even slept for an hour or so. However, none of them had to be told to stay on alert.

Upon daylight, Bravo Six swept the frontal area with the Recon Platoon and found no more he expected. They collected a few pieces of insignificant equipment including rifles, pith hats, grenades, small perfume bottles, and pieces of bloody clothing, but no bodies. Even at times of great disadvantage, the North Vietnamese were well-disciplined soldiers and could recover quickly. The U.S. Army G4 intelligence staff would evaluate what had been found and would make educated guesses about the aftermath. Bravo Six would only ever know a little more than his own riflemen would.

At noon, choppers came to take Bravo Company back to the Badger position. After three more days of no further action, the battalion companies returned to their "home" in Hau Nghia province. The NVA had obviously withdrawn to their Cambodian sanctuary.

Before falling asleep that next night, Bravo Six meditated about that NVA encounter. He reconstructed it for the worst. He envisioned too many attackers to shoot. He saw himself unable to help his men or even save his own life. Moreover, that is the way it would have to be. How could he honorably be the only survivor? These young Badger soldiers are his "ship," and he the captain. He'll be there for them and he'll go down with them. Then, of course, he prayed with praise for what didn't happen.

CHAPTER EIGHT

AN IN-HOUSE BATTLE
AT TRANG BANG

Trang Bang village was the largest rural community of any of the tactical areas that the Badger Bravo Company had been assigned. Its lively main street with a lively market row, large Buddhist temple, stockyard, and foodstuff bazaar complemented the many rows of well-constructed homes that also boasted several upper class concrete dwellings with expensive orange ceramic tiled roofs and ornate landscaping. Trang Bang was even assigned a MACV unit and a military district magistrate who enjoyed an impressive office by Vietnamese standards.

This town was also to be world famous for a napalm bombing that was blamed on the Americans. Liberals scored another victory(?) for what was actually misinformation. This author had information that the fight on

June 8, 1972, was all Vietnamese! No Americans were involved and actually almost all had already left the country. A Vietnamese pilot mistakenly directed the napalm bomb at a crowd of civilians running from a Cao Dai temple. At some time all Americans have seen the photo of the severely burned young naked girl pitilessly wandering down a road in horrible pain. It is an iconic picture that will always remind us of needless wartime suffering. At the hallowed Washington D.C. Memorial Wall on Veterans Day, 1996, Jan Scruggs himself stated that it was an American bombing. It's interesting that he is also involved in the related Kim Foundation that collects contributions to help the Trang Bang victims. It's also incredibly interesting that Reverend John Plummer of the Methodist Church claimed on that same day that he was the American who ordered the bombing even though he had been in no position to do so and actually had had no authority to do so. Is this a lie conveniently connected to another lie? If you follow the money trail, the truth may become obvious. Hopefully, it's only conjecture. Let's return to our story.

In the public market of Trang Bang, Bravo Six was amazed to see the open market sale of small dogs and piglets in baskets, plucked live chickens and ducks, colorful peculiar fruits and vegetables, and vendors hawking steaming or grilled exotic victuals that were sometimes unrecognizable and easy to resist. Such was common fare all through Asia. Here, one could sample Banh Trang Phoi Suong, a local dish famous all over South Vietnam. It could be described as a pork noodle soup complete with rice paper and local greens. Bravo Six was skeptical of these unfamiliar victuals and easily preferred Army mess hall fare. However, he sometimes did eat rice and other well-cooked victuals presented at a social gathering .

The great current event was a national election. For president, General Nguyen Van Thieu was running with Nguyen Van Ky as prime minister. The opposition was almost nonexistent. Actually, in Vietnamese politics, if anyone else showed any viable opposition, he would later have to run for his life, maybe even during the campaign. The Viet Cong really didn't want the common people to vote at all. Any facsimile of Western democracy would be at variance with the proposed fascist government.

To alleviate the people's fear of using the ballot boxes, American units were placed near all the polling sites. Bravo Company was bivouacked near Trang Bang. The voting turnout was predicted to be high and hopefully uneventful. That was the job of Bravo Six. He immediately ordered daylight patrols at irregular times throughout the surrounding area to make military presence known to both the local populace as well as the Viet Cong.

Less frequent night patrols were designed to instill 24/7 confidence. Well rehearsed drills to respond to probable enemy disruption made Bravo Six confident that these local Trang Bang voters would cast their ballots in peace. On election day the Viet Cong did not show up anywhere in Hau Nghia Province. President Thieu would continue to serve. His make-believe competition wouldn't have served anyway. This democracy certainly wasn't perfect, but the people actually voted and the success of pacification would eventually bring power to the people. At least, that was the plan and the long range hope.

The success of the election day mission made everyone feel a welcome calm throughout this operation area, but Bravo Six had no inkling that an incident that could have been calamitous to his reputation was about to spontaneously emerge at squad level in the third Platoon. An "in-house" anomaly is impossible to predict and can severely test one's grit and fortitude.

Unlike in some other units, racial relations had not been any kind of problem in Bravo Company. Bravo Six credited that to several Negro and Latino sergeants who were strong leaders. Because they were professional, fair, and constantly considered the welfare of all their men, they were respected and appreciated. Besides that, Bravo Company was busy enough with dangerous combat exercises that taught all the men to be grateful for the close companionship of whomever they could trust beside them. That is not to say that a few individuals did not harbor subdued prejudices about a category of others or even all others different than they. Circumstances and a series of related incidents could possibly precipitate an emotional outburst not limited to a verbal assault.

A strong squad leader learned to notice potential interpersonal difficulties and took action to diffuse the trouble before it progressed to a dangerous physical confrontation. The First Squad of Third Platoon had an ongoing difficulty with the Alpha fire team. PFC Apollo Newsome was a tall muscular light-skinned Negro who exercised a disagreeable attitude about the division of labor and responsibility with his two white and Latino teammates. His size and strength gave him a perceived notion that he should be able to "boss" them. Daily verbal retributions and threats of physical retaliation caused everyone in the Third Platoon to share the discomfort of Platoon Sergeant Laird that this situation could escalate into a serious altercation. With firearms and other combat equipment in the hands of everybody, internal fighting could not be tolerated. The fire team leader tried to discuss the matter with them, but he only aroused the scorn of Apollo Newsome who assumed any criticism toward him was biased. He also then blamed his teammates for "whining to the man" behind his back.

Apollo Newsome, besides exceptionally large and naturally muscled, wasn't particularly bright but had always excelled in athletics and physical skills. Because he fancied himself as the "main man" of Bravo Company and was never challenged, he was resentful that the newly arrived Hector Lobo (nicknamed "Wolf" was being spoken of as "a mean ass to avoid."

Because Apollo made a demeaning remark about Wolf" that brought a sardonic guffaw from those who heard, Apollo felt obligated to demonstrate his preeminence. He approached Wolf and confidently told him to steer clear of him or get his ass kicked. Wolf stood up to him and loudly growled, "Who in a pig's ass do you think you are?"

That brought an "uh-oh" from the onlookers that prompted Apollo to roughly shove him. Wolf didn't fool around with anybody no matter how silly the circumstance. He kicked Apollo in the groin and simultaneously grabbed him in a headlock. His Bowie knife was pressed to Apollo's throat and was already drawing blood. His usual demeanor was such that Apollo could have died then had he not pleaded, "No! No! Let me go! Please! C'mon, man. Please!" Anyone there would understand the fear on Apollo's face.

Apollo escaped with his life and Wolf didn't go back to the stockade, but Apollo had lost his esteem and afterward began to strike out at his fellow soldiers in recompense. He would lash out quickly at any imagined cue. All knew that a "blow-up" was sure to happen.

Bravo Six was not aware of this incident. Such episodes were best handled at the platoon level where they happened. Sgt. Laird kept an eye on Apollo at all times but thought it would be better to only intervene if an altercation erupted that was beyond the control of the squad leader.

To bring his squad into compliance with the Third Platoon's defense plan, the first squad leader ordered his fire teams to dig a three man fox hole. Of course the labor was to be shared evenly, with the men relieving each other at agreed intervals. PFC Ditmeirer, the short, stocky rifleman in the alpha fire team with Apollo Newsome and PFC Fidel Chavez, had been digging for an hour. He was tired and anxious to be relieved by Apollo who wouldn't even need a half hour to finish the "lazy T" shaped fox-hole position. Apollo was with three of his friends from Second Platoon.

When Ditmeirer approached him with the entrench-ing tool, Apollo not only wanted to show his displeasure about being interrupted but also saw a chance to impress his friends by deriding the white boy who was known to be favored by his squad leader and platoon sergeant. "Get that fucking thing away from me and get back in that hole. I'll let you know when you've done enough."

Those words cut deep with Apollo already on shaky ground with his fellow teammates. Ditmeirer was espe-cially annoyed when Apollo struck the tool which sharp-ly hit his knee. He was insulted and embarrassed and noticed the mocking eyes of those who witnessed. He vented his rage by shoving the tool into Apollo's chest and shouting, "You get your big ass over there and do your own work. You ain't my boss!" Apollo reacted vio-lently by shoving Ditmeirer to the ground and then kick-ing his rear as he rose to his feet.

The fight was on. Ditmeirer was a rough character in any ordinary crowd, but he stood no chance of beating the much larger and stronger Apollo. However when en-raged, he wouldn't back down no matter what physical beating he was sure to suffer. The first salvo of punches quickly landed Ditmeirer painfully on his back. He then grabbed the entrenching tool and viciously swung it re-peatedly to hit Apollo wherever he could find an open-ing. Apollo suffered the sting of several sharp blows as he tried in vain to grab the tool. The hoots and howls of the onlookers along with the general noise of such a raucous battle caused Sgt. Laird to come quickly to see what was happening in his platoon. He immediately saw that the extent of this altercation was beyond the ability of the fire team leader and even the squad leader.

Sgt. Laird was not surprised that Apollo was one of the actors in this brutal quarrel. He was also disappointed that he was obviously going to have to discipline two men of different races for fighting. His fellow black men had given him so much pride. They had been good soldiers and were comfortable working with the others of different races. His platoon knew that he should be credited with promoting a sense of teamwork with such a mishmash of men in a challenging situation. Because Apollo was such a recalcitrant, Sgt. Laird was facing a no-win situation. He knew that no course of action would be successful with Apollo. However, he had to diffuse the situation. The only reasonable thing for him to do was to grab Ditmeirer and take the entrenching tool from him. His back would be to Apollo but at least the weapon would be put out of action. Maybe Apollo would be glad to escape that treacherous tool and perhaps the blame for the disruptive fracas. However- *no such luck!*

Apollo grabbed Sgt. Laird by the shoulders and flung him aside to continue his battle with Ditmeier. Laird could only right himself and look about for a suggestive solution. Apollo could easily trounce Ditmeirer now that the entrenching tool was out of play. He would punish this gutsy white boy as a message for all who watched. Ditmeirer did the only thing he could do to stave off the punches. He grabbed Apollo by the waist and fought a hopeless wrestling battle

Sgt. Laird quickly ran to Bravo Six when he saw him approaching the scene. Not much explanation was needed for Bravo Six to understand that he would have to use his authority to stop this dangerous scuffle, especially with Apollo involved. Bravo Six bellowed in his best influential tone, "Hey! Knock it off! Right now! Both of you!" When neither responded to his command, Bravo Six grabbed both by the fatigue shirt sleeve and barked, "Stop right now!" as he pulled to separate them. Ditmeirer relaxed his hold, but Apollo never lessened his aggressiveness. Even with Bravo Six attempting to push him back, Apollo strongly resisted and continued to punch at Ditmeirer.

Bravo Six spoke as roughly as he could, "At ease! Right now! Back off!" Apollo attempted to push Bravo Six aside to get at Ditmeirer. When Bravo Six grabbed Apollo and shouted, "Knock it off, soldier!" Apollo allowed his ruptured temper to carry him into a forbidden self destructive act. He punched Bravo Six hard enough to knock him to the ground.

Because he really didn't want to engage in serious fisticuffs with one of his rank and file soldiers, Bravo Six rose to his feet and told RTO Forney to call for a Military Police arrest squad. Apollo was beside himself with unbridled emotion. He was slobbering, whining, wild-eyed, and frustrated of the unfinished fight with Ditmeirer and an obvious aggressive blunder with his CO that was surely going to land him in the stockade. Because no degree of apology was likely to save him from at least some punishment and his reputation still not yet regained, Apollo foolishly chose to show all thereabout that he could "whoop" his renowned company commander who was nearly as tall but probably fifty pounds lighter in brawny weight.

The only warning of Apollo's charge was an abbreviated shout from RTO Forney, "Look out, Sir!" The warning was cut short as Apollo's sudden bull charge met the unsuspecting CO with a fist to the chest combined with a back slam knocking the wind from Bravo Six. He was barely cognizant enough to quickly roll away from an ensuing kick or crushing body lunge from his attacker. As much as Bravo Six anguished, he was going to have to defend himself from this crazed brute. Apollo successfully landed on Bravo Six in a sitting position and began pummeling him with his fists. Because Apollo was high on his chest and Bravo Six was now clear-minded enough to respond, the frantic CO was able to use his arms to force Apollo over his head and roll away to escape, but the fight was now inescapable.

Apollo again quickly charged with his right fist raised. This time Bravo Six was ready with a counter action. He feinted a fearful deference and then readied his counterpunch at the last second. With his weight shifted to his left foot, he stepped forward to unleash his best "straight right" with all the power he could muster. The timing, aim, and force of the CO's fist met Apollo's clumsy rush and staggered him with a smashing whack on his nose. Apollo wobbled in shock and pain but immediately continued his ungainly assault. His violent course of action left no room to suspend anything. He must win to at least salvage his street-level honor.

Bravo Six surmised that the onlookers appeared to be more interested in "looking on" than stopping this unlikely and obviously interesting brawl. Not that he had much choice, but he decided to throw himself headlong into a nasty scuffle that was likely to get him physically hurt, in trouble with his superiors, and probably both. The two enraged combatants stood toe-to-toe and punched each other at every opening.

The scant minute that they exchanged punches seemed to be an hours to Bravo Six. He was getting the worst of it. He attempted to gain advantage with several hard body punches but Apollo wasn't showing any distress. Although both had landed some good shots, Bravo Six knew that he couldn't last much longer and was certain to lose.

As if providence was aware that Apollo would be an undeserving and doubtful winner and Bravo Six would be satisfied to discontinue this ridiculous altercation, Apollo back stepped over the edge of the nearby canal embankment. His fear of water caused him to grab Bravo Six for support which caused both to tumble into the murky four feet deep channel. Bravo Six immediately realized that

Apollo was panicky as he thrashed his arms, breathed in gasps, and stumbled for balance on the muddy bottom. Apollo's response to a crashing blow to his forehead was only to duck his head to avert another punch.

Bravo Six quickly used this opportune advantage. He grabbed Apollo's tousled "fro" and used both hands to shove Apollo's head underwater. Because Apollo lost his footing in the mud, Bravo Six was able to use his upper body weight to hold Apollo underwater long enough to cause Apollo to shudder in fright. As Apollo's head was allowed to break free of the water, Bravo Six unleashed the hardest punches he could still muster to Apollo's agonized face. Again he went under briefly as he was caused to fall back. Bravo Six had a punch ready, but this time the panic-stricken and demoralized Apollo held up his arms and pleaded "No more. Please! No more!"

It was over. Bravo Six waded to the bank where several of the wide-eyed soldiers reached to pull him to dry ground. Although he heard many voices expressing delight with this outcome, Bravo Six only recognized the raspy voice of Rahskle who had rushed to "cover" his captain's perilous predicament.

Rahskle only viewed situations in his own personal perspective. He had previously considered testing his mettle against Apollo, but was glad that his commander that he regarded so highly was able to "whoop the ass" of this big mouth bully. "You done good, Captain! Damned good!"

Apollo pulled himself out of the canal and lay on his

stomach with his arms over his head. He appeared to be crying but he wasn't. No amount of bravado or jive jargon was going to mask the torment he was suffering. He had nothing left. Not only was he sure that he was going to the stockade, but his reputation was beyond repair. Again he got his butt kicked when he was the aggressor. He lay in subservient disgrace and wished to be anywhere else. The redoubtable bodyguard, Rashkle, knowingly stared at him.

Bravo Six was bruised and bleeding about his face but wasn't seriously injured. After he doused his face with water, the medics applied a butterfly patch and a couple Band-Aids to his face. Other than an obviously bruised rib as indicated by the already discolored skin and a bloody scraped ear, his hands were sore and already swelling from the shock of his own punches. An offer of assistance from a medic to Apollo brought only a scowl and a wave of his arm to get away. He was bleeding profusely from his nose and mouth but would otherwise feel fine the next day, save for a couple knots on his head and an obvious contusion on his right cheek.

Bravo Six wanted to minimize the after effects of this anomaly in military discipline. A serious rough and tumble fist fight between a company commander and one of his squad soldiers was a travesty of institutional rapport. If not handled wisely, it would become a news item to travel quickly from company to company in every echelon of every command throughout War Zone C. As with every story passed on by mouth, it would be callously edited to the detriment of Bravo Six. Nobody would know anything but the version that they preferred. This was the gut wrenching low point of Capt. Smithe's career. His next move had to forestall any "negative spin".

He thought of it first, but here they came. His platoon sergeants were admittedly a strong reason for Bravo Company's success. Subsequently, they were a strong reason for his own success. All three, Sgt. Mueller, Sgt. Laird, and Sgt. Tiega, were professionally superior and functionally dependable to the extent that no one needed to ever supervise or evaluate their decisions or performance. They could "talk" to Bravo Six. The three of them could discuss an issue completely outside the bounds of deference or resentment.

The old sage Sgt. Mueller took the lead. "Sir, we want to handle this whole thing within the company. It would be better for us and you." Bravo Six was pleased to hear a suggestion that this volatile situation could be handled "in house." He responded with a tone of respect and regard. "How will that work"?

Sgt. Tiega explained, "Apollo has just lost everything. Being a soldier was the best thing he ever had in his life. His attitude was misguided in his attempt to find a social place for himself. He has had his ass kicked a couple times now and has nothing left. He has nowhere to go and the stockade won't do him or anyone else any good. We think that he needs us more than anything right now and he knows it. Let us talk to him. When he starts to 'soldier', it will be good for him, and us, and for you. Okay?"

Bravo Six was impressed but not really surprised that these three denizens of dangerous circumstances were offering yet another course of action that could brilliantly succeed or conversely cause organizational disaster. If the denouement proved negative, they knew that they would suffer as well as Bravo Six, but they also had confidence that, as always, their own determination and capability would force a desired outcome.

Bravo Six spoke with as much faith as he could project. 'Okay. Take over. He's yours. I admire your nerve and your faith in humanity and yourselves. I would trust you three with any task. Good luck with this guy."

Tiega and Mueller motioned for Laird to come with them for discussion. Even in combat, it was rare for three top NCOs to have such a strong relationship when working together.

Bravo Six thought, "What the hell! It might work, and it's better than anything else I have right now." He still wasn't forgetting Apollo and the canal.. Right now he could be hurting much worse, both physically and socially.

Providence now handed him a coincidence that would need a blessing as well as luck. RTO Forney received a radio message that Bravo Six was to attend a command staff briefing at 0700 hours. As bad as he now looked, he knew that tomorrow morning he would probably look a little worse. All eyes would be fixed on him and the room would be buzzing with speculation and guesswork. He would be "up front' with the questions, but would tell no more than needed. Col. Langham, was sure to query him and would expect an inclusive explanation.

He was right. His facial contusions had matured with the expected swelling and discoloration. His left eye was nearly shut with only a dime-sized brightly bloodshot opening near his nose , and the scrape on his right ear was exaggerated with a weeping scab. He was the focal point of the room. Few were daring enough to query him directly, but all were wondering who or what could have severely mauled the ballyhooed Bravo Six. He would have been much less self-conscious with a bullet wound. No reference was made by the stately Wolverine Six. As always, he reviewed the command situation with the circumstances, explained what was expected of the major units, and allowed a couple questions. He then made a sharp exit as sudden and dignified as his entry. One had to rise to attention quickly to honor him.

Col. Langham called Bravo Six aside to get the story. Surprisingly, he motioned Badger Six away when he moved to join them. Col. Langham often liked his information from the bottom to top. After Bravo Six explained with no reservations, Langham advised a court-martial. Bravo Six then appealed for resolution within his company. He wanted to give his platoon leaders a chance.

"Sir, I'm looking for a win-win resolution. I won the fight, but it can also be a win for that soldier and the morale of the company. Let's let those sergeants go through their paces. I believe in their experience and expertise with these matters. There's nothing hurting me that won't heal quickly, and within a couple days my company will heal."

With that familiar omnipotent expression he again backed his idealistic young commander. "Okay. Let me know how it works out. I'll talk to Badger Six. Good luck!"

Bravo Six was glad for that development. He went straight to Sgt. Mueller to give him the go ahead. It was already done. Apollo was told that he was being given a chance to escape the stockade. They added that stockade time was considered "bad time" and would be added to his time in the war. Apollo didn't have to be convinced that the stockade was no picnic. He said that he didn't want to go and would accept their terms.

He had to apologize to Ditmeirer, Sgt. Laird, and to Capt. Smithe. From that point on he would "soldier." Everybody would cooperate with him because they really did want this huge man on their side. If Apollo relapsed, Bravo Six would bring charges against him. The fact that he had been given a chance but failed would work against him. The three profoundly dour sergeants also added in harsh earthy language that Apollo would be facing their full fury if he let them down. He believed them. From that point on, his demeanor and "people skills" dramatically improved. Bravo Six was pleased and relieved that Col. Langham had obliged his request. Reggie Trainor was right. Bravo Six kept falling into onion patches and emerging smelling like a rose.

Several evenings later he lay awake and marveled at how fortunate he was to profit from such a perilous, career threatening situation. Badger Six and the antagonistic Major Domsavich only looked without expression at his injuries but not actually at his face and never mentioned or questioned the whole affair. The story must have circulated in a manner favorable to him because other officers often congratulated him on sight in various informal manners without soliciting an explanation. Within Bravo Company the affair wasn't talked about and normal combat business returned. The only injury to Bravo Six that refused to go away quickly was a buttonhole in his upper lip caused by a punch to his teeth. Was it good to have your "clock cleaned" now and then? Probably, but don't plan for it, he thought.

Bravo Six knew that Reggie Trainor would be eager for a complete narrative and he actually was anxious for his visit. "Okay, let's have it. How did you fall into the outhouse and come out like a petunia again?" Of course, Reggie liked the story and wished that he could have seen it. When Reggie said, "Okay, you done good", Bravo Six felt proud of those words, coming from his best friend. That night Bravo Six prayed in gratitude for his fortunes and asked for strength to continue. This war wouldn't be over any time soon.

CHAPTER NINE

AMBUSHED BUT VICTORIOUS

O ld dogs, children, and drunks, and, sometimes, American soldiers can foolishly stumble and accidentally roll the right way-something like that. Such was this tactical drama enacted often, as in probably every war. A tiny defunct village named Song Trang Chu lay on the west bank of the historically navigated Vam Co Dong River in battle weary Hau Nghia Province. This hamlet's only historical fame reflected its location within the broad end of the infamous Ho Chi Minh Trail. It was the suspected transit home of a well-equipped Viet Cong light infantry company that could strike vulnerable targets anywhere east within a ten kilometer radius and then scurry back to hide across the Cambodian border.

The Wolverine 2nd Brigade intelligence officer had surmised this place to probably be a discreet guerrilla rally point and supply cache. Any civilians there were actually living in a tactical "free-fire zone" as designated by MACV and ARVN. The Badger Battalion was ordered to probe the area and initiate a "search and destroy" mission. At 1430 hours helicopter squadrons deployed both Alpha and Charlie companies about a half-kilometer west of the river. Because they met immediate resistance, the best they could do was to consolidate their platoons and find adequate cover. By happenstance they had landed in the enemy's main travel route to Cambodia. The treacherous light weapon fire spewed from several outpost units that were probably also close to panic.

Much to his dismay, the career ambitious but unpredictable Badger Battalion commander was caught on the ground with Alpha Company. He preferred to circle a battle scene in a helicopter while barking threatening commands to the already harried company commanders. Rarely did he first let them go through their paces and then execute his own job of determining which tactical option was best to guide the mission. Nevertheless, his unpopular tactics had usually been unexpectedly successful and hard to challenge.

The Badger Battalion had already run several "touch and go" sorties on the west side of the Vam Co Dong that morning with negligible results. Now, as both companies landed, expecting another routine check of terrain, they found themselves fully engaged and "pinned down" in the tactical snare of the patient VC who had planned their trap all the way back to "leaking" the information about their operations in this area. Because of their haste to get things done, high-ranking American commanders were easily duped by the militarily unsophisticated but tactically expert Viet Cong guerrillas.

The incoming barrage was heavy and steady enough that Alpha and Charlie companies could do little more than return light fire and try to jointly consolidate their position. This, of course, was not the crux of the sinister Viet Cong plan. Bravo Company was in reserve on "ready alert" at an abandoned Japanese airstrip because they had been literally up all night on a high priority ambush mission that yielded nothing. Even that was part of the enemy's overall plan. It was 1430 hours when Badger Six called for the ten helicopter "Hornet" attack squadron to transport Bravo Company to the battle area to relieve the beleaguered Alpha and Charlie companies. What appeared to be a logical reaction to an American tactical snafu was the final piece of the VC tactical puzzle that would hopefully culminate in the destruction of an American infantry company.

Bravo Six was battle savvy and experienced enough as a Badger officer to know that his company was going to a "hot landing zone." He had been listening to the unit radio and knew that Badger Six had been suckered into the enemy's trap. The "coup de grace" would come as surprise annihilation of an unsuspecting relief force (Him!). The Viet Cong were masters of long range tactics and had the patience to complement it. The bulk of their force and their best fighters would be waiting in ambush at a predetermined landing spot that would look like a natural place to deploy. From camouflaged concrete bunkers and profoundly discreet slit trenches cut into the currently overgrown rice paddy between the chosen LZ and the river, they could immediately overwhelm the sixty American soldiers with devastating firepower and severely disable the helicopter squadron that would hardly have a chance to get airborne again. The American soldiers would be at a disadvantage just getting off the choppers in an unfamiliar place.

Since Bravo Six didn't really know where he was going, he had allowed the squadron commander to pick an LZ. Of course that adroit but anxious pilot chose the small open field very near to the river, which would place Bravo Company only about a half kilometer east of the other companies. Normally that would be an expedient choice, but as they approached the area, Bravo Six worried about the brushy plot next to the river and to the immediate north that was also dotted with the dozen houses of Song Trang Chu hamlet.

He made a gutsy but expeditious decision, just as he had never been afraid to do before. He ordered the squadron commander to land in the overgrown rice paddy beside the river. It could possibly have been tactically disastrous, but he wanted his men to have ready cover should they be engaged. Thus, the enemy plan was luckily disrupted. Instead of this relief unit landing where the waiting ambush would be a combat picnic for the VC, the victims of their own devilry would instead have to escape a face-to-face confrontation with these comparatively huge Americans.

By happenstance, Bravo Company had actually landed atop the Viet Cong position. Sixty soldiers of perhaps the most experienced heliborne infantry company in the 25th Infantry Division had leaped from their helicopters to immediately engage in close quarter fighting with almost equal a number of confused and startled guerillas. As the panicky VC were exiting the camouflaged concrete bunkers, the frenzied Americans were assaulting them with gun butts, kicks, and anything else that would gain a life-saving advantage. Only a few guerillas were shot. The enemy only wanted to escape and the Americans only wanted to avoid shooting each other.

Hand-to-hand fighting was almost unheard of in the Vietnam War. Moreover, it is actually rare in any modern warfare. Instructions to prepare for that sort of frantic fighting, yelling, and running to gain an advantage would never be found in any military training manual. No orders could be given (or understood anyway) by either side. The free-for-all lasted less than a minute but seemed a much longer time for those who were there.

The physical size and unexpected aggressiveness of the Americans caused the outclassed Viet Cong to break contact and bolt to the cover of the wooded hamlet. Only a few returned gunfire. Sgt. Tiega of Second Platoon called to Bravo Six that some VC were holding bare-chested women behind them as they escaped. The answer of Bravo Six and several willing riflemen quickly put an end to the VC supposition that their overt coward-ice would help them. Several of those sacrificial women found later were dressed in black pajama uniforms and laden with backpacks. Their shirts had been ripped open in the desperate attempt to identify their gender and thwart American fire.

The ten helicopters lifted off but not without damage. Most had taken hits and two didn't go far before losing power. Fortunately, those were able to set down across the river. A crew chief and a co-pilot had been wounded.

The squadron command airship suffered a nerve-shattering experience. During the melee, one coura-geous VC, armed only with a hand grenade, had jumped aboard the Bravo command helicopter as it struggled to lift off. He obviously intended to toss the grenade into the cockpit and probably would have succeeded in de-stroying the aircraft and possibly himself (He probably thought that would please Buddha). However, in the confusing frenzy of disembarking, the Bravo Company platoon RTO hadn't yet disembarked and grabbed the ambitious VC to become the hero of one of the most un-usual war stories of the whole theater of operations. To abridge the danger, the terrified pilots broke away from the squadron and flew top speed straight for the Bam Nam base.

The brash RTO was slightly larger than the guerrilla but was physically hampered by the radio backpack. However, he did manage to violently throw his fierce foe on his back. And, because the viciously writhing VC was still armed and very strong, the RTO first planned to force him out the open door. Probably sensing his hated adversary's intention, the desperate guerrilla quickly altered his resistance to include tightly gripping with his arms and legs while savagely biting and head butting. All the while the RTO had to keep that grenade in mind should this VC decide to end everything for them all. Thus the outlandish struggle continued while the pilots radioed their base, forced the helicopter to shudder at maximum speed, and repeatedly twisted their necks to view the battle behind them that held their fate.

Upon landing at Ban Nam, waiting MPs in riot gear very quickly disarmed the VC and handcuffed him. That heroic RTO was treated for minor injuries and nervous exhaustion. He was later awarded the Bronze Star Medal for his gallantry. He also was heard saying that his high school wrestling skills had been decidedly helpful.

That wiry young man had wrestled all through his school years. Although he had always complemented his talent with resolute practice and staid determination, the competition in his famed Iowa athletic region was always more than he could overcome to gain a championship for himself. The honor that had eluded him remained an ever-present burr in his psyche.

In considering the circumstances of this all-or-nothing personal battle with a redoubtable enemy campaigner of the war on freedom, he was contemplating how close he was to death with failure but even more how honored he was with victory that saved four crew members of a UH1B helicopter. This Bronze Star Medal for valor was going to mean more to his life than any trophy of any level of competition. That night he prayed that he might be deserving of his fortunate consequence and that Bravo Company would survive the denouement of the Song Trang Chu crisis.

At the battle scene, Bravo Six was running about to organize his badly disarranged and frightened assault force. He very quickly organized his three platoons in a square three-sided position with the river on the eastern side. Sgt. Laird's hard-core Third Platoon guarded the strategic north side toward the hamlet. Second Platoon with the command group secured the west flank with First Platoon protecting the south side. Now an attack would get Bravo Company's "A game." Once organized, Bravo Six had little fear of his unit being overrun. Even these fiendish guerrillas wouldn't be willing to suffer the required casualties to penetrate this skirmish line of veteran defenders.

The foot high levee bordering all three sides afforded excellent cover. Actually, the escaping VC had joined the awaiting assault force to overrun this relief company had they been overwhelmed as previously planned. Now both sides were faced with a dangerous dilemma.

Two dead and four wounded Bravo soldiers had to be evacuated. Two Third Platoon squad leaders were missing and presumed dead. Forty-five minutes passed before a "dust-off" (MedEvac helicopter) could be landed and protected by cover fire. By then, one of the wounded had died and another man in Second Platoon was hit in the leg.

The dust-off safely left and Bravo Six braced for the impending action that was sure to happen. All could sense that the VC campaigners weren't finished for the day.

Badger Six was still with Alpha Company that had consolidated with Charlie Company. Seeking to consolidate all his forces for their safety and his ease of command, Badger Six radioed Bravo Six to link with the rest of the battalion to form a defensive posture for the night. Even with three hours of daylight remaining, Bravo Six asserted his preference to stay put rather than run a gauntlet of gunfire over open terrain. Of course he lost the argument.

At the insistence of Badger Six, Bravo Six ordered his platoons to begin crawling across the weedy terrain as Badger Six had suggested. Of course the enemy spotted them immediately and the rapid firing caused three more casualties. One of those was a very dedicated and popular medic who had tried to get to the first man wounded. In his haste to aid his fellow soldier, he had probably crawled a little too high because he took a bullet through his butt cheek. The loss of this particular medic was difficult for his fellow soldiers because Rupert Byers was a soldier that anyone could come to for moral support. They had lost more than just a medic. His popularity was rooted in his ability to take care of both physical and emotional needs. He later healed and returned to his unit, but this would not be the last Purple Heart Medal for this God fearing courageous soldier.

The platoons had moved fifty meters when Bravo Six radioed a brief but terse message to Badger Six that he was staying put and could defend himself for the night. After a brief silence, Badger Six answered "Roger." He had wanted tactical protection for all his companies. This obstinate company commander who had often raised his ire was now even countermanding his authority! However, could a severe Bravo Company defeat now overshadow the self-imposed tactical quandary of the harried Badger Six? Nonetheless, Badger Six had to admit to himself that Bravo Company was an integral part of his command and his career. He knew that obstinate young company commander had little respect for him, but he took solace in feeling that Bravo Six was the only one. The end of that story may be fast approaching.

The VC were now firing through small portholes from inside several two-foot- high dike locations around the hamlet. Russian AK 47's, American BARs, and various carbines were aligned in cross fires about knee high. The Bravo Company soldiers, now over the initial shock of the engagement and under fire, were hastily preparing their personal defensive positions. The remaining medics treated several for superficial shrapnel wounds, including Bravo Six who had just picked a nickel-sized, fiery-hot chunk of metal from his right thigh. Then suddenly, all rifle fire and the B-40's ceased. Were the VC commanders ready for their next move to salvage a victory before evacuating the area?

With daylight soon gone, Bravo Six was crawling to visit the remaining fretful fifty-one men of his beleaguered command. These frightened soldiers who all received at least an assuring pat understood the unspoken encouragement. He instructed the platoon leaders to have everybody loosen his boots. If overrun, they could kick them off, swim the river, and wend their way toward the lights of Bam Nam. He knew that probably none of them would make it, including himself. The Vam Co Dong River was much too wide, too deep, and too unforgiving for exhausted and terrified soldiers. At least, it was a plan, however unrealistic. No other options could be surmised.

Bravo Six was again on the radio paying lip service to Badger Six and listening to things that he already knew when the expected assault began. Badger Six interrupted his own sentence to exclaim that his position was being hit with rocket and mortar fire. He was savvy enough to realize what was happening. His tone mellowed as he warned, "Get ready. They're probably coming for you!" He even sounded somewhat sympathetic.

Even as Bravo Six replied "Roger. Wilco," the north side of his perimeter began receiving very heavy small arms fire, along with B-40 rocket, and 40-millimeter mortar fire. The VC would want the Americans to keep their heads down and not be willing to return enough fire to hamper their advance. Sgt. Laird allowed only light return fire because his frightened soldiers couldn't clearly see the enemy and their ammunition supply would soon become critical.

Realizing that the enemy advance was methodically getting closer, Bravo Six surmised that the enemy may be pressuring him to move his company farther downstream. A VC assault typically came fast from all sides. A base of fire on one side and an assault on another was not their style And, why were they so intent on keeping his company separated from the other companies? They may think that they could overrun him if he were forced into a less advantageous position.

The enemy fire was steadily advancing on that north side and showed no sign of subsiding. The Bravo soldiers continually wriggled to flatten their bodies in the damp turf as they heard and saw bullets tearing through the top of their small protective earthen dike. Bravo Six could see that only the steadfast bravado of his young infantrymen was saving his position from collapse. Even as some beside them were crying out from wounds, these mostly teenage boys held their places and returned fire the best they could. Sgt. Mylar's squad was receiving the brunt of the action but never faltered. Even the VC must have heard a couple of them yelling, "Fire. Shoot." Four riflemen from First Platoon made a gutsy run to reinforce the desperate north side defenders.

Bravo Six was determined to defend this square quarter acre of riverfront estate. It was now priceless to the lives of his small command and obviously also important to the Viet Cong guerillas. He crawled close behind Third Platoon, and to force a break in the action, he ordered that they all start throwing grenades.

These unexpected explosions practically in the face of the VC stymied their advance and saved a few rounds of ammunition.

Again, the assault stopped as suddenly as it started. A frontal attack against these doggedly determined Americans was proving too costly to gain them any advantage. The break didn't come too soon.

The sergeants passed out what ammunition remained. They also took some from those who were out of the action and received a few magazines from the First and Second Platoons. All in the company knew that they needed each other to win the day- or they would die. Captain Smithe was well aware that the courage and resolve of many of his soldiers in the second and third platoons were the real reason that his company position was not overrun.

The young American soldiers who bore the brunt of this and the previous ferocious action of the day were unnerved to the point of mild shaking, but none showed any sign of losing their resolve. Miraculously, those hit during this assault had suffered only superficial wounds. No more "dust-offs" would be able to come anyway. Now the shadowy dusk was challenging the tactics of both sides. Bravo Six radioed his situation to Badger Six and apologized for cutting him off as he demanded information during the attack.

Badger Six then suggested that command headquarters be briefed on a need for "Spooky" (the Air Force air-to-ground aircraft that could deliver rapid fire support all night). What the Hell! Bravo Six thought. He just might get this marvelous weapon popularly dubbed "Puff the Magic Dragon". Spooky(it's radio call sign) always defines the seriousness of any situation. Why should Bravo Six believe that Badger Six would have completely informed him of everything?

As the night loomed, Sgt. Laird crawled to talk to Bravo Six. He knew that his big captain always at least listened to his comments and requests. With subdued emotion, he explained that he wanted to look for the bodies of his two missing squad leaders who had inexplicably charged toward the enemy. Laird was a short, black, non-descript, but very competent and conscientious young sergeant who wanted to find (probably the dead bodies) of those two white squad leaders who had become very special in his life. Because Sgt. Laird had been so loyal, Bravo Six told him to go if he must, but also warned that he couldn't come to rescue him or even alter his defensive plans to help him. (You'd have to know Capt. Smithe and Sgt. Laird to understand why that request was allowed in this extreme venue.)

Laird removed his shirt, tied his neckerchief around his forehead, and entered the hell-laden darkness. Never doubting his cause, he crawled to where his young squad sergeants would likely be lying. Both those brave soldiers were "acting jacks". They were corporals in official rank, but were doing the job of squad sergeants without official promotion as yet. They could wear the rank insignia because they had demonstrated all the necessary responsibility, expertise, and leadership abilities.

Sgt. Laird was an exceptional platoon leader who was always shorter that any of his men, but was probably a better father than most of them ever had. He constantly monitored their weapons, their performance, and even their personal hygiene. He cared enough to advise them on anything, and would even help them write to their families.

Laird was very glad to have Bravo Six as his company commander. And Capt. Smithe knew that Laird couldn't work well with a second lieutenant nor did he even need one. Of two emotionally fragile lieutenants previously assigned to Bravo Company, neither lasted longer than three weeks. One, a nemesis of Sgt. Laird, was reassigned after twice lying to cover his incompetence. Laird knew that Capt. Smithe wouldn't assign him another one. There was almost no chance of a second lieutenant appearing who could keep his mouth shut long enough to gain experience in handling a platoon before assuming leadership.

Laird crawled, slowly and silently, and was amazed that he was not afraid. He felt that he couldn't be killed because of his unselfish quest. He had made good soldiers and good leaders of those two boys who had trusted him. He just couldn't leave their status unknown. Stripped to his waist, he carried only a knife and Bravo Six's 45 cal. pistol. His muddied ebony skin was at least as good as any camouflage material as he slithered through the wet weeds.

After thirty meters he spotted a supine body on the matted grass with the face silhouetted against the dim sky. It was Sgt. Beard. His close friend Sgt. Roye lay nearby. They were on their backs from being searched. Their weapons and ammunition were gone. Their dog tags were also missing-a VC souvenir item.

Satisfied that both were definitely dead, Ward's mind first wavered between remorse and consideration of protecting the bodies. He was not afraid but intrinsically knew that he should get back to his platoon. They would need him if anything else happened. Besides, if the fighting again broke out, he would be in the line of fire of his own platoon.

Then, three meters away, a phantom-like human rose to his knees to adjust some sort of equipment. Ward felt the electricity of shock and fear as his stomach rolled inward and his facial muscles tightened. Next he heard a voice whisper, "Phai am lang" (Be very quiet) as more human forms rose to their knees and began moving southward. His mind screamed, "My God! I have actually joined the Viet Cong!"

Being so small, dark-skinned, and without a shirt, any who looked his way must not have suspected him. Ward's mind raced desperately through alternatives, but only after about ten seconds, a hand lightly shoved his shoulder. A guerilla leader, trying to get his frightened unit moving, thus caused Laird to involuntarily do what he hadn't considered and certainly wouldn't have done on his own. With the darkness as his only ally, he calmly half rose to his knees and began sneaking away in the company of his enemies.

As Laird fought to control his terror, he crawled as rhythmically as they did without any attention. He knew that his only hope was to wend his way to the outside left and rear of the group and then somehow break away. He estimated twenty guerrillas in this group, but where were the others? Any moment, one might ask him a question or order him to do something.

If discovered, he would make a dash toward the river, but the sounds would cause the Bravo soldiers to open fire. As if he had any choice, he forced his mind and body to continue with the reckless masquerade and even felt an alternate sensation of enjoying this brush with surreal misfortune.

Finally after about seventy-five meters, he slowly lowered his chest to the ground and lay motionless. The beguiled VC guerrillas disappeared into the night without their phantom compatriot. He had played this scene better than any Hollywood actor could have. A kitchen cockroach would have congratulated him.

Laird had eluded his unwitting captors, but had become a prisoner of his anonymity. He estimated that his location put him in danger of being shot by the Bravo second platoon soldiers. He probably wouldn't find Beard and Roye again and could even encounter more Viet Cong. Laird knew that he had no alternative but to lie very still until daybreak. Never had he ever thought so clearly. All his life, he had been too small, too dumb, and too poor.

As much as he had always been humiliated by all others in Haut Bois (locally called "Hot Boy") Mississippi, he was even lonelier now. After he had volunteered and arrived in Vietnam as a PFC, he served three tours of duty and was promoted four times. No one refers to him as "Pee Wee" anymore, and he is well known as one of the best at his job.

It wasn't that he was homesick for the black neighborhood of Haut Bois. For the first sixteen years of his life, he hated the nickname "Pee Wee" but it seemed to fit him as a runt.. His three older brothers were taller than average and even his sister, a year younger than he, was a little taller. All the residents of his hometown were black and poor, but none lived poorer that Rosie Laird and her children. Their three-room row house had never had plumbing and was wired for only one light fixture and one outlet. Pee Wee shared a bedroom with his three brothers and slept on an old smelly single mattress on the floor.

Many of Rosie's neighbors had little more, but they did their best to keep their children clean and in school. Rosie, however, kept nothing clean, including herself. She rarely prepared a hot meal for her children and cared little about anything except the old television given to her by a "friend" in lieu of the usual fee for her personal affection. The TV reception afforded only one channel clear enough to enjoy. The TV society they viewed appeared as a different world. Was everybody rich out there? Even the black persons on the programs were unreal.

None of Pee Wee's siblings ever improved their lot in life, but he was always different. He used to stare at the beautiful social worker and wonder about her home. He admired his school teachers and wished that he could do better for them. He especially liked his sixth grade teacher who coached several sports. Mr. Kovich saw something in Pee Wee. He made him an athletic assistant so he could shower at the high school. Several times he gave Pee Wee a "leftover" team T-shirt and some clothing from his children. He trusted Pee Wee with all his keys and talked to him about responsibility and staying in school to improve himself. The athletic bus trips were his best entertainment. All the team trusted him with their wallets, watches and other valuables.

Rosie died when he was fourteen. He and his sister were the only ones still at home. They both cried when the social worker took them to a far away orphanage. Now he lived cleaner and ate better, but the new school was very impersonal. He wasn't athletic enough for any sports and couldn't make any better than a "C" in any of his classes. As he was constantly insulted in Haut Bois;, now he was mostly ignored and very lonely. To his dismay, his sister had immediately told everyone to call him "Pee Wee" He'll never forget the local U.S. Army recruiter who arranged for him to "join up" on his sixteenth birthday. He told him that some of the most important men in history were no taller. If he worked hard, the promotions would come fast. He would be "Sergeant Laird" and be saluted.

That was 1964. Sgt. Laird was now serving his third year in Vietnam, and he is not "Pee Wee" anymore. Well known to be one of the neatest and best at his job as an infantry platoon sergeant is an honor known to only a few.. That's why he was not panicky while alone in the weeds of Song Trang Chu. His platoon was only a little over a hundred meters away. Come daylight, he would be home.

Before Laird left, with about an hour and a half of twilight remaining, Bravo Six had been interrupted by a familiar voice as he was again reporting to Badger Six. His helicopter gunship pilot friend, Rand Kniter, was on the way and wanted instructions. He had been off duty and lounging with other pilots at their tiny officer's club. When he heard on the radio scanner that his close friend, Capt. Smithe, was in bad trouble, he also heard that artillery support was out of range and all aircraft were waved off. Kniter was well liked and respected as a pilot. When he began talking of what he should do, instead of laughing and daring him, the others warned him about authorization. They also knew his mettle and that Capt. Kniter would not hesitate to rescue one of them.

Kniter sat silently for several minutes, stewing within an aura of anxiety. He suddenly added a shot to his half empty beer, drained the bottle with one continuous gulp, and slammed it down hard enough to dent the bar. He sharply pointed with both hands at his friends and made an angry prediction, "You're going to hear me on that radio! I don't give a damn!" As he left, the silence was pregnant with veneration and self-reproach.

Kniter ran to the maintenance pads and lifted off a high-tech fighting machine that he had learned to master and love as part of himself. Foolhardy or not, he was throwing himself into his big friend's fight. Besides, this was probably the battle that he had long awaited. He meant to get into the middle of all this romantic excitement. Bravo Six would not run the gauntlet of fame without him.

As Kniter approached the battle scene, he announced himself on the Bravo radio frequency without getting clearance through the Badger frequency, or for even being there at all. Badger Six monitored everything but only took notes for future use.

"Bravo Six, this is Stinger Alpha. Where are they, Buddy?"

"Stinger Alpha, thanks for coming, but it's too hot for even your gunship. How about just observing for me?"

"Bullshit! I'm going to blow their asses off!"

Bravo Six already knew what must be in front of Third Platoon. Kniter might discover what lay waiting in front of the first and second platoons.

"Friendly cherry smoke out (the enemy might know and duplicate red). Recon by fire that wooded strip to my southwest. Fly high! Fly high!"

Kniter came at full speed and angled sharply downward. As he crossed the river he fired four rockets. As they exploded, he saw several VC scurry for cover. Instead of veering off and reporting, he continued at treetop level with his rapid fire machine guns cutting through almost a hundred meters of small trees, heavy brush, and about a hundred well-armed guerrillas.

These weren't the poorly trained NVA conscripts from the North, who, when surprised by aircraft, would scatter or half-heartedly return token fire. Most seasoned Viet Cong would fight viciously in any situation and were used to doing it in the face of overwhelming opposition.

As Stinger Alpha released the full fury of his raging gunship, he could see a couple scores of guerrillas. No less courageous, they rose to fire into the face of his assault and even after he passed.

No doubt Kniter caused a significant number of casualties; he had even seen some go down. But, he would not make another run that day. Although the VC didn't know, Stinger Alpha was steadily losing power and could fly only about a half kilometer to land before his engine completely stopped. He was rescued almost immediately and a recovery helicopter then later brought back his gunship.

The Stinger gunship was afterward a big attraction for a few days before it was scrapped. Kniter miraculously was not wounded, but one could scarcely find a square meter anywhere on that aircraft without bullet damage. All the glass was gone, along with the fuel and oil. He had named it the "Widow Maker". It had been just that, but Rand Kniter still was. Reggie Trainor used to say that the VC had the balls of a brass monkey. Another pilot joked that Kniter must have found all the brass monkeys out there. Some opined that they would have been with him, but they knew that was only in spirit.

After arriving back at Bam Nam, Kniter ran back to his friends at the officers club that he had left only forty-five minutes ago. Listening to the scanner still, wildly anxious friends greeted him with cheers and supportive questions. Stinger Alpha was an instant celebrity and loved it. Now he sat with a beer to savor his freshly kindled popularity among those who wished that they could have done the same.

Kniter and his friends continued to monitor the scanner. The worst of the Song Trang Chu battle was maybe yet to come. They would be up very late.

The looming darkness, as usual, was on the side of this bold enemy. American helicopter assault troops usually carry only a few grenades and all needed rifle ammunition. The VC would probably be crawling close enough to throw their own grenades over the small defensive dike. Bravo Six knew that he had better take a chance. He requested to speak directly to the S-4 supply officer back at Bam Nam. He explained to Major Reno that he wanted a supply chopper to come to the battle scene with lights out and hover at a thousand feet. Bravo Six could then flash his strobe light to fix his position. The chopper could drop to two hundred feet and throw out four cases of ammunition and four cases of hand grenades.

Major Reno didn't criticize or even question the

request as staff officers usually did. Furthermore, he went with the helicopter to ensure speed and performance. Emergency situations such as this were good indicators of worthiness and attitude. He had it all. Those staff officers whose efforts are aimed at only self promotion should emulate Major Reno.

Bravo Six could only hope that no one would be injured as the heavy boxes dropped through the darkness. The Bravo soldiers fired a covering burst that also helped the chopper crew to aim better. All eight boxes landed within five meters of the light. The pilot reported muzzle flashes outside the perimeter but he took no hits.

The platoon and squad leaders were able to give every man a double ration of bullets and grenades. And, as a gesture that he cared, Major Reno had taped several boxes of Hershey bars on each container. Confidence and morale quickly elevated. A simple gesture can be tremendously effective.

Bravo Six received a call from "Spooky." Now he was sure that the usually insensate headquarters staff must be thinking that he was really in desperate trouble. Everyone knew that "Spooky" was an Air Force AC-47 converted cargo plane from the WWII era. Outfitted with 7.62 mm Gatling guns, it could spray the ground with 6000 rounds per minute. Spooky could also light the area to near daylight with flares, but that might only help the enemy at the moment.

Bravo Six, this is Spooky. Are you familiar with me? Over."

"Roger that and welcome. I'll fix my position with a light. Over."

Bravo Six knew that a few VC would probably be in the surrounding trees and could even have a radio. He placed his strobe light in the middle of his position and quickly rolled away from it. The pilot identified it, but no snipers fired. That worried Bravo Six. It meant that if they all weren't leaving, they may be massing for another assault and wanted him to think that they had left.

"Spooky, this is Bravo Six. Show me what you can do on a radius of a hundred meters from my spot. Remember that a friendly unit is about a half kilometer to my west. Over."

"Roger. Here it comes!"

Bravo Six yelled "friendly fire" to his platoons and almost immediately a conical veil of continuous red tracer bullets encircled the Bravo position creating a rare, beautiful sight in an atmosphere of ugliness. All the Bravo soldiers could have imagined themselves inside a Christmas tree.

Not only did that demonstration possibly cause a few enemy casualties, but it surely gave the Viet Cong another reason not to attack. The Bravo soldiers had another reason confidence should be replacing fear.

"Spooky, this is Bravo Six. You're right on, buddy. Can you hang around awhile for me? Over."

"I have you fixed and I'll be with you all night. Don't hesitate to call. Over"

Bravo Six was glad for this high-tech support.

However, he knew that if the VC managed to rush at very close range, Spooky would be little help.

Another factor was a growing concern. Following that uneventful ambush mission, this was the second night with no sleep for most of his men. Some of these tired boys would intermittently doze, no matter what. Bravo Six suspected that the enemy had also woven that into their strategy.

Now the long wait began. After two hours of black silence, Bravo Six decided to probe the enemy for a response and get his company fully awake. At his voice command, every Bravo soldier threw a grenade in unison. That sudden semi-circle of explosions even caused Spooky to ask what was happening. Bravo Six smiled that Badger Six probably just had a near coronary attack.

Soon after that, a few restrained enemy voices sounded like probable complaining or bickering. Small groups could be heard running short distances. The Viet Cong were possibly confused or even experiencing a breakdown of leadership or morale.

Thereafter, all night, grenades were intermittently lobbed into the darkness when anyone thought enough time had gone by for the guerillas to creep close enough. The Bravo soldiers were caused to stay alert, and, as the hours passed, they even gained enough confidence to shout insults to taunt their distraught enemy.

Bravo Six knew that the enemy would have to be gone by daylight, and they wouldn't attack now unless they could run through his company and have enough time to get at least close to the Cambodian border. Some of the odd noises indicated possible problems with casualties. It was 0500 hours and the advantage was fast approaching the American side. Bravo Six knew that victory was at hand, but his company was only feeling relief.

At 0530 hours Bravo Six heard the brigade commander radio to Badger Six that he was on the way. As his chopper passed low over the Bravo position, Bravo Six waved back to him. The sunrise allowed each platoon to send a fire team to look around. Sgt. Laird signaled his return.

Col. Langham landed to heartily congratulate Bravo Six. He quickly led him around the quarter acre perimeter to spread the glory to his men. Before he left, he commented that it was the "neatest and most orderly" post-combat perimeter he had ever seen. He was also anxious to report to the division headquarters. An exciting story about a victorious engagement on such a large scale for his morning report at command headquarters was interrupting his sleep.

One of his companies had handled probably the largest Viet Cong unit in the area. Twenty-three dead guerrillas lay in front of Bravo's position. The VC had also lost a valuable staging base and most of their munitions and quartering supplies. Because they take with them as many of their dead and wounded as they can, their total casualties could be much higher. Bravo Company had lost seven dead and twelve wounded.

After quickly making an inspection of his three light platoons, Bravo Six ordered a sweep of the small buildings of Song Trang Chu. A variety of expected items were found: a few weapons, backpacks, scraps of bloody clothing, tire-tread sandals, perfume bottle nightlights, empty containers, and the usual conical hats. Three more bodies were found dressed in black pajamas with blue neckerchiefs. One was a female with a stomach wound and her throat cut. All the paraphernalia along with the great amount of food supplies were thrown into the river along with dishes, pots and pans, and large storage crocks. Because this had obviously long ceased to be a peaceful civilian hamlet, all the buildings were burned. They were still ravaging the area when the "Little Bear" squadron landed to heli-lift them back to Bam Nam. It was time for showers, beer, and retrospection.

The morning debriefing was full of good news. The intelligence staff reported that the Song Trang Chu battle had involved a reinforced company of approximately two hundred Viet Cong along with about fifteen women and a few children. To carry out a diabolical battle plan, they had rallied at this transit headquarters, and then planned to retreat to Cambodia for rest and new orders. The report from Cambodian sources was "hard" information. The "Song Trang Chu Company" had lost fifty-two casualties: forty-two dead and eleven more seriously wounded.

Col. Langham surmised that Bravo Company was blocking the escape of these desperate Viet Cong who had actually only succeeded in tactically trapping themselves. Whatever, they had suffered enough to keep them in Cambodia for a while. Two Air Force F-105D Thunderchiefs, each laden with six 750-pound bombs pounded the Song Trang Chu location the next day to destroy any hidden caches and ruin it as a staging area for a long while.

The Viet Cong usually won when they could pick the time and place. Their tactic of "One slow-four quick" (plan, then move, attack, scavenge and escape) always worked well if they could intimidate their targeted unit and execute with enough speed to avoid artillery and aircraft.

Two weeks later, several of the Bravo soldiers were decorated for their courage, and they certainly deserved it. Also, Bravo Six had never seen so many Purple Heart medals (He didn't get one!) awarded at one ceremony. Captain Smithe was also quietly encouraged by an understanding staff major to recommend his gunship friend, Rand Kniter, for at least a Bronze Star Medal for valor. Somebody reviewing his case would need a reason to think that he should get a medal instead of a court-martial.

He did request the Silver Star for his brash friend, but was happy to settle for the Bronze. Award requests were usually downgraded and all high level commanders would rather attend an awards ceremony than a court-martial. Bravo Six was present along with probably every other command pilot to see Kniter honored with rowdiness at the club bar that night.

This battle had been a close call for the Badgers, and severely tested the resolve of even the most experienced combat veterans. Many could have been blamed for much had fate been more fickle, but winning the day always helps. The altruistic hero wasn't the maligned scapegoat today.

Badger Six was not rebuked for his professional incompetence. To protect himself, he had joined those who personally revered Bravo Six for carrying the day. Captain Smithe received no official recognition but was very happy just to be the headstrong "fair-haired favorite" of those whom he thought mattered in the Wolverine infrastructure. Captain Smithe knew that he was not personally intelligent enough to warrant his acclaim, but "dumb luck" and the grace of God conquers all. Whatever, he would continue forward aggressively. His prayers that night were more involved than usual.

CHAPTER TEN

RISKY RECREATION
IN SAIGON

The Badger Battalion was not expected to leave Bam
Nam Base for about two weeks. The format of operations in War Zone C was changing and creating new
missions for all the major tactical units. The Wolverine
Brigades of the command would especially have to
be the forerunners of whatever new scheme the G3
Operation Staff decided to initiate. For at least a week,
Bravo Company could rest with revitalization and repose. The old lifers would say, "Don't bet on it!"

"Delta Six" Reggie Traynor, "Alpha Six" Jerry
Bartam, and "Bravo Six" Hasel Smithe had previously
planned to take an R & R (an allowed five day Rest and
Recreation break) together. Of course, since this had been
discussed during a few beers, Bravo Six figured that it

would never amount to anymore than "bar talk" usually did. He knew that the three of them would likely have difficulty scheduling an R&R together.

Reggie Trainor was a fantastic finagler. Even with this short notice, he managed matching leaves for Bravo Six, himself, and Rand Kniter. Their close friend Alpha Six, Jerry Bartam, was now dead, but Captain Rand Kniter, the renowned gunship pilot, who helped to save Bravo company at Song Trang Chu had often been attached to the Badger Battalion and preferred the bawdy but honest social camaraderie of the likes of Bravo Six and Reggie Trainor. He was a good match for them. When seen together, Rand was always in the middle, but he was cautious to actually never socially come between them. His heritage was one of the blueblood tradition but not the stuffed-shirt type. His family's old money allowed them a much-heralded lifestyle of patriotic projects, adventurous travel, and heroic quests. He was handsome, ivy-league intelligent, and, of course, somewhat aristocratically debonair. His family was already ballyhooing his success as a combat gunship pilot, but Rand thought that he was yet to go over the top as a standout pilot for his family. Although not yet realized, his bravado at the Song Trang Chu battle was his starburst of glory with the Bronze star to show for it.

Bravo Six supposed that his company really did not need him here at Bam Nam for now. He may as well go. He bought a shirt and a pair of denim jeans from a mess hall sergeant close to his size. As per the advice of the worldly wise Reggie Trainor, something offhand on the anticipated agenda could make casual civilian attire more comfortable and appropriate.

The next morning as he dressed to meet Reggie and Rand at the officer's mess, he experienced an emotional wave of embarrassment and trepidation. This sudden fearful uncertainty was a flashback of his past introversion. He had often experienced an inability to relate to strong personalities in a social or working interaction. At the least he imagined that he lacked the charisma and persona to be a lead personality in a dynamic communal experience. Real or not, was he again demanding too much of himself? He would have to learn to relax for his own mental fitness. He must loosen up... and wit would take care of itself in a fast crowd. Instead of being a dump truck in the fast lane he was going to enjoy this "man's vacation" as Reggie called it.

The three were halfway through breakfast before Bravo Six thought to ask Reggie about where they were going. Reggie answered "Kuala Lumpur" with a furtive smile.

"Kuala Lumpur?" Rand asked.

Bravo Six laughed. "I don't even know where it is."

Rand opened his hands to express his relaxed joy. "What's the difference? I'm ready to go anywhere. But by the way, where the hell is it? Malaysia?"

Reggie was laughing and bubbling with the confidence of one who enjoys any social challenge anywhere. "Kuala Lumpur is the capital of Malaysia. I don't know a thing about it. That's the bad news.

However, Singapore is only about a hundred miles away and that has to be good. Anyway, Kuala Lumpur is the only place I could get for us.

Bravo Six chuckled and was already relaxing. "That's what I thought. As long as you know what to do to get there and get us back, I'll be happy."

"Don't worry about anything. Right now we have to be on the tarmac at the transit pad at 0800."

Rand broke in with an ultimatum. "No helicopters! No helicopters anytime or I'm not going! I mean it. I've got to stay out of them whatever it takes."

Reggie just smiled sardonically and stared at him for a few seconds. Then he snapped his response. "Okay. I'll get us there by truck. Don't worry. I'll be right back. Be ready."

As Reggie started for the door Rand winked and impishly grinned at Bravo Six "He thinks we'll get to Saigon early enough to raise hell with the 'tea whores', but we can't afford that kind of trouble." Bravo Six was also smiling but he was wide-eyed with uneasiness. "You're trying to outmaneuver him, but that is what will get us in trouble. I know him too well. When he says that kind of stuff, I worry a lot! It's hard to tell what he's doing right now. Let's just go along and enjoy whatever. Give Reggie a free rein and he'll take care of us."

Rand acquiesced and didn't want to be a stick in the mud. "He's probably going to get us on the armed convoy that goes to Saigon every day. We'll get there in time for dinner in an Air Force officers' club. No need to worry."

"Forget that! C'mon! Reggie's out there in a jeep waving for us."

"What? Why the hurry? He didn't steal it, did he?"

"Maybe. Don't ask. I didn't think he would sit around waiting for a convoy. C'mon."

Bravo Six and Rand jumped into the jeep as Reggie popped the clutch and headed for the main gate. He knew the MP guarding the gate cared more about incoming traffic than anybody leaving. Roger waved and the guard saluted. They were on the way to "no matter what"!

Rand looked at Bravo Six on the back bench loading a shotgun on his lap. "What the hell's going on? Surely you guys don't think we're going to drive alone to Saigon! About half the road is gray (not in continuous control of friendly forces)."

Reggie laughed and blatantly reminded him. "You don't want to go by helicopter!"

"You guys are crazy. That shotgun isn't enough. Where the hell did you get this jeep?"

Bravo Six knew enough to go along with Reggie's effervescent style. This surely was dangerous, but after all, this was Vietnam! An exciting escapade full of different dangers would be a refreshing diversion for these battle weary captains who should be able to handle it and enjoy it. Go for it! He also wasn't going to be Bravo Six for awhile.

He now was himself and resigned to recharge his resilience. Reggie had nicknamed him "Chug" after he easily outclassed the field in a rowdy beer speed drinking contest at the makeshift Badger officer's club.. He really never drank very much at a sitting, but chugging a one liter mug of beer was an easy game for him. "Chug" had thereto been his tag at the ad hoc officers' club and at the NCO (sergeants) club.

Chug was now cutting seatbelts from a length of rope and laughing wildly. "Hey, Rand. Here! Tie yourself to the seat. No need to worry. Remember?"

"Yeh. Don't worry. You're both crazy. Why are we going so damned fast and why are you trying to hit the holes?"

Reggie grinned like a Cheshire cat and answered "mines".

"Oh………shit." Rand Kniter had done nothing but fly his helicopter in this war, and he was well-known throughout the 25th Division as one of the best air-to-ground combat support gunners around. He knew just enough about the ground war to realize that he really should be frightened right now. All he could do was hang on and hope that nothing would happen. Reggie and Chug were enjoying this with an outrageous passion, but poor Rand was out of his element and was rendered helpless for the first time in his career.

Reggie continued to drive as fast as he dared over the roughest part of the two lane dirt road while native pedestrians, mostly with animals and carts, often scrambled out of the way. He and Chug knew that the VC planted mines in the best parts of a road where light vehicles were more likely to travel. Also, these were usually mines that were detonated only by the weight of motor vehicles.

Speed was only minimally helpful avoiding the full effectiveness of explosions but was more tactically important for giving snipers and bushwhackers less time and a more difficult target. As they traveled, several times they passed small groups of military vehicles probably going only short distances. Also, Reggie and Chug knew that a mine could be hand-detonated by waiting ambushers watching for an easy target.

For fifteen kilometers Reggie intermittently increased his speed and sometimes negotiated a pothole briefly in mid-air. He even appeared angry as he sounded his horn and waved and swore at any pedestrians or traffic slow to clear the way. Chug knew that his madcap friend was actually enjoying this hell bent for leather scramble. It was unnecessary and even senseless to take such a chance in only a single jeep, but Chug was only half as frightened as he should be. His in-depth experience in the rigors of this war had slowly lightened his regard for personal prudence. Stupid and nonetheless irresponsible, he would rather die by challenging the enemy-even this way.

Chug held the shotgun ready as he constantly scrutinized the landscape ahead. His expectant expression might have made one wonder if he actually hoped to spot the enemy lying in wait. Thirty kilometers passed but the anxiety never faded.

Rand could only cower in fading hope as he gradually wiggled lower in his seat to where he could hardly see the road over the sandbags lying across the flattened windshield. He probably didn't care anymore that he was going to Saigon or where Kuala Lampur really was.

Chug raised his head a little higher as his eyes fixed upon a scene about a hundred meters ahead on the left. An old woman there was hurriedly switching a bullock while a child was pulling at the nose ring of a water buffalo to force it behind a building.

Nearby, a clump of trees extended close to the road which bordered a flooded rice paddy on the right. Chug next saw a tell-tale movement at the edge of the trees and yelled at Roger. "**Get off the road! Get off the ....!**"

In Vietnam, infantrymen learned not to question shouted orders. With a deep ditch on the left, Reggie had immediately swerved to the right into the rice paddy, hit second gear, and floored the accelerator of his before Chug could say it twice. As water and mud splashed overtop the jeep, a deafening explosion on the road pelted them with dry dirt and stones.

Rand twisted his head and torso even lower and didn't care that he now couldn't see anything but the dirty dark OD (olive drab) metal floor. Reggie and Chug had instinctively ducked their heads but only for an instant. Reggie grimaced with a horrible smile and never let up on the accelerator as he forced the 4x4 jeep through the muddy paddy and back toward the bank of the high crowned road. He already knew that they escaped the brunt of this ambush.

Chug had immediately begun blasting 00 buckshot at the base of the brush and trees. He had seen a guerrilla turn his head just before the explosion. As Reggie shifted to first gear to help the straining jeep struggle to the road surface, Chug fired his fifth shell at three guerrillas now running to their rear. He had left the fifth shell in the chamber out of combat prudence from experience. Chug was reloading and still watching for danger as Rand sat up and momentarily looked surprised that they had survived unscathed. Then he let out a string of loud curses and profanity that of course caused both his unruffled companions to roar with delight.

"Shit! You stupid crazy bastards! You're both out of your simple-assed fuckin'minds! We're going to die, and you don't have brains enough to care! Stupid shits! Stupid fuckin' crazy bastards!"

Reggie let up on the accelerator. "You want to walk?"

"Go to hell!"

"Only about twenty more 'klicks'", Chug sarcastically assured him.

"You kiss my ass!"

"I have to watch the road."

"You both think this is funny 'cause you're too stupid to know that you're crazy! If we get to Saigon, I'm flying back to Bam Nam! Why did I ever think that you two could handle a simple pleasure trip! I don't give a shit what you jerk heads do. Count me out and don't talk to me anymore!"

Reggie was chuckling. "We're jerk heads!"

Chug also was snickering. "You're a jerk head. I'd rather be a stupid crazy bastard. That sounds more fun."

Rand sat aloof . Reggie and Chug said no more but knew that he would eventually calm down. After a few more kilometers Reggie gradually slowed as the road improved and the passive security of American installations appeared. The traffic increasingly grew heavy with a conglomerate of civilian and military vehicles.

They commented about the now concrete highway congested with monstrous military vehicles intermingled with the archetypal wooden-wheeled pony carts and oxcarts. The three-wheeled cabbed motorcycles and school bus type excursion coaches were overcrowded sometimes with people even standing on an outside rail. Rand again joined the conversation as they entered the outskirts of the largest city in South Vietnam.

Reggie stopped at an American Military Police Compound. Even there, as anywhere in Saigon, a small gang of ragged little boys instantly appeared to "protect" the jeep. The smiling moppet-faced spokesman repeated several times, "Watch your jeep. Four hundred piasters."

Reggie shook his head. "Too much."

He had expected a price haggle. However while the others pointed their index finger and made a hissing sound (the tires), their dirty-faced leader quickly changed to the sardonic expression of a street-wise hood as he forewarned, "You be number ten beaucoup dingy-dow!" Reggie and Chug knew that they didn't want to be "no good big dummies" so a deal was made for 'two now and three later. Their chuckling as they all chortled "Hokay! Hokay!" would have worried even the Mafiosi.

However, as they checked the shotgun with the desk sergeant (who had been inside watching), they also accepted his advice to park the jeep inside the compound to avoid "losing" part or all of it somewhere downtown.

Rand still harbored emotional strain from that firefight on the road. Even with his excellent record of effectiveness and dependability in combat, right now he couldn't share the calm objective composure of Reggie and Chug as they reported the ambush and supplied the requested details. It seemed no more than a common bar room brawl to them. They didn't appear to even notice the sergeant's quizzical tone as he pondered why they had been in that situation. After so many firefights, Rand surmised that one must become hardened to the trauma and fear of close-range ground assault. They all had no problem with effectiveness in this war , but now Rand was convinced, however, that he was much less vulnerable in his gunship helicopter than they were on the ground.

Rand suddenly stopped his companions while leaving the station. "I know I said at Bam Nam that I didn't want to travel in a helicopter. Now I don't want to go anywhere in a jeep even if Reggie's not driving. I've heard about Saigon traffic."

Reggie spoke coarsely but without annoyance to avoid another diatribe from Rand. "Well, hell, we can't walk everywhere, 'grandma.' Our plane doesn't leave until five in the morning. We have a whole day to look around and do something."

Chug was now loose and in a fun mood. "Yeh. We've got to take in Saigon. It's still morning and this is a wide-open city."

"I hope you're thinking taxi instead of bicycles. I don't want...well I don't know." Rand was desperately trying to figure how to guide these two into a controlled tour of the sights and possibly a three-star restaurant of fine oriental cuisine catering only to Vietnamese intelligentsia and international notables. Maybe he could swing a few hours of downtown cocktail lounging complete with floor entertainment, casino gambling, and alluring ladies of assignation. Surely his well-educated but bourgeois companions could follow his lead and be comfortable with the amusement of the affluent.

Chug interrupted him. "Hey- a rickshaw?"

Rand's face lit with delightful disbelief. "Really? They have them here? Now that would be oriental charm that I could appreciate."

"Of course. Just like old Shanghai. They've been modernized a little, but they're still the first class way to go. Reggie knows and he'll go."

"Yeh. Hot damn, Rand! What do you say?" Reggie really didn't know but didn't care. He just wanted to get this pleasure excursion on track and under way.

Rand agreed. "Okay, let's get a good tour of the city and then have a sidewalk lunch."

Chug and Reggie didn't want to laugh at that anticipation. They really did like him and felt that he would
come around eventually.

Chug had also moved closer to Reggie's mind-set
and wanted to help get things moving. "You got it. You
and Reggie put the jeep into the compound and I'll talk
to these kids. They can get anything."

Chug paid the little imps enough to challenge them
into getting a big tip for bringing in a rickshaw. They did
seem a little perplexed about this special assignment but
guaranteed satisfaction. They really were resourceful. It
was their continued subsistence. Within no more than
thirty minutes, a rather bizarre vehicle, for anywhere
but Southeast Asia, motored directly to them. The "rickshaw" was a motorcycle with a three-person automobile
bench seat mounted in the front. Except for a single long
seat belt, the passengers had no protection. At least it
had the comfort of armrests and a metal bar footrest.

The inharmonious engine barely idled as the driver
dismounted to assist his passengers. He held his tiger-
striped cotton western-style hat as he smiled, repeatedly bowed, and extended his hand to help them aboard.
Chug and Reggie scampered into position, leaving the
middle to Rand. He was apprehensive to be sure as he
joined them and further wondered about the now sober-
faced driver leaving without any instructions. Unlike his
laid-back companions, he didn't appreciate the mystery
of the situation.

As they entered the highway the traffic continued to

be a mish-mash of military trucks, staff cars, buses, taxi-cabs, bicycles, motor scooters, and various wagons and carts. The suburban streets of Saigon were a continuous marketplace. Selling, bartering ,and trading of wares and foodstuffs including livestock extended even to some of the streets. Everyday traffic was so heavy that even the traffic police had to be protected by stacked truck tires. They weren't really controlling the traffic anymore than one could manage the running of the bulls in Spain.

The driver joined and cruised with this impromptu parade that appeared to hurry everywhere but stop nowhere. Soon the three awestruck captains saw the Presidential Palace, the great statue commemorating the ARVN soldiers, the busy Saigon docks, and the modern downtown specialty shops that were so unlike the Vietnam these three had known for the past five perilous months.

Reggie called the driver "Tiger" because of his hat. The driver smiled, of course, when Reggie told him that it was time for "bom-de-bom" (beer). After only a few more blocks, they stopped at what was unmistakably one of the more popular bars of the city. Complete with a neon illustrated marquee and a barker on the sidewalk, one could be reminded of Bourbon Street in New Orleans.

The cabbie was told to wait. Inside they were not surprised to see a brass-railed bar with decorative mirrors and about a dozen mini-skirted girls "painted" for hawking pleasure but presently outnumbering the customers this early hour. This really wasn't what Rand had in mind, but upon seeing other Americans at the tables, he didn't object. It looked both clean and rough enough to suit Reggie. Chug was glad the beer was bottled, cold, and American Budweiser, even if it was expensive.

Three smiling young girls lightly danced to their table and asked what was probably the most commonly heard question in the city. "You buy me Saigon tea?" It really was just tea served in a shot glass for the illusion of being whiskey. The whiskey price covered the girls' commission and the companionship of a female who was a professional at allowing just enough "petting" to keep your interest and to encourage you to buy more tea.

Reggie had spent his early youth basking in the bars of Tucson and Tijuana. As expected, he took the lead.

"You number ten girls! Beaucoup ugly! No good boom-boom (sex)! You stay in kitchen!" Then he pretended to spit on the floor. Two cautiously sat with Chug and Rand, but the one who knew she was a "knock-out" and recognized a "good time Charlie," laughed as she pummeled Reggie's premature balding head with her palms and rattled off a long string of insults in her best broken English. Roger caught her by the waist and lifted her almost over his head before plunking her onto his lap. Her laughter was then spiked with a scream that launched two hours of ribaldry that even Rand enjoyed.

All three girls giggled through the banter of improvised Pidgin English and proved to be delightful experts in seductive teasing and erotic tomfoolery. They also took their turn with the other girls in topless go-go dancing which of course elevated the revelry. Not to Chug's surprise, Reggie "inspected the kitchen" with his very anxious bubbly playmate. After three rounds of beer and "Saigon tea" every fifteen minutes to satisfy the manager, plus a platter of spiced crabmeat and shrimp over brown rice, they said their good-byes.

Chug certainly enjoyed those easy hours of bawdiness, and even Rand, tipsier than the other two, had mellowed and veered into near rowdiness. He was surprised to see the rickshaw still waiting outside. "I'll be damned. He's still here! Hey, Tiger. You're my main man. Gimme five!" The driver didn't understand but bowed and smiled again to load his partying passengers. He knew that they would return and he knew that he was going to be paid. A "deadbeat" wouldn't want to see his victim again in this city and he wouldn't escape the victim's friends either.

Rand didn't notice that Reggie winked at Chug and nodded a signal to the driver who also acknowledged with a nod. Immediately the rickshaw contraption charged into the traffic and continued to dash menacingly and career wildly block after block through the forbidding intersections.

Rand had gripped the seat belt and pushed against the footrest as if applying brakes. "Oh-h, shit. Somebody's gotta be crazy. This son-of-a-bitch must be a VC!"

The determined driver drove as if the throttle were stuck wide-open. He weaved through the traffic to pass them all and even intermittently used the sidewalks. One could be reminded of old Hollywood's hilarious Keystone Cops' scenes as they leaned hard to avoid upsetting while several other vehicles just swerved to avoid losing bumpers and fenders. Carts, displays, and containers were upset, and even a few people were knocked down. One poor fellow stood fast with outstretched arms to protect his vegetables, but bumped heads with Rand as he landed face-down atop him. The furious huckster was flailing his arms in a rage and got one good punch to Rand's forehead before Chug flung him rolling onto the street.

Reggie was gasping and coughing with laughter as he signaled the grimacing driver to keep up the speed. Chug was in tears as he nodded approval at the driver and laughed at Rand as he continued his tirade of screams, insults, threats, and even short prayers. He didn't even remember that he was sick enough to barf over the side.

After several more blocks, suddenly the rickshaw stopped, and the driver quickly unsnapped them. Chug paid him well. He smiled and pointed to a large ornate door as he sped away-probably to hide.

Rand blamed Chug, but this time he wasn't actually angry. "You stupid bastard! This is the second time today that I almost got killed. What did that cost you?"

"Two thousand piasters (twenty dollars)."

Reggie took out his wallet. "Here's half of it. That was a blast! What's next? Now I'm thirsty again."

"I can't believe you guys. I can't believe myself. I'm laughing and I should be running for my life. Hey, please. No more of this extreme shit."

Reggie put his hand on Rand's shoulder. "I can't believe that the star gunship pilot of our whole command is still wimping and complaining."

"I'm supposed to be resting! Let's do something somewhere . An MP squad is probably looking for us right now."

Chug led through the heavy carved door. He knew that what would be inside probably wouldn't disappoint either of them. A plump successful-looking woman greeted them in excellent English. She described the services and prices, gave them wooden tokens for what they paid, and assigned girls to guide them.

This was probably the best massage parlor in the city, complete with a classic steam room and colorful tiled showers. The sauna alone would have rivaled the best in Finland. With a towel about their waists and their valuables in a plastic bag, the three captains could hardly see each other as a young girl poured boiling water over steaming volcanic stones in the old world fashion. From there they showered in separate stalls with pungent lime soap. Chug thought about all those baths in water-filled bomb craters near the Vam Co Dong River.

Again they were led by the same young guides who took their tokens and smiled courteously and seductively. The massage room had linen partitioned stalls with freshly-sheeted cots. None of the three were surprised that the same girls were also the masseuses.

Chug had heard about the Japanese, or somebody, walking on the customer's back. This girl weighed probably no more than eighty pounds. She steadied herself by grasping two pipes running parallel near the ceiling and sang a lively Vietnamese song as she used her heels and toes to sharply knead his back. He couldn't help a few grunts of pleasure.

Then, back on the floor, she worked hard with her tiny hands from his neck to his toes. Still singing, she used her lithe, rippling fingers and palms to chop with clicking noises, to swirl with constant directional changes, and to knead every muscle as if counting while caressing. It was Chug's first professional massage, but how could any be better?

The "love pat" on his butt cued him to rise to a sitting position. Now she stood before him with the smock open. Nothing masked her native buff. She spoke daringly yet somehow demurely with a passive tone and seductive pout as if offering herself as a sacrifice for his satisfaction. "You want short time?"

Chug was twenty-six years old. He hadn't been with a woman for almost a year. The charms of her naked young womanhood awoke and stimulated his virility. A pang of passion filled his loins as he sucked in a sudden breath. All he had to do was nod his heavy head.

She was neither innocent nor naïve nor even a little uncertain of her proposal. However, she was too young and too small to provide other than a shallow, sordid, and licentious sexual release. That fresh doll baby appearance was also a factor in his decision. If she had been less childlike, he may have indulged.

Chug responded negatively but was careful not to insult her. He also gave her a substantial tip which most likely was the greater part of her daily compensation.

He met Rand in the foyer who said that he had taken the "extra" but was now afraid for his health. Then Reggie joined them and gave a full explanation of why he was now more "relaxed" than they. Also, he said that he was awfully hungry and thirsty again.

The pot-bellied proprietress recommended the "Estaminet Chez Nous,", just down the street, as an excellent dinner lounge. She said that many Americans patronized it. She then added, "Be nice to 'Dessie' and she'll be nice to you. Tell her that I sent you." They took her advice and were glad for it. Upon arriving, Rand described the overwrought European atmosphere as Casa Blanca "in drag." However, he noted that the excellent chateaubriand meal and service would have rated at least a two star anywhere.

During the recommended mint cake with chocolate sauce dessert, Rand engaged in conversation with three trendy American couples at an adjoining table. After introductions, they advised him about a gambling casino of his probable liking.

Upon leaving, the three men chugged beer for the tip. Reggie had to mention that his friend "Chug" was probably better than their champion. Being both polite and sporting, they responded with a round all around bet at two to one odds. Chug handily won to the delight of the women. They paid and then taunted their abashed friend as they left.

At least four of the remaining patrons were Australians at the cabaret bar offset from the dining room. None could know that Chug, Reggie, and Rand were officers wearing barely presentable civilian clothing.

While the others watched, one approached and called them "mates' as he challenged Chug, who was now ready for such sport. He stood to meet this burly long-mustachioed sergeant who looked him over as he spoke.

"We have a man more the match of you, mate. What do you say to the sport?"

Chug smiled as he conspicuously scrutinized the others at the bar and answered for them to hear.

"He must have left, or maybe he's not here yet, huh?"

Reggie reveled in such bar play, but Rand was too cautious to laugh as loud.

The anxious Aussies smiled but didn't laugh. They were of the "Outback" hard-living breed and relished any such encounter more seriously, especially with pretentious Yanks.

"He's here, mate. But maybe you wouldn't like a go at our game."

Chug knew to expect something rough and probably somewhat unfair, but he didn't want to disappoint Reggie. "What's your game?"

"The winner of the beer guzzle can drop his man. Are you with us, mate?"

Chug surmised that the winning drinker could punch his opponent. He had heard of it. He also noticed that this Aussie's tone was growing in intimidation and each of the other three looked to be stalwart ruffians. At this point maybe he'd better not say no.

The Americans at the other tables were aware and awaiting Chug's response. Reggie and Rand were uneasily silent and not too inebriated to realize a possible set-up for skullduggery. They could easily be suckered into a bad beating in a back alley and left with empty wallets.

"I didn't hear you, mate. Are you for us?" Chug would have answered then but for a feminine interruption. She appeared from behind one of those oriental beaded partitions. Obviously Eurasian, probably French and Vietnamese, she was certainly the better for it. She stood every bit of 5' 10" and was built like a West Virginia detour. That and her full-featured face with exaggerated high cheeks and drop-dead magnetic almond eyes were stylishly offset by expensive clothes and jewelry. She needed only to speak softly to command full attention.

"Pardon me, gentlemen. Let us make this more interesting. I will bet fifty dollars on this American." She already knew the potential malevolence of these Aussies and knew people well enough to read the confidence in the tall muscular American. It was a win-win bet for her. If they won, these Aussies would quickly splurge their money on celebration.

Chug had almost gasped at her bombshell appearance and now he was resigned to whatever it would take for her attention. "And I will not do it for nothing." He then caught the Aussie off-guard with a hard finger jab and added his own wager. "If you will also cover my fifty dollars, you're on."

Rand and especially Reggie were not only mesmerized with the macho plot of the developing international high drama but were also awestruck by this fascinating femme fatale who ingenuously mocked the spirit of Mata Hari.

The Aussies were caucusing and still hadn't disclosed their champion when the temptress called their hand. "What's it going to be? Is your mouth bigger that your purse?"

You're a bit hard on us, Dessie."

"Put up your money or go find an easier mark," she demanded.

Chug figured that she knew these four sergeants to be scoundrels and probably didn't like them. Maybe she was also quick to see the mettle of this bold brawny American who was now looking much more challenging than before to these rough opportunists.

Finally the contender was revealed and the bets were secured with the shaved-head bartender who projected a disdainful indifference.

The Australian challenger, a broad-faced curly blond, was a thickset unsightly man in his early thirties. Previously content to let his friend verbally exploit the situation, he now spoke loudly and angrily to "psych" his opponent. "You lose when I have finished and you haven't, mate."

Chug took a step forward and smiled as he spoke his confidence. After all, he had never been bested at chugging, and, he knew that he certainly would like to show off his best punch to this "Dessie" as they called her. He easily maintained an unyielding eye contact without blinking and growled his own daunting message. "Then maybe you'd better quit now...boy!" That caused several onlookers to groan in delight and approval.

One of the Aussies volunteered a rule. "You can't punch 'til I signal your beer be gone, mate."

They stood ready at the bar, each with a one liter mug of draft lager. The "referee" held a hat one foot above the bar. The other customers had left their tables to stand near for a better view. Reggie and Rand voiced encouragement to Chug. A few other Americans also barked supportive comments and wagered with each other. The Aussies were silently worried about their money and their local reputation. This strapping Yank could be a troubling yeoman. Their practically unchallenged reign of rowdy hooliganism could be compromised.

"Dessie" was the street name of the tall siren who had hopeful faith in Chug and stood behind the bar for the best view. She was Desiree Hoa Hau (beauty queen) Barbour, the second daughter of a French Colonel and his Vietnamese mistress. They both had died in a café terrorist bombing in Tay Ninh City. Her sister hadn't been seen for five years but was rumored to be with the Viet Cong. Dessie had become her own woman. She was well-noted to be street-wise and business-wise. This place was only one of her establishments, and these unruly Australians had often caused offended customers to go elsewhere. She also was aware that her sensual feminine charms could be even more intoxicating to a virile young man whose courage was already whetted with beer and whiskey. Only a few had ever been successful with her. Dessie was no whore, but she was a lascivious woman in the strong sense of that word. Just before the hat dropped, Chug noticed her elliptical bewitching brown eyes projecting a silently seductive communiqué. Now the stakes far outweighed the ante for him.

The hat was still in mid-air when the Aussie's mug touched his lips. Chug was not a heavy drinker, but in drinking games, he could naturally bypass the normal swallowing procedure. With innate control, beer could pour down his throat unimpeded by even a strained gulp or painful gag. During spontaneous small parties involving the drinking of a few beers, Chug was invariably challenged by an acquaintance or someone's friend just for the fun of the contest. But now, in this wartime social situation, the fun was more on the serious side and even smacked of danger. As in every rowdy sport of physical consequence, he knew that it would be better to win.

His mug hit the bar first with nothing but foamy drizzles left streaming to the bottom. The referee slapped the bar to signal his successful finish and then a second later signaled the same for his opponent with an obvious inch of beer remaining. The Americans raised their arms but were withholding any celebrant cheering pending the trophy punch.

For no more than a few seconds, Chug struggled to get a breath and clear his weepy eyes as an enormous burp burned through his nose. As he maneuvered to deliver his best wallop in accordance with his victory, an unperceived and heretofore unprecedented heavy fist crashed into his left cheekbone just under the eye. He had been in a few difficult fights, but this was the hardest he had ever been hit. The force of the stinging blow snapped his head and deeply buckled his knees to land him reeling onto his back. Because his brain had been rocked to a near concussion, the bar scene melted, waved, fluttered, and faded as he lapsed to near unconsciousness.

Even as he fought to maintain his senses he instinctively knew that the worst next move would be to violently assault his opponent in reckless retribution. He slowly rose again to his posture at the bar and questioningly looked at the referee, as the silent onlookers stood stymied with anticipation of pending violence.

The referee smiled nervously as he met Chug's glazed eyes that were sullen above his bleeding cheek. He explained without apology that both could punch when they finish. The first finisher could punch first and he had nodded the finish. Chug hadn't acted so the other did. Of course Chug realized that this had been planned to be a win-win contest for them no matter the outcome.

All the Aussies rudely snickered at this big Yank learning their game the hard way, but the American crowd, increasing in number, remained silent and confident that their hero of the moment was not finished.

The blood of a small open cut reached Chug's neck and shirt, but he paid it no mind. He only glared at his opponent as if blaming only him, and ordered the contest to continue.

"Fill those mugs again. This time we'll know the winner!" Chug was still sorely determined but knew that the game would be over if he got hit like that again. These ruffians couldn't be trusted with their "rules" and had to be met on their own terms.

Another liter would be harder to chug, but the Aussie saw the Yank as no bigger himself and suffering with a painfully bruised cheek besides. Knowing that he couldn't back off, he nodded and smiled confidently as he exhorted, "This time we'll bloody well know, mate."

Chug glanced at Reggie and Rand meaning a warning that they should be ready. He also took fleeting notice that Dessie and her bartender had just shared a smile of assurance. They all knew that Chug wasn't really playing a game anymore. These scoffing Aussies were venomous as Viet Cong and would have to be hurt badly enough that their "rules" wouldn't matter anymore.

Both mugs were tipped before the hat hit the bar, and the crowd again shouted support for Chug. The Aussie was strenuously struggling to gulp but was only slowly succeeding.

Chug drank in long forceful gulps with no regard for his burning throat and breast. He drained the mug and slammed it on the bar for the astounded referee who obliged the finish. With no loss of momentum Chug swiftly snaked his arms and torso to his best posture of power. The desperately determined Aussie had his eyes tightly closed and his mug only two-thirds empty when Chug exploded with all the collective might his muscles could muster. His right fist led an uncoiling unconscionable assault straight to the bottom of the Aussie's trembling mug. True to his former boxing training basics, he followed through from the dull thud of the impact to subjectively drive the mug right through his enemy's skull. The Aussie's head hit the floor first.

All eyes flashed to the terra cotta tiled floor where the mangled nose and gaping mouth spewed moans and whimpers through bubbled blood and beer. Chug painfully belched beer through his nose and wiped at his tear-flooded eyes as he fought to recover from the blinding nausea. Reggie and Rand joined him, and braced to meet the forthcoming vengeful attack of the three remaining cursing Aussies.

One drew a knife and another broke a bottle. Reggie raised a chair and Rand did the same. He was decidedly helping his raucous friends as if he had a choice. Chug's throbbing right hand was bleeding and useless, but he reached for a bottle with his left.

Then two familiar metallic clicking sounds froze everybody. Dessie held a .25 caliber pistol at her side, and her heretofore-indifferent bartender was aiming a nickel-plated sawed-off double-barreled shotgun. Dessie spoke through a contradictory oriental smile unpleasantly tainted with French arrogance. "You lost. Get out while you still can."

The Aussies knew that downtown Saigon was no place to call a bluff. They hesitated only long enough to threaten Chug. "Look for us, mate. You have bloody hell to pay." They gathered their friend, who had recovered enough to rise to his knees, and started for the door. The agonized Aussie pointed to Chug as he strenuously stepped to the doorway. His mouth and nose would sorely remind him about this brutal Yank for at least a week, but his ego would never completely forget.

The bartender distributed the winnings and returned to his duties as if nothing had happened. A very young kitchen maid mopped the blood and beer without even glancing at anyone.

Reggie slapped Chug on the shoulder and proclaimed his approval. "You done good, Buddy. You're internationally famous now."

Rand congratulated him in a more reserved manner. "You beat him fair for sure, but that overkill won't be forgotten."

Reggie was still snickering in delight. "Don't worry about it. They made the rules, and they lost their own game. We probably won't see them again."

Dessie was wiser, or at least more cautious. "They won't come back soon, but they'll be sure to watch for you. Don't fight them. You can stay here tonight."

Also, even if this sharp-featured, hard-hitting American wasn't as handsome as she could demand, he appeared to have every other physical quality a woman desired. And, that was complemented by a savage will to win which matched her own successful business style, necessary to even survive in increasingly savage Saigon.

Dessie was pleased but not really surprised that Chug had bested those despicable Aussies. She probably understood men better than most women. Chug had started for the restroom to clean his wounds, but he was willing to accept Dessie's offer to tend his throbbing hand and cheek.

She led him to what was obviously her office and bedroom. Nothing in that boudoir was cheap or in bad taste. Everything was as clean, well coordinated, and stylish as she was. A large portrait of her mother and father, both elegantly dressed and imperially postured, commanded the only wall without a mural. The artistically carved teak frame would have impressed any of the world's master craftsmen. Dessie displayed no photos of her sister nor did she even mention her when Chug complimented her handsome parents.

Chug sat waiting on a richly upholstered Queen Anne chair after Dessie removed his bloodstained shirt and rang for a girl to have it laundered. Now the almond eyes of that noble Eurasian face grew soft and amorous as she skillfully applied a butterfly bandage to close the split skin of his swollen cheekbone. As she finished, she shifted her eyes to meet his which caused both to silently disclose sensual secrets about their mutual veils of inhibition and pretence.

They aggressively but passively sought to heighten the breadth and depth of their carnal passion. For two hours they cavorted and caressed with reciprocal care for the innermost intimate pleasure of each other. Chug was not as experienced, but Dessie easily aroused, engaged, and finally exhausted the entire sexual potency of his manhood. While in the final euphoric embrace of post coital repose, Chug mused that the spirits of Mark Antony and Cleopatra were probably now envious. He knew, however, that he had no better chance for a long term relationship with Dessie than what those immortal lovers had been afforded.

Dessie was emotionally relaxed for maybe the first time as a woman. Her bi-racial hybrid vigor had endowed her with physical charms that would be cheapened with any but the most exclusive cosmetics. Likewise, her superior intellect and ingenuity could never have been corrupted by the facetious affections and deceptive endearments of a romantic swindler. The rigors of Saigon society had not yet allowed a partner to share her life. Chug was disparate in comparative attributes but attractively virile, unassumingly honest, and unselfishly gentle. Nevertheless, she knew that in a few months he would be fourteen thousand miles away…or maybe dead.

This paradoxical evening of vulgar victory and exquisite intimacy was destined to be cherished only as a gratuity of the gods. If it was, however, a diabolical deception of the devils of despair, those demons should have chosen a lesser man and woman. Chug and Dessie reluctantly returned to the bar to begin their goodbye.

All heads turned and smiled. Rand was the first to speak. "Ho! Ho! Ho! Your wounds must have been more serious than we thought."

Reggie chuckled and brought a beer to Chug. "Chug just had major surgery. Let him rest."

Rand then explained that he thought maybe they should stay the rest of the night at the MP station to avoid any more trouble. They mutually agreed. Chug offered to pay their entire bill for dinner and drinks, but Dessie indicated to the bartender with a discreet nod of her head that it was, without recourse, on the house. Their public goodbye hug and kiss amounted to little more than a loving husband routinely leaving his wife to go to work.

Chug was the last of the three out the door. He looked back to wave and saw Dessie staring at him pensively with those luminous eyes. His lips parted as his face flushed with a fervor of frustration, but Reggie quickly reached back to roughly snatch him away.

Chug said, "Thanks for the rescue,." to his worldly friend, but during the taxi ride he knew that Dessie was going to be an indelible memory. Another time…another place! Well, maybe it was for the best, anyway.

Everything during this excursion had been a remarkable experience and this taxi ride was no less unusual. Vietnamese taxicabs were made for the average local citizen. Reggie and Rand were quite cramped but the taller Chug could not even get his feet on the floor.

This driver managed traffic with the same audacity as did as the rickshaw guy, but they weren't surprised and weren't going far anyway.

The desk sergeant at the MP station had surprising news for them. He had routinely reported their arrival to their command headquarters at Bam Nam. The duty officer there had stated that both the Badger battalions had just been ordered to convoy deep into the jungle area of War Zone C north of Tay Ninh City.

Rand was quick to ask about the obvious. "Did they say anything about our leaves?"

"No, sir."

Reggie looked to Chug and spoke very seriously. "They'll be gone for a couple weeks. S2 must have something good on a big VC or NVA concentration."

Chug said what the other two were already thinking. "I'm going back."

Reggie laughed. "To Bam Nam or to Dessie?"

The desk sergeant's face lit up. "Dessie! Holy shit! No wonder you're beat up! If you gentlemen had trouble with her, you're lucky to be alive."

"Not with her, Rand explained, "it was some discord with some of her Australian customers."

"One have a big black mustache? Another with curly blond hair and a wide silver

bracelet?" He winced as they affirmed. "They were after your money and probably also your blood. What happened?"

Reggie now smiled with pride. "We got their money, and the blond one looks worse than Chug here."

The desk sergeant was glad but concerned. "I don't mean any disrespect, gentlemen, but you were smart to come here for the night. If those goons find you again…"

He broke off his sentence and shook his head as a sympathetic warning. "And, it would please me to dispatch our helicopter to take all three of you to Bam Nam right now. You know you'll get another R&R."

Helicopter! Rand winced but was glad for a chance to get back to familiar territory.

Chug spoke earnestly, "I just have to go back to my company. But you two do what you want."

The desk sergeant interjected, "I'll get your jeep back there sometime soon. You'll have my receipt to show."

Reggie looked at his watch. "Almost midnight. Not even a full day, but it was a damned good day. What the hell, Rand. Let's go back." Rand nodded.

In less than an hour they landed in Bam Nam and were tired but relaxed from their exciting diversion. They parted for the night as closer companions.

Reggie had chosen not to tell them that they really didn't have legitimate passes and that he had stolen the jeep. That can be covered if anyone really cares.

Chug woke the ill-tempered Major Domsavich just to aggravate him with a report. He was more disappointed to see Chug than impressed with this consideration, but he said nothing except mumble a cool acknowledgement.

The next morning, Badger Six said nothing to Chug about foregoing his vacation, nor did he even mention his injuries. However, he really was glad to see him. He was admitting to himself that he did need his obstinate but awkwardly effective Bravo Six.

Chug was Bravo Six again and wasn't sorry to miss Kuala Lumpur. That madcap one day trip to Saigon wasn't very restful, but it certainly was refreshing.

Now his unit was heading for what might be the "big game.". The primary objective was the confirmed location of COSVN, the Viet Cong's Central Office of Viet Nam, and General Thanh's headquarters. If there, he'll surely be guarded by several battalions of crack VC and NVA regulars. Depending on the outcome, this could be the deciding battle of the war. Bravo Six wanted to be there...up front!

Before he slept, Bravo Six had plenty to pray about.

CHAPTER ELEVEN

THE JUNGLE CAMP CHALLENGE

All available mobile units of the 25th Division were mustered to a ready position north of Tay Ninh City. Both the Wolverine Brigades would be coordinating on the same operation.

This was Operation Junction City, thus far the largest of the war. The general headquarters of all the Viet Cong units was hidden within an approximate 1000 square kilometer section of dense jungle bordered to the west by Cambodia. Friendly units would surround that area, with the 25th Division to push from the South. If successful, the Americans and ARVN would destroy the enemy's command center, their base of operation, and much of their supply system.

It was a massive move. Truck convoys traveled all day with preparations and supply interests new to most of the men. The G2 reported large base camps of Viet Cong and North Vietnamese.

The section assigned to the Badger Battalion of the Second Brigade was very similar to the rainforests of South America. This was the dry season, but the jungle always consisted of very tall trees forming a thick canopy with their top foliage constantly struggling for places in the sun. What light that reached the ground grew an odd assortment of tangled ropelike vines, now mostly dormant and brown from lack of moisture.

Every squad was issued a machete. They traveled in single file, slowly, with much effort. The tedious snarled undergrowth afforded very few normal steps. In two days, the Badger Battalion traveled only four and a half kilometers. Very little wildlife was seen, but small slowly running streams were a change from the tidal canals and swampy drainage of the Plain of Reeds section of the massive Mekong Delta.

The intelligence report had probably been right because small enemy units began to engage the Second Brigade forward units, obviously to impede their progress. For five to ten minutes automatic rifle fire would graze the ground about six inches high in overlapping fire lanes. That way the enemy soldiers didn't have to expose themselves or even aim, and the Americans couldn't easily maneuver. Then, the VC would withdraw before any mortar or artillery fire could block their escape. Every advance unit suffered a few casualties.

Nothing startling happened that first night, but all

the Badger soldiers had a feeling of pending strife. All night, friendly heavy artillery and jet fighter-bombers pounded the jungle for several kilometers ahead.

The next morning brought a sure sign that the enemy was desperate to slow the American advance. Another battalion to the east was attacked by small unit cells of Viet Cong guerrillas running and firing kamikaze-style at the Americans. A few even had large round anti-vehicle mines tied to their chests. The Americans suffered only a few casualties but were flabbergasted at this lunacy. Every dead VC had pot in his possession and probably a few had been drugged with something even stronger. None of the Americans would forget the eerie screams of those crazed attackers and their ludicrous smiles as they wildly charged to their death.

The next morning Badger Alpha Company was the advance unit when machine gun fire from left and right began raking the whole column. Only two soldiers had been hit, but the intensity and volume, combined with a terrain disadvantage, made maneuvering impossible without risking needless casualties. The Alpha soldiers stood fast and were glad to just "hug the ground" while Bravo Company moved to engage on the left flank. Bravo Six, however, was suspicious of a malevolent set-up.

Bravo's second platoon engaged the machinegun on the left flank and brought an almost immediate silence with a volley of intense M16 rifle fire. Sgt. Tiega called Bravo Six to the scene. It was a shocking reminder to the Americans who immediately saw that they were on the right side.

A young NVA soldier, his plight now over forever, had been chained at the waist to a tree. He had been left with a pile of corroded ammunition to postpone his inevitable fate. This wretched creature had probably been sickly or an incorrigible and then put to use as a delaying obstacle for the American advance. The Bravo soldiers felt pity and sympathetically commented about this "expendable" human. To say that he died for his country would be a paradox.

Bravo Six radioed Badger Six for a "halt in place" without giving an explanation. He would want a lengthy explanation anyway. Sgt. Lee, the interpreter, was hurried to Bravo Six. He called to the other machine-gunner after he finally quit firing. He called him "Dai Lien" (machinegun) and repeated "Phai im lang" (Be very quiet! Don't move!) several times because of dialect differences. Sgt. Lee then told the desperate man that the Americans knew about his situation and would be fair with him if he surrendered. The "dai lien" answered back that he would cooperate in any way if he was not tortured or killed. He then sat with his hands raised and smiled with oriental humility. Bravo Six went along with the point squad to make sure that nothing went wrong. This one also had been bound to a tree but with rusty quarter-inch steel cable. . The terror of the trembling, comparatively small soldier subsided quickly when Bravo Six shot off the bolted metal clamp and gave him water.

This foreign "Dawi" (captain), the biggest and strongest man Ngo Le Duc had ever been close was the first savior in his life. Never having a family to speak of, he had always been a scavenger on the outskirts of society in Hanoi. He had subsisted only by sharp wits, a wiry body, and a will to survive. Once, while cramped in one of those concrete one-person bomb shelters, and hungry again because the American bombers had tightened the economy severely, he decided to make a desperate move. He would join the war in anticipation of steady meals and a daily routine with some real consistency and purpose. However, he lacked the necessary community commitment to blindly embrace the wartime goals and had already developed too much of a spirited nature to obey and respect his zealous superiors. He had been struggling with Vietnamese civilian laws all his life and now was suffering military authority. Fate had consequently sentenced him to die as a "persona non grata," useful only in his death throes.

He wanted to tell all he could to this straw-haired, blue-eyed foreigner who just may be a beginning link in his quest to somehow get to Thailand where he heard that he could get a new start. He munched his first Hershey bar and volunteered information even beyond the questions. Bravo Six called Badger Six just six minutes after the halt. He was quick to tell him that he had a prisoner who claimed that a large base camp was only about one kilometer forward. Anxious for personal involvement, Badger Six moved on to the huge abandoned camp with Charlie Company, secured the area, and called for Col. Langham. Here were buildings, pavilions, and other structures of various types untouched by the artillery and air strikes. Everything was carefully camouflaged among the trees and covered an area big enough to house a couple thousand troops. The advance of the brigade just may have missed this huge strategic find, but Badger Six, true to his jaundiced mind-set, never reported anything about Bravo Six and his prisoner.

The Badger Battalion moved on to their previously assigned positions about a half kilometer north. Bravo Company, reinforced with the Recon Platoon, was left to search, inventory, and destroy the camp since the prisoner's information could make the job much easier.

In case of attack, Bravo Six established a comprehensive defense posture. Then one squad from each platoon alternated to search the area. The enemy's delaying tactics had allowed them to salvage everything they could carry. However, Duc, the prisoner, knew the locations of large underground caches of food, clothing, munitions, and miscellaneous supplies. These were hidden too well for the slightly lazy and unenthusiastic American searchers to find. Duc was so glad to be alive that he readily pointed to anything that might please these kindly Americans.

That afternoon, the enemy food supply for War Zone C became severely diminished. Hundreds of fifty pound sacks of rice were cast into a stream. Hundreds of five liter cans of cooking oil from China were punctured and burned along with numerous cases of condensed milk and powdered milk, and probably a ton or more of salt-cured pork. The Chinese foodstuffs were labeled "Panda Brand.".

Besides food, about forty barrels of kerosene, many rolls of black plastic sheeting, salt, and hundreds of black uniforms with "flip-flop" shoes with tire tread soles were destroyed. Lots of odd items became souvenirs, but Bravo Six and his platoon leaders were infuriated to find some new U.S. Army equipment and a few shipping crates with New York stamped on them.

To the disgust of all with noble intentions, the traitorous black market was operating throughout South Vietnam. Devious American civilians and corrupt Vietnamese officials embezzled an estimated one-fifth of all American war supplies. Even some Playboy magazines and American whisky was found with a supply of the usual oriental betelnut chaw used for psychotic entertainment. All the bamboo structures would be burned the next morning because Bravo Company was staying that night before joining the rest of the battalion.

At the north end of the camp, one Vietnamese man was found bayoneted in the back beside a Cambodian woman with her throat slit. Photographs were taken for possible identity, but the motives would likely never be known. The end of another story was revealed when the First Platoon discovered a crashed Huey helicopter about five hundred meters outside the camp with three dried leathery bodies. The enemy had scavenged everything worthwhile and had mutilated the bodies. The dog tags were missing, but the nametags over the left breast pocket gave one a feeling of long-lost buddies. Now their families would have at least some of the closure they desired.

Fearing a possible massive attack, Bravo Six carefully checked his platoon's positions and helped his artillery liaison lieutenant plan close emergency barrages. The lieutenant also plotted an H & I (harassment and interdiction) pattern to discourage enemy movement and to let the Viet Cong know that he was there and ready for them.

Bravo Six and his platoon leaders knew that they could not stop a determined attack in this venue, but they had to at least convince the enemy that any attack would be met with a punishing defense. No one had to explain to the soldiers in their slit trenches that they may be attacked by too many VC or NVA for them to shoot fast enough. Every man was glad for the extra supply of ammunition and grenades brought by the supply helicopter just before dusk.

A few of the less experienced soldiers thought and talked about the worst and even advised each other. Some even boasted of how many attackers would die trying to get them. However, the true nature of one soldier surfaced. He calmly and resolutely took aim with his M16 rifle and shot through the instep of his left foot. He said nothing but uttered whining involuntary cries of pain and anguish as he writhed on the ground and grabbed at his foot. The medics quickly cut off his boot and sock and tried to comfort him as they bandaged the quivering foot and worried about the continued bleeding.

PFC Lee Roy McGowan had watched and finally his sense of right and wrong caused a twist in this devious plot. "What the hell did you do that for?"

A medic chided him. "Hey. Let him alone."

"He shot himself! I saw it! That was no accident! I saw it!"

Now the agonizing soldier faced his accuser with shouted anger. "Kiss my ass, McGowan. You ain't nothing."

If any code of loyalty existed among the troops, or even their races, McGowan was having none of it. "You're a sorry-assed mother fuckin' nigger! You ain't fooling nobody, you asshole!" McGowan then had to be restrained as he tried to kick him.

The squad leader, Sgt. Eli, told everyone to shut up. He and Platoon Sergeant Mueller reported to Bravo Six that it was probable that the wound had been self-inflicted and not an accident. The sweating and suffering, but perverse soldier, told Bravo Six that he wasn't saying "nothing because "everybody always knows everything anyway."

PFC Knopley then spoke. "I saw him, too, sir. He was just sitting there holding his rifle steady at his foot and it went off. I think he did it on purpose, too."

Bravo Six felt sure of what had happened and he despised it. He probably could have gotten a "Dust off" , but would he also be able to explain about the security risk because of the overall situation? That sniveling coward was going to have to stay all night. At the least, he would have a scar on the top and bottom of his foot that would require a fancy lie back home. Bravo Six also decided that paperwork should show a court-martial conviction for a self-inflicted wound to preclude him from finagling VA compensation.

Nonetheless, this way his punishment would be severe but natural. Bravo Six was causing this feint-hearted young man to regret his foolhardiness. He would have to always live with dishonor from combat service that could have been a rare honor for himself and his family. Now he was even without a weapon as he sat distraught and quiet. With anger, remorse, and pain, he wished for a second chance at his decision.

Bravo Six was more interested in another man who sat in deep thought. The prisoner, Duc, was pondering his situation and wondering about his prospects. These strange-looking Americans had been fair to him thus far and he would not betray them. He didn't mind that his feet were tied just far apart so he couldn't run or even walk fast. Bravo Six was feeling a personal responsibility for this unfortunate stray from civilization. There wouldn't be much room for this urban North Vietnamese alien in the war-torn intolerant and struggling economic system of the South. Most likely he also wouldn't even want to return to Hanoi, Haiphong, or any other place in the North. He may even have a bad time in a prison camp or a Chieu Hoi (repatriation) camp. The underground communication system reached into all places.

Bravo Six radioed Badger Six to request that the

Division G2 intelligence officer come to this position at daylight for an immediate interrogation of the prisoner and an on-the-spot inspection of the camp lay-out, along with materials discovered and destroyed. However, Badger Six wouldn't want high-level exposure of his incorrigible company commander who was largely responsible for the best success of the operation thus far. Moreover, he knew that Bravo Six would be sure to somehow enlighten the right brass about his own disregard for potentially strategic intelligence. In addition, Col. Langham would probably accompany the G2 if he came. He radioed Bravo Six that he would let him know in the morning. (Yeh, right!)

With no moon, the camp seemed to disappear, leaving no one but the two or three defenders scarcely discernible beside each man. The blackness, combined with a feeling of vulnerability to a possible massive attack, caused a strict self-discipline for noise and light. Those at forward listening posts knew that they would surely perish, but the indeterminable blasts of interdicting friendly 155mm artillery fire brought an assurance of instant indirect formidable fire support.

How could the jungle be so quiet? A Hollywood film director should be here to apologize for all those noisy Tarzan movies with squawking birds and frightening growls. Most of the soldiers on alert contemplated this feeling of void. The human senses were useless. It was like hiding in a coffin, and everyone knowing that you are there.

SP4 Randy Quinn sat beside his sleeping teammates at their 81mm mortar positions. This was only his fourth month in the war, but he had adjusted quickly to the rigors of his job and the social demands of this transient but unyielding squad fraternity. Oddly enough, here he felt a spiritual freedom unknown before in his nineteen years. He sat alert, but relaxed, without any drowsiness. Ironically, the eerie black silence was soothing and peaceful to him while he served his turn in a three hour lonely security watch for his own squad.

Randy thought clearly about his stormy childhood. His tenth grade unwed mother had been pregnant to a handsome twelfth grade athletic rebel. He was an intelligent but borderline student, often reprimanded, and always more interested in the fascination of unruly parties with rock music, pot, and the constant peer pressures of fads, fights, and downtown follies. She had been falsely enamored with his hip charm and cool disposition.

The infatuation had brought the gamble of unchecked passion and its sobering consequence. Devastatingly, she quickly learned that she wasn't "good enough" for him or his family. Already ostracized by her own family, she quit school, worked as a waitress, and lived with a sympathetic lonely aunt in a small but comfortable mobile home. Soon after Randy's birth, she left town without notice and never returned. Baby Randy was left with his struggling, widowed great aunt. Already distraught with her own adverse fortunes, she expressed little concern for anything other than his biological needs.

As he grew, Randy developed close ties with the more spirited neighborhood children but viewed adults as a peripheral group only to be tolerated. At school, his friends were much more important to him than the teachers. Throughout his teens, he was handsome, witty, and athletic enough to be very popular but unlucky enough to get caught more times than the average. Even the food and shelter of his "home" seemed to be slowly slipping away. The school and community officials, uneasy about his behavior, never penetrated his fierce aversion to adult supervision or charitable assistance.

Halfway through his senior year, his girlfriend, he had taken so closely into his life, suddenly and involuntarily married one of his best friends. He had never known that she was pregnant until another friend living next door to her, telephoned him that same night with the disheartening news. The next morning he sat quietly on the school bus and then walked down the school halls as if seeing no other students. Outside the principal's office, he sucker-punched his newlywed best friend with a right cross that split his lip and spun him to the floor. Crying guttural whines and moans he savagely continued to beat the cringing boy with a whirlwind of punches. A teacher and the vice-principal pulled at him, but they quickly became the new victims of his rage. His ex-girlfriend along with other onlookers pleaded with him to stop. He met her eyes for a moment and then broke her nose with a punch that he has never regretted.

He then fled the school and went straight to the local

U.S. Army recruiter, who was pleased to arrange his future. He had previously spoken with that amiable sergeant and liked his disposition. He understood Randy and had explained some very agreeable traits about the everyday life style and learning opportunities of the service. The Vietnam War precluded any problem with his lack of a diploma. Now, after a few fast phone calls, Randy was on his way to Fort Benning, Georgia.

From the beginning, he got along well with the toughest of the officers and sergeants, and preferred the roughest recruits who gave no quarter to weakness. They respected his erudite expertise with weapons, his natural and unabashed military bearing, and his fervent desire to be the best at everything. Two promotions came fast, and one day he asked to be sent to Vietnam. He wanted to experience this challenge that many others were fearing and avoiding. He also wanted to do some real fighting-especially with the 81mm mortar that he had mastered so well. All on the base who knew him marveled at his proficiency with setting up the tube on its base plate and bipod. He could calibrate and align the sight in record time. Dropping the rocket on the money was one of the few things that made him smile. Although he couldn't explain it, that high-tech indirect fire weapon felt like part of his essential nature.

Now, here in this dark jungle, he was watching for a slant-eyed horde that had better not give him half a chance. As the hours passed, he prepared for the worst and chose not to waken his relief man. If he was to die, he would go in style and not miss any part of it.

Twenty minutes later, Randy's mouth dropped open when he heard a staccato coughing sound somewhere south of the perimeter. No one knew more than he that a communist 82mm mortar rocket was arching high through the dark sky and would very soon burst on contact somewhere in the Bravo Company area. Even with his nerves already fraught with fears and excitement, his fine-tuned expertise caused him to simultaneously begin the "one thousand, two-thousand," seconds count to determine the range of that gunner.

Upon the heavy ripping "wroomp" sound of the exploding enemy rocket that landed harmlessly just beyond the south perimeter, Randy leaped to his waiting weapon. He mentally calculated the probable range of the enemy gunner and was adroitly calibrating the firing adjustment when he heard the second heavy "cough" from the same place. Before waiting for permission he resolutely pulled one powder bag from the fins of a mortar rocket, jerked the safety pin from the detonator in its nose, and prepared to drop it into the tube. Sgt. Gomez had jumped from his sleep and immediately signaled to fire when he saw that his most competent gunner was ready.

The second enemy mortar blast landed just north of the Bravo perimeter which told Randy that his enemy opponent was adjusting his range and would probably now "bracket" for effect as he listened for sounds of effectiveness. That course of action was almost as good as having a hidden spotter directing the fire. It was a difficult tactic but not impossible. With practically no room for error, these skilled technicians actually savored this perilous challenge to their expertise. Randy's own rocket sent back its ripping report of detonation, and the battle was on. Most likely only a single enemy mortar team was assigned to harass Bravo Company and hopefully cause a few casualties. Of course, maybe it was a probing tactic or a diversion. In any case, an effective response would foil this initiative and avoid casualties.

Better for both than blindly firing at a general area, a dramatic duel developed between two weapon specialists. In a war pitting thousands against thousands contesting dissimilar ideologies and pursuing conflicting goals, two determined top professionals of deadly indirect weaponry were competing to prove their prowess in a game demanding a precision performance for survival. It could be likened to a 19th Century championship boxing match that would finally be won by a knockout or the inability of a contestant to continue. As is often the case, the indomitable contenders, even in war, train and spar endlessly to finally meet in a deadly duel with a destined opponent to determine the paragon. Never mind that neither have any reasonable ulterior motive, nor that they ever met or ever will. The two contestants are anxiously willing to grievously injure or even kill the other to win. Probably the enemy gunner was apart from his parent unit, but Randy had to win before one of those diabolical rockets was correctly adjusted to cause Bravo Company casualties and maybe cause a concerted attack. With no thought of his own safety, he listened and counted seconds and calculated and calibrated as he zeroed in to finally fire a knockout barrage.

The VC gunner had fired four expertly adjusted but thus far ineffective rounds before Randy went for it by firing a flurry of five rounds meant to "splash down" in a diamond pattern. The subsequent silent seconds finally proved to count out the enemy contender. The VC gunner was dead, wounded, or running for his life, and Randy had won. Bravo Six immediately congratulated him and then made a note to later recommend him for the U.S. Army Commendation Medal for excellence in his job specialty.

Long range artillery support had been available and protective area barrages had been expertly planned. However, even as competent as the attached liaison lieutenant was, he would have readily admitted that the 105mm or even the much ballyhooed 155mm howitzers couldn't have confronted this particular problem with the speed and accuracy of an 81mm mortar expert. Not only did Randy Quinn spare Bravo Company the agony of probable casualties, but he thwarted the enemy's desire to harass Bravo Company anymore that night.

Randy had always been a good fighter. Society rarely rewards such a talent. However in Vietnam, his overall job performance, his execution under combat stress, and his excellent soldiering attitude in general earned him the Bronze Star Medal for competence as well as the Commendation Medal as recommended by Bravo Six. A solid success experience often cures a young man of his errant ways. Randy Quinn ultimately retired from the

U.S. Army after twenty years of exemplary service and the rank of master sergeant. With a substantial savings, he was able to invest in a hunting lodge in the Canadian Yukon. No one would have predicted how satisfying his life was thereafter.

Dawn came and nothing more happened. Just after the mortar battle, one shy soldier had sought some privacy in the jungle to answer an urgent "call of nature" and then was afraid to go back to the perimeter until early daylight. Similar incidents have been tragic.

Bravo Company would now be moving farther north by helicopter to secure a new bivouac area for the rest of the battalion. The other Second Brigade Battalion had fought a running battle with small bands of VC, obviously to again cover an escaping unit. The enemy was not going to make a stand anywhere. An air strike hit that VC camp later to hopefully get any missed supplies or, perchance, some returning soldiers.

The command level operations staff was sometimes the enemy's good friend. Their foolish good ol' boy decisions caused missed opportunities. When a First Brigade Wolverine Company surprised a platoon size VC unit and had it pinned down, the CO's report was received by the G3 operations officer who ordered that company to stay in place while he arranged for "covering" artillery support from his friend at a little used fire support unit. Of course the reaction time of this inept unit gave the VC time enough to manage an escape from almost certain annihilation. Such bungled tactics were common and certainly didn't help those who were serious about the war effort .

That requested G2 officer never came to interview Bravo Six, nor had Badger Six even called for him. As disgusting as that was; now Bravo Six had the prerogative of his prisoner's fate.

Sgt. Lee now asked Duc if he wanted to be free. He said that he did and told Sgt. Lee that he wanted to go on his own. Bravo Six nodded his approval and gave him a compass to guide him through the jungle to the west.

It was fascinating to watch him prepare for probably his most important life journey, resulting from his most traumatic experience. He donned the familiar sandals made of rope and tire tread, black pajama-like shirt and trousers, and a rag tied around his head to appear as a Viet Cong. Two pairs of socks stuffed with rice, salt pork, and rock salt hung from his cloth belt. He asked for nothing and was still a bit apprehensive about his strange, benevolent captors. Randy Quinn handed him a large folding Buck knife. As he accepted the gift and shook Randy's extended hand, they saw something mutual in each other's eyes. Then some others stepped forward to give him something and shake his hand. He readily accepted a small red "ditty bag" full of candy bars and money with a bigger smile and the traditional bow. Duc waved as he left the perimeter. Bravo Six stood tall as he watched the little vagabond enter the jungle. He felt good when his company command group told him that he did a good thing. Ngo Lee Duc would live forever in his store of memories.

Two days passed without orders in the new battalion bivouac and then all returned to Bam Nam. Not many of the enemy were known to be killed during that whole operation. It was unofficially known that the Junction City operation area had not been effectively surrounded nor had the participating units been coordinated correctly. Nevertheless, the enemy had been forced to abandon their hidden base camps at great cost in supplies, operating materials, and confidence. Also, confirmed intelligence reported that General Thanh, commander of the Viet Cong COSVN (Central Office of Vietnam Nam) died from injuries during the operation's area "carpet bombing." It was February 1967 and the Communist "Dau Tranh" (doctrine of struggle to unify South Vietnam) was not going exactly as planned.

However, maybe Ho Chi Minh wasn't very worried. He had stated in 1965 that the war would not be won on the battlefields but in the big cities of the USA. Even the U.S. news media appeared to cater to that segment of American society that also ghoulishly enjoyed the supermarket tabloids. This victory wouldn't be reported any better than that of the battle at Hue, the 1968 Tet Offensive, the siege at Khe Sanh, or many other large scale successes. Actually, one had to look to small unit level to find any enemy combat victories, but even there the Viet Cong suffered many more defeats.

The Badger Battalion rested for a week to prepare for the next mission. Everybody had clothes to put in order, letters to write, and equipment to maintain.

Weary bodies needed showers, real beds, and, for some, "downtown" entertainment. The village of Bam Nam, namesake of the huge nearby Army base, gladly accommodated the Americans with any desired amenities, legal or otherwise. Once, Bravo Six was deeply embarrassed when he took a large bag of dirty clothes to a local establishment with a large signboard that said Ho My Ho Laundry. Two girls tugged at him to stay, but the cruel laughter of the others caused him to hastily return to his jeep. Rahskle, his driver, begged forgiveness, but couldn't contain his amusement. Only he could get away with that.

Of course, almost everybody of every rank enjoyed the psychological repose of a few beers and relaxed conversation among their colleagues at those lightly-constructed buildings designated as Post service clubs (drinking places). Especially at the officers' club, the camaraderie usually never went beyond the level of good-natured ribaldry. However, the spirits of strong young men, tempered by the emotive demands of combat, are easily mixed with the deceitful spirits of strong drink. A catalytic challenge involving the mystique of masculinity could incite these sworn gentlemen to angry physical discourse.

A "green beret" captain of the U.S, Army Special Forces arrived in Bam Nam the next morning. He was from the area of the next operation and was requested to brief the command staff on that terrain and advise them on what to expect of the indigenous Viet Cong. Later that afternoon during the battalion operation order, Bravo

Six observed that this Captain Solomon must have been well received due to several references to that exceptionally big man of impressive military bearing.

However, that evening at the officers' club when this tall and very powerfully built black captain met the usually friendly and unassuming hospitality of the battalion company and platoon grade officers, he revealed his persona façade. He practically announced a crude dislike for grunts (infantrymen) and probably also any white officer not respecting his superiority. Already watching for such an opportunity, when he learned that Lt. Darrel Wagnal was a new platoon leader of Bravo Company, his general derision now narrowed to a degrading verbal attack on that flabbergasted lieutenant.

Wagnal, only two months in the country, was of average size and build. He was outranked besides and could only sheepishly stare with his mouth open, as if to speak. Then, in a show of derision, he suddenly tightened his lips, flared his nostrils, and turned away in disgust. Solomon viciously dug his fingernails into Wagnal's cheek. He jerked the abashed lieutenant's face close to his and spoke in a tone meant to rob this pitifully discomposed young officer of any remaining dignity. "Don't you ever turn your head when I'm speaking to you. You understand me, boy?"

Wagnal sensed the glaring silence of his cowering fellow officers and decided to relate his disgrace by answering with a subdued acceptance. However, the disgrace was shallow as all present rather sympathized with his hopeless predicament.

Solomon then broadened his attack to leave no doubt about his real target. "Tell me, boy. Is it true what they say about Bravo Company lieutenants?"

"Wh…what's that…sir?"

"I was told that they don't miss their girlfriends because their company commander is so nice to them. Is that true, lieutenant?"

Wagnal then realized that that he was being cruelly used as a pawn. This egotistic bully meant to bully not him but Captain Hasel Smithe, whose imposing reputation had undoubtedly reached the periphery of his own area of operation.

Sensing that he could now get away, Wagnal rose from his stool and spoke loudly with renewed self-respect as he nodded toward his commander who sat at a nearby table with Captain Reggie Trainor. "Ask him that yourself. I'm leaving this bullshit!"

Bravo Six had been calmly observing and was not surprised that he was suddenly the new target.

Solomon spoke to him with a smile that also served as a sneer. "What about it, Smithe? You really have any balls?"

Bravo Six knew that even with his amateur boxing experience, he was physically outclassed. Solomon would also be too experienced to fall for a sucker punch. Even if he could land a solid first punch, this big jerk probably had the gumption, as well as the superior strength to recover and persevere. He no doubt was also expert in hand-to-hand combat and would show no mercy in asserting his dominance.

Bravo Six knew that he could fight well enough to at least save his pride and the respect of his fellow officers. However, he could be rendered physically unable to accompany his unit in the next field assignment which could cost him his command position. In any case, Badger Six would not be sympathetic in considering that such an impressive guest had to fistfight with his least favorite company commander who threw the first punch. He would no doubt lose the fight and suffer serious collateral career damage. All this streamed through his mind in five long seconds following Solomon's insulting question derisively meant to emasculate him.

Captain Reggie Trainor, beside him, also knew that Bravo Six was in a no win situation. Even if Bravo Six could beat Solomon, it would have to be a very fierce, bloody battle, leaving his friend to bear the brunt of the blame.

"Not now," Reggie mumbled to him. "Go to your bunk, and I'll send for you. Trust me."

Bravo Six rose to his feet and spoke as he turned to leave, "I'll see you all later."

Before he got halfway to the door, Solomon sharply called his name. He turned his head to see Solomon smack his lips to throw him a kiss. His ears burned with anger, but without even changing his bland expression he continued out the door as he heard a few guttural murmurs and groans reacting to Solomon's crude challenge.

Bravo Six lay on his bunk and contemplated his embarrassment. It was tough for him to rationalize that he had done what an officer and gentleman should have done. What was more important-his command or his ego? Self- respect often has to face a double-edged sword. Reggie, and maybe a few others, would be able to later convince anybody who cared, that his honor was respectfully unmarred.

Back at the club Solomon was reveling in his victory. The drinks continued to flow while Reggie charismatically maneuvered eight of his fellow officers into cajoling Solomon to relate tale after tale of glory and gore about Green Beret exploits. Probably at least some of it was true, but most of it, of course, smacked of Solomon himself. Then Reggie led the group into a few macho drinking games that served to cause all to drink more and faster. Two hours quickly passed, and finally Solomon had to go outside to throw up even more violently than three others just before him.

The big captain's sallow face told Reggie that his ruse was working well. He immediately sent a sober lieutenant to quickly fetch Bravo Six and Lt. Wagnal. One would suppose it smart for the Bravo commander to have stayed in bed, but he was too much a plebeian to resist Reggie's call for the counterattack. Lt. Wagnal had fallen asleep and would rather have not complied, but he went anyway to humor his colleagues.

Bravo Six marched into the club straight for Solomon who was now taking Reggie's calculated bad advice to settle his stomach with ginger brandy. The gaggle of functionally inebriated officers backed away a few steps but certainly weren't going to leave. All could sense the growing electricity of a pending climax to an exceptionally exciting evening.

Solomon looked weak and certainly felt weak. His stomach was very queasy and his bowels were loosening. His lips felt numb and wet as he breathed in short sucks through his mouth and continually snorted with his runny nose. This "grunt" captain now looked bigger and stronger and hell bent to fight. He suddenly knew that he had been hustled and was going to pay for his stupidity.

Bravo Six would still be in trouble with his superiors if he actually had to maul this bully, should he be stubborn. However, if he could decisively force Solomon to cower, without actually hurting him, he would still achieve a victory bound to be ballyhooed by those who cared about such masculine balderdash. It would certainly be better than the earlier disgrace that would have cost him his knightly honor among his peers and would have caused Badger Six to smirk with vindictive pleasure.

Bravo Six stood close in front of Solomon who sat on a stool facing him with his elbows resting on the edge of the bar. "I said that I'd see you later. Now let's answer your question about my balls." Bravo Six snatched that green beret and stepped back to balance a punch. Solomon rose to his feet but did not attack or even speak.

Bravo Six then tossed the beret to Reggie and continued his assault. "C'mon, big shit." He shoved Solomon hard against the bar and stared savagely at a face searching desperately for a nonviolent discourse. He then offered him an alternative that would not jeopardize his vindication. "You apologize to my lieutenant or take your best shot right now."

Solomon thought hard about his chances of respectably surviving this climactic turn of events but couldn't imagine anything less than some conspicuous bruises that would have to be embarrassingly explained at Special Forces headquarters. His big muscles felt flaccid and his mind was so fogged with the debilitating booze that his martial art skills would be clumsy at best. Five seconds after that tenacious ultimatum, he knew that he had better make his move.

"Hey, lieutenant, you have my apology." He spoke in a conciliatory tone almost void of inflection. Unaccustomed as he was to humility, this cut deep into his self-worth.

Bravo Six turned and started out before anything else could happen or be said. The others followed and shouted the usual slang expressions to tout his success. He acknowledged their compliments with a brief hand wave and then headed straight for his bunk. He was relieved and happy for his success even if it did mean that Badger Six and Major Domsavich were probably correct about his proletariat lack of refined intelligence.

Before falling asleep, he thought about the Viet Cong and realized that he had just done what they had mastered. He had beaten a bigger, stronger enemy of superior firepower by lulling him into overconfidence and then attacking at his weakest posture. Those dirty little guerrillas out there would have been proud of him.

At daylight, Reggie woke Bravo Six to go to breakfast. He gave him that green beret and told him that last night couldn't have gone any better. He laughed when he said, "Just as always, you found a rose in an outhouse."

Bravo Six liked Reggie and cherished their friendship. This shrewd abrasive man had little time for most people, and none ever fooled him for very long at anything. He was comparatively short in stature and prematurely bald but built like a fireplug. He was unusually worldly, intensely chauvinistic, and in some ways, an old-fashioned idealist. Certainly, nobody could be more loyal. If you were one of his few friends, you were as a part of his body. Women liked his company, but knew that he would be a terrible husband.

"I'm going to give this beret back to him." Bravo Six smiled as he waited for Reggie's expected response.

Of course Reggie smiled at the thought of his brash friend attempting to force his own ending to the affair. "He'll have a hangover, and he really doesn't like you. It might go bad."

"Yeh, but it might go all right. I'd rather not have him for an enemy. Let me approach him alone…"

"Okay, but remember that he has a lot of pride." Reggie was still smiling as he imagined Solomon leaping from his chair to punch Bravo Six. He would enjoy watching an early morning donnybrook in the mess hall.

Most of the battalion officers were already eating.

Solomon was sitting with Badger Six, Major Domsavich, and Colonel Langham who had come to be briefed on the command operation plans. Of course, this high level table company was bound to influence Solomon's response to Bravo Six who was brazenly walking straight to him with his beloved beret.

Bravo Six made sure that his facial expression and the tone of his words and voice inflection would not cause Solomon to think that he was making fun of him. "You left this at the bar last night". He held it out to him as one would return a hat to a stranger in any other situation.

Solomon hesitated about two seconds before taking the beret. He blandly said, "Thanks." Then just after Bravo Six turned, Solomon called to him and offered a respectful salute. Bravo Six, of course, courteously returned it. They then shook hands and briefly wished each other good luck. The heavy aura of reconciliation about them caused the few who didn't already know to speculate about the night before. Colonel Langham surmised what had brought on this odd scene and smiled in remembrance of his youth as a feisty lieutenant in Korea. Badger Six and Major Domsavich, knowing Bravo Six, also figured what had probably happened but only glared in disgust that their nemesis had apparently effected such a positive impression.

Reggie shook his head in disbelief as Bravo Six joined him at his table. He smiled as he quietly spoke. "You're a charmed son of a bitch. If I had your luck, I could rule the world."

CHAPTER TWELVE

CHICANERY AND CONTRARIETY AT HA CU CANAL

The picturesque horseshoe bend area of the Vam Co Dong River in the upper Delta below Tay Ninh City had been rich in sugar cane and pineapples. A few impressive concrete homes with orange ceramic- tiled roofs were scattered about the area along with now unkempt cemeteries of elaborate gravestones and wrought iron fences., The most impressive building was a small but beautiful Buddhist temple on the outside curve of the river horseshoe. Nearby was a rustic operational sugar processing factory of three buildings.. That particular local business was seasonal, but the location just had to be beneficial to transient Viet Cong.

Americans had never been there. The Viet Cong had taken control of the entire municipal area with no functional local government remaining for about a dozen large and small villages. The roads had been cut and all bridges destroyed. Viet Cong strength was estimated to consist of up to several hundred experienced and well-equipped partisans. The vicinity had been previously bombed and then probed by ARVN reconnaissance forays that had met heavy resistance.

The Badger Battalion had been given the mission of quelling hostile resistance to allow the U.S. Army Corps of Engineers to rebuild and reopen the roads and canals essential for revitalizing the local economy. The first two days were spent about four kilometers east of the river. The three companies leap-frogged with heliborne assaults against light resistance from fleeting guerrilla cellular units sent to tactically occupy them. Only Charlie Company was successful enough to report three body count.

This show of force would have probably been enough to cause the insurgents to at least temporarily abandon the area. They would not be beaten, but their propaganda would suffer for awhile. Bravo Six would have argued that the enemy had to be hurt badly enough that the populace could work with some confidence. However, he would never have agreed with the plausibility of his mission for that night. Badger Six and Domsavich may have decided to get rid of Bravo Six the easy way?

Bravo Six knelt, glaring at Major Domsavich while holding his map and grease pencil. Sp. 4 Forney, the unflagging company RTO, stoically sat at his side scrutinizing the strain on his captain's composure. He also contemplated this almost middle-aged major explaining an operation order as if he were rehearsing it for a B grade movie. He tried to imagine this averaged-sized but tough-talking major in a drunken stupor at the bar back at Bam Nam base. The story was that he had been purposely taunting the formidable Bravo Six in hopes of awing his own anticipant colleagues watching from a side table. The story was that Domsavich had tempted the exasperated Bravo Six to "take his best shot." Bravo Six, not really fully inebriated but beer buzzed enough to cross the line of composure with this dunderhead, let go with his best straight right. Forney wished that he could have seen that shocked field grade pretender spasmodically fall backward over a table full of lieutenants and then unceremoniously spit out a sequence of sundry expressions through the blood streaming from his smarting nose. His only threat as he left was, "I've got you now, boy!"

Colonel Langham advised Major Domsavich that his requested court martial should be handled by him. An altercation with both parties drinking in a bar cannot easily be explained and usually weakens any case for aggravated assault-even when one is a superior officer to the other. When one voluntarily subjects himself to the composure debilitating effects of an intoxicant, the benefits of rank are eroded and can even become a detriment. Colonel Langham also knew that Major Domsavich, in his most important field grade assignment as a battalion

S3 operations officer, was experiencing the last throes of losing an overdue promotion before his retirement from an unimpressive career. The incorruptible and unshakable Bravo Six was the nemesis of the "perfect" performance that he and his equally impotent immediate commander, Badger Six, imagined that they were achieving. They would relish a court-martial for Bravo Six. Although Domsavich always projected a front of importance, it was obvious that his adjunct position of S3 Operations Officer was the epitome of his lackluster career.

Badger Six gladly signed off on the paperwork and forwarded it to Colonel Langham who would officially review the case "without prejudice". As expected, he chastised Bravo Six for lack of good judgment, conduct unbecoming an officer, etc. He also reminded him that he was commissioned to fight only the enemy. He almost lost his official composure and practically apologized as he presented Bravo Six with a copy of the official reprimand that would be in his personal file. He knew Capt. Smithe wasn't sorry for his actions and the whole affair would be no more than a chuckle to the division commander who would also review the matter. Lt. General Hought would also remember the mettle of this brazen captain who boldly effected the rescue of Alpha Six. General Hought himself was called the catalyst of that victory and became the three-star hero of those rank and file soldiers who knew about it.

Col. Langham was right. The general returned the paperwork without comment. It was hand- carried by an aide who advised that it be trashed.

RTO Forney, during that forty-five second stream of consciousness, had been barely listening to the details of Major Domsavich's operation order. He knew it was to be that night, but he ordinarily didn't care about the logistics anyway. What did catch his attention was Bravo Six's interrupting and disquieting question.

"Why aren't you looking at me?" His tone was unpleasantly terse.

"Captain, I'll look at you if and when I want to. You just tell me if you understand this order. Maybe Badger Six should read it to you."

"Is this order from you, from Badger Six, or both of you?" Bravo Six spoke as if he were involuntarily condescending to a disgusting child.

Major Domsavich tightened his already stern mouth and dropped his pretense of composure. "Are you telling me that you don't want to go?" Domsavich flashed his eyes at the wide-eyed Forney and spoke again as if sensing victory. "Just say it right out, Smithe."

Bravo Six surmised this as a no-win situation designed to damn him or physically eliminate him. By refusing to go he would probably lose his command or at least his reputation. By attempting such a foolhardy mission he would probably suffer a devastating defeat which could easily be spinned as incompetence. Of course, the great possibility that he would be seriously wounded, or killed, along with a high percentage of his company, would be a bonus for these two self-centered unscrupulous schemers.

Bravo Six countered with his only chance to endure. "Of course I'm going." His distinctive half-knitted brow and wry smile complemented his gruff confident tone. This natural demeanor was plenty to rebuff the hatred glowering in the sultry major's face, now ruddy and slightly twitching. Bravo Six spoke again to cut off any hope of this impotent oppressor regaining control. "You're welcome to go along on this one."

"Get out of here."

"I want a complete operation order in your handwriting."

"Why?" His tone was now a reminder of when this wretched man had attempted to bully him that night at the club.

"You know I have a right to it. This is important, and I want it. I also want to see Badger Six before I leave tonight."

"I'm sure he wouldn't mind saying goodbye to you." The disembarrassed major inflected his words to retain a degree of offense.

Again Bravo Six countered while glaring very directly. "How about you saying good-bye?"

"Get going and don't screw up, Smithe."

Bravo Six walked as he wondered about preparing for this difficult mission that not only would be under great disadvantage but was also unnecessary and extremely dangerous. He was sore afraid for himself and the soldiers depending on him.

As RTO Forney strode beside the only officer he had

ever admired, he now read a message on his command-er's face that evoked a frightening uneasiness. "Is this going to be bad, sir?"

Bravo Six spoke without changing stride. "Yeh...but we're going to meet it head- on and win."

Forney said no more and drifted into his own thoughts and anxieties.

Bravo Six watched the faces of his platoon leaders as he explained that Bravo Company was to travel in boats two and a half kilometers down the canal after dark. Then they would walk two kilometers down a pony cart road to surprise the suspected Viet Cong rally point and transient camp at a small sugar processing factory. Sgt. Phillips and Sgt. Mueller looked at each other as experienced veterans would. They knew that the noisy boats would surely either draw close sniper fire or alert an encampment of any size. The attackers could be am-bushed instead. The combination of handicaps and in-consistencies was unbelievable. Intelligence staffers had reported a high probability of a company-sized guerrilla unit in the area with weaponry and supplies to counter the American maneuvers. The terrain was unfamiliar and probably mined and booby-trapped. Although most units of the Wolverines were experienced in daylight he-liborne operations, no unit had ever attacked a prepared enemy position by boat or any other way after dark. Even the present location of the enemy was unfamiliar. Bravo Company would have no advantage except blind guts and the probable shock of a stupefied enemy.

The disdain for Badger Six and S3 Domsavich was mostly unjustified. Bravo Six's own ego and earned reputation was in direct deference to their personalities, learned perspectives, and tactical judgments. His opposition to them probably wasn't fair, but he would only say, "I gotta be me." However, that is not to say that those two were honest and without culpability. Their shared decisions usually smacked of personal advantage.

Bravo Six decided to take only the First and Third Platoons. He further customized them by taking only the riflemen, his best 90mm rocket team (bazooka), and six selected riflemen from Second Platoon. With only two boats, he could simplify his execution, lose a boat or evacuate wounded enroute. Human noise and movement would also be more easily controlled to compensate for any loss of firepower.

The forty-eight men stripped themselves of any unnecessary items, muddied their exposed skin, and checked their weapons, ammunition, and hand grenades carefully. For the first time they were wearing soft caps on an attack. And, for the first time, they feared that their commander might be attempting too much with too few who were mostly too inexperienced and too scared. They would go, but probably not without Bravo Six. A common response to the grumbling was "Ain't he straight?' or "Ain't he there in the thick? Get your ass in gear! We goin' to give 'Charlie' the shit!"

PFC Herb Wolfe was thirty-one years old and much more experienced in combat than even his squad leader.

He also muddied his fatigues and hair and further tied strips of black cloth around his elbows and knees and rifle for camouflage, protection, and emergency bandaging. A while back, others in his squad wondered as he tore apart the shirt of a VC that he had personally killed.

His squad thought it odd, or at least unnecessary, that he always put another bullet into any VC supposedly dead. It probably had something to do with his irritating habit of never taking anybody's word for anything. He was barely personable enough without having any distinguishable personality and would never be accused of talking or laughing too much. Being too assuming about his generosity with his cigarettes, soon after his arrival, had caused a couple of loud "home boy" bullies to suffer a stinging backhand and then lose the ego-soothing game of staring to bluff retaliation.

Herb Wolf was nick-named "Lobo,", but nobody would be surprised. Besides his name, his physique was more sinewy than muscular. The heavily pock-marked cheeks on his ill-favored face were complemented by a long bulbous nose. His unsightly hair was even in some wrong places.

A new soldier asked a short-timer (almost ready to go home) about Lobo's battle preparation. The response was respectful of the man who was now napping. "Because he's smart, boy. He's a survivor. You gotta be smart or tough, and he's both. Now if you want to be smart, give him plenty of room. He ain't to be questioned or pushed. Got it?"

"Man, I don't think I even want to be anywhere near him. He must be a bad dude."

"It'd be better to be near him. He's seen more action than most, and he's better than some of the best. They say that he's more of a killer than a soldier. Most guys think a little about killing, but he just does it. Be glad he's on our side! Just ask the others about him and Apollo. That affair was a real ass kicker!

Then why is he still a PFC?"

That question caused an immediate chuckle. "He ain't exactly a model citizen. That's why he gets transferred so much. He came here from the stockade. Sgt. Phillips asked Bravo Six to go get him. He said that he and the others would be responsible for him.

The new soldier looked again at Lobo and thought he was fortunate to be in the same squad. This ugly misfit of polite society was no doubt of the bulwark of the infantry. All he needed was a little more room than most others.

Bravo Six watched as the tide slowly gained momentum up the ancient canal. Bits of flotsam on the brackish water made him wonder about possible activity downstream. No matter, his prior fears were now jelling into audacious anxiety.

The dusk was yielding to the darkness of a half moon, and the wind was a slight but steady draft toward the ancient Vam Co Dong River. For thousands of years this pristine pearl of the Southeast Asian tropics had been intermittently interrupted by the fickle antics of mankind.

Now Americans were probably becoming a chapter of the history of Japanese, French, and others to fight and die here.

Bravo Six knew that he was most likely heading into the denouement of his command or even his life. A lesser chance existed for a validation or even a victory. To go out with a whimper or a qualm wasn't his style. Be it a bust or a boon, he was determined to run out the show. The were now walking to him, and this side of the battle would begin.

The tall but slightly built Badger Six always spoke with as much arrogance as a pseudo-intellectual could muster. "Any problems, Captain Smithe?"

"No sir. We're in the ready position."

"Why are you taking only two platoons?"

"Mobility and control. They're reinforced." Bravo Six spoke confidently but with a detached tone. "And I'd feel better to be with the tide instead of against it."

"We know what we're doing. I just hope you know what you're doing. Why did you want the S3 to write the order?"

Bravo Six glowered at the stolid major but spoke to his commander; "Did he write it?"

"Yes, but I want to know why."

Now Bravo Six had to force a finish. "I want you to sign it. You don't mind, do you?"

"You know you're playing games way out of your league, Smithe. What are you going to do with it?"

"I don't know for sure. I just want it. This is an important operation for me." Bravo Six thought that a bit of nostalgic camouflage wouldn't hurt.

Badger Six handed the yellow note paper to Bravo Six while Major Domsavich continued his reticent and glowering posture.

"It is important. Damn important. Don't screw this up. I'm not even sure that I should send you." Badger Six pointed at him as he spoke with a slight lisp.

Bravo Six smirked at that comment as he quickly seized the paper while he had a chance. He then spoke with angry derision and an indirect threat. "I had hoped that you two were sending me because I was the best for the job. Everything will go right or the three of us will be dead wrong."

Badger Six understood and spoke angrily as he turned away. "You'd better know what you are doing." The two connivers left silently. They knew that Bravo Six just threatened to kill them, but they were confident that if Bravo Six survived, which they doubted, incompetence under pressure would be easy to charge. His disrespectful response aside, they also doubted that the signed operation order could become a determiner if Bravo Six were already disgraced. It would probably be lost during the fighting anyway. The brawny, usually taciturn, and always fortuitously lucky Bravo Six surely couldn't also be shrewd enough to use that paper to his advantage. If necessary, they would have him summarily incarcerated for their own protection.

The two open-hulled boats arrived on time. They were proficiently piloted by armed operators who had probably volunteered for a real combat mission. Both pilots and a third one, their crew chief, (a substitute pilot) would appreciate and deserve the Bronze Star Medal that Bravo Six was destined to recommend for their valor. The unusually silent Bravo soldiers boarded the inboard-outboard powered boats and assumed a posture reflecting stealth infused with apprehension.

Now Sgt. Mueller shouldered up to Bravo Six, "C'mon sir, what's going on?"

"As you may have guessed, this is probably 'payback' from Major Domsavich for me punching him in the mouth and getting away with it."

"Not probably. This *is* payback! That mealy-assed bastard would do anything no matter how cowardly and that colonel isn't any better."

"I think you're right, but now I have my whole company paying for my foolishness. I'm sorry I did this to you."

"Sir, you did just what I would have done. You got away with it because you are you! That's what burns his ass more than anything. This is a foolhardy mission, but don't forget what kind of guys are going with you. I've got some feeling that we're going to do all right. We can put a bad whipping on some VC tonight. Let's go show them and everyone else who we are."

Bravo Six flushed with delight. "Mueller, I love you, man. I love all these guys." He was glad that no tear exposed his subdued emotions.

The grizzled battle-wise sergeant gave his up-front commander a shoulder punch of confidence and ended the talk with a verbal boost. "Forget love and let's give 'em hell!"

A slight mist felt cool as the task force cruised past the repetitious dense array of equatorial trees and huge ferns shrouded in a nocturnal haze. All of nature appeared to be silently moving aside to allow these noisy intruders to challenge those other inharmonious evil creatures.

The heavy drone of the engines surely could not have been mistaken for anything other than what it was. Bravo thought disquietingly that an outgoing tide could have carried them at the same speed in virtual silence but he knew that wouldn't have fit into their plan. He couldn't help scrutinizing both banks for an ambush although he knew that nothing would be obvious. He was glad that he stressed the importance of preponderant return fire. He had also instructed the pilots to gun the engines to scramble ahead. A clever tactic of the Viet Cong in ambushes was to allow the targeted convoy to pass their initial main elements and then open fire while the convoy units were trying to reverse themselves to escape a smaller fusillade just ahead.

Nothing was happening and only about a half kilometer from the crossing Bravo Six ordered the boats to stop at the right bank but to continue running the engines.

Sgt. Monroe's squad was sent ahead by land to reconnoiter the road landing site and secure it. Milton Monroe hadn't been much of a soldier for his first three months of combat, but accidental glory changed his life. He had discovered a large cache of 82mm mortar rockets camouflaged in a rice paddy dike. An exposed nose cone made him curious enough to dig away the loose dirt. That, along with a sudden shortage of squad leaders, catapulted him into a position of responsibility that unveiled and kindled his leadership abilities. This mission was his first solo assignment, and success would solidify his status as one of the company honchos. He had established control of his squad and had earned their respect. Now he was determined to prove his prowess to Sgt. Mueller, to himself, and to anyone else that mattered. Maybe he would even get a medal.

Monroe's squad found the crossing. His men lay prone and quietly alert as he scanned the area with a Starlite scope. In the eerie green light reflected in the lens, he spotted two men sitting on the road at the water's edge. His heart pounded in response to his realization of his responsibility. He had to determine this leg of the company's mission. His breathing steadily labored and his nostrils flared as he whispered to his men that they would sneak up on these two apparently unprofessional but still very dangerous Viet Cong sentinels and silence them. Milton knew that Bravo Six wouldn't want to abort the mission for two sentinels, and the terrain would disallow an alternate route to avoid their attention. He also knew that any gunshots or one of them escaping would ruin the mission. Milton and his seven young riflemen very slowly stalked through the tropical weeds and grasses toward the two unsuspecting guer-rillas. None of these eight Americans, barely out of high school, had ever done anything as gutsy or ever thought they would. Considering the responsibility and the danger, probably none would have volunteered. But here they were, on their hands and knees, performing a semblance of a child's prank-this time for keeps.

As they approached within ten meters they could see rifles and a cigarette butt passing back and forth. Monroe figured that the two lackadaisical guerrillas were high on "Maui Wowie" (marijuana) and possibly thought that the steady din of the boat engines was probably a far away generator.

Their senses were dulled to the extent of accepting any night noises as harmless. As the two slackers sat staring at the water and mumbling a conversation, the squad suddenly rushed and pinned them to the ground with only limited scuffling and a muffled cry of surprise and anguish. They were gagged, their hands tied behind them, and their necks tethered to their feet.

Herb Wolfe was in that squad. That's a big reason why Sgt. Monroe had been given this mission. Lobo, as he allowed everyone to call him, wasn't even a fire team leader, but when he stated his opinion, as he rarely did, everyone listened carefully. He quietly advised Monroe that the bigger prisoner, who continually twisted his arms and grumbled, could cause a dangerous problem. Monroe knew what Lobo would do and worried about the affect on the other squad members. However, he also knew that

Lobo was right, and besides, he wanted to keep the faith of this fighting man, even if he was a potential problem himself. Monroe decided to let Lobo have his way. He whispered, "Make damn sure he doesn't."

Lobo at least gave the squirming captive a chance by pointing a finger at him in a universal "be quiet" gesture. Noticing no immediate response, Lobo grabbed the prison's long coarse hair with his right hand and the nylon rope binding the feet with his left hand. He walked into the waist high water and completely submerged the doomed guerilla. Then, afterward, he calmly walked out alone and knelt beside the other prisoner who had been watching. This one fully understood that lying quiet was in his best interests. Monroe later reported one body count. No one ever asked how a VC died anyway.

It was over. Sgt. Monroe had instructed his men well, and they performed perfectly.

He secured the landing with his own sentinels and "broke squelch" on the company radio with Morse code for okay. He felt proudly professional and anxious for the task force to arrive. Knowing Bravo Six, he was confident that all his men would later receive a commendation. Surely there'd be something extra for him, too.

RTO Forney acknowledged the coded signal, and Bravo Six waved the boats forward. That's when he noticed a familiar face smiling at him. It was hard to believe that someone could be daring, adventurous, or even curious enough to "spit in the face of dishonor" and maybe death, again. Whatever prompted Reggie Trainor, his audacious Delta Six friend, to practically stowaway aboard a miniature fleet on a mission foreboding a fatal outcome, could only be understood by one as spirited as he. This time the gallant and crazed combatant would challenge the enemy again as ordinary rifleman do. Bravo Six appreciated the raw courage and faithfulness of some of his colleagues. He would do the same for them, but he always seemed to be the one in the path of a calamity. One could bet that Reggie would be heard of again on this mission.

The boats met Sgt. Monroe at the landing, and Sgt. Mueller and Sgt. Laird immediately organized the task force to traverse the three kilometers of treacherous distance along the ancient cart path leading to the sugar factory.

Monroe's prisoner was left in one of the boats and guarded by the crew chief. They returned to the battalion base at the same speed to maintain the noise level. The pilots had performed perfectly and would not be forgotten at the next honors formation.

Bravo Six moved his entourage with growing confidence. The point squad and flankers warily but steadily led with a cautious stride. The movement order was the same. If attacked, charge forward out of the firing to regroup and defend. With good execution, it would take a force twice their size to overpower them.

The pristine nocturnal silence continued undefiled and that dire dank scent of the monsoon tropical Delta had become even more herbal. The fifty-five earnest young American journeymen arrived two hundred meters from the comparatively small Buddhist temple unmistakably outlined on the dim Delta skyline. No sign of enemy presence could be detected but those two sentinels had been there for a good reason. Bravo Six signaled his force to proceed as planned. Sergeant Laird's Third Platoon moved to the left of the objective to set up a base of fire if needed.

Bravo Six helped lead the First Platoon in a slow silent assault to the temple grounds and the adjoining buildings. If they received effective gunfire, then the Third Platoon would provide flanking fire support from the south. That would allow the assault force to deploy and call for the pre-planned artillery barrage or continue with an overrunning attack, depending on the resistance.

Captain Reggie Trainor stealthily walked in a slight crouch close by his friend. He would go anywhere and do anything with the unassuming Bravo Six, his favorite partner for banter and beer. Together they were both incorrigible and formidable, but those in the know often said that the bawdiness and spontaneity of both negatively overshadowed their stalwart character and charisma.

Onward they advanced to where something would have to happen soon. Bravo Six felt a different variety of "butterflies" in his stomach. This small assault force could be approaching maybe a hundred Viet Cong cunningly waiting for the right time to open fire at "spitting range" to ravenously slaughter them without mercy.

This mission had him out of sync with his tactical ability, and the enemy could play out a master plan well within their expertise. Never did he wish for the right expectation of the enemy as he did now. Whatever, he would play it out.

Then the enemy was discovered, as any attackers would prefer. A lead soldier almost stepped on an enemy sentry. He had been either hiding in fear or caught napping. As he and two others quickly pointed their rifles in the wide-eyed and open-mouthed face, Sergeant Phillips began to gag and tie him. The unnerved guerilla began to plead with a low wail. One soldier tried to clamp his hand over that moaning mouth, but the anguished VC began writhing in near panic. Sgt. Phillips moved quickly to quash what could cost the mission and many lives. The heavy thud of his steel-plated M14 rifle butt as it crudely jolted the VC's forehead repulsed the younger less experienced soldiers, but they were glad for this veteran's help. When the pitiful young guerrilla again began groaning, now in severe pain and shock, Phillips finished him with another, even heavier, stoke that clearly fractured his skull.

Bravo Six had watched the incident and then studied the temple and the two smaller buildings now only about forty meters away. No activity could be seen. As pre-planned, he raised his hand to signal "get set". After everyone acknowledged with the same sign, he signaled for a swift rush to the buildings. After running about twenty meters, he saw what had to be several men asleep on the ground. His next command might as well have been shouted at a speeding bullet heading for an unsuspecting but potentially dangerous target. His attack force was practically already there.

"Charge! Charge! Get 'em!" Bravo Six fired a burst into a rising guerrilla and then started waving and yelling loud blatant encouragement. He fearfully hoped that he wouldn't find that he had asked too much with too little. All the subordinate Bravo leaders were shouting with many of the riflemen joining the uproar. The violent assault was as effective as hoped. This reputedly experienced Viet Cong unit had been lulled into confidence and contentment. Such complacency was a rare flaw of Viet Cong leadership. On the other hand, Americans normally just didn't do things this way.

The Viet Cong considered American tactical movements easy to foil or avoid with a minimum of casualties. But now these clever guerrillas were caught sleeping in and around a building without effective security. A three-quarter moon also favored the Americans.

The attacking young Americans had been apprehensive at first but quickly became inflamed with a joyful masculine fever of an easy victory over a highly rated enemy. These usually skillful and savage guerrillas were awakening and rising to the variegated rustling sounds and sharp shouting voices of seemingly huge and powerful foreign soldiers brutally grabbing their smaller enemies now weak from bewilderment and terror.

Because both sides were mixed during the melee,

shooting was more limited than usual. With the darkness and confusion a few VC were escaping, but most other luckless guerrillas were being ruthlessly manhandled by two and three captors almost too willing to punch, kick, or twist the limbs of any who slightly resisted. No one was encouraging the violent fracas more than Reggie Trainor. While showing no pity for any VC he could seize, he continuously barked at the Bravo soldiers who were trying to subdue a struggling guerrilla. "Slam him down! Kick him in the ribs! Break his fuckin' arm! Do it!" He was obviously a major factor in the overwhelming devastation of this esteemed Viet Cong unit.

In only about two minutes, the fury and frenzy and intermittent firing subsided. Bravo Six established a collection point for prisoners with his bodyguard, Rahskle, in charge. Then he ordered Sgt. Mueller to make a head count and organize a defense with Third Platoon. He also reminded him that RTO Forney had radioed for them to come in from the south.

Rahskle and Reggie Trainor organized the prisoners. Because of the limited visibility, they were made to lie spread-eagled aside each other, regardless of injury. Sgt. Laird sent a fire team from his platoon to help guard them. Of approximately fifteen to twenty Viet Cong, nine were known dead and seven were prisoners. At least three were known to escape. Of the prisoners, one was suffering an obvious dislocated elbow, three were bleeding from head and body wounds and still another had a probable broken nose. All had been maliciously manhandled. Sgt. Lee told them that the medic would treat their wounds at daylight, but if they moved now they would be shot. The dead were thrown face down atop one another and guarded as preventative insurance.

Any injuries among the Bravo soldiers were only a few slight bruises and scrapes that they seemed to value as proof that they had actually physically grappled with the enemy. Those injuries certainly qualified for the Purple Heart Medal. These beaming combatants were already trading brief spirited tales among themselves as the members of a football team would after a surprise victory. Several were recommended for a Bronze Star Medal for valor and all received letters of commendation. Their hometown newspaper later received copies of the citations.

Rahskle, with two riflemen, had charged into the other smaller building to kill two male and one female VC and capture another unarmed female. While leading her by her long black hair, he helped to calm another resisting captive with his signature punch to the kidney.

The temple had previously been ignored as a target due to the supposition that even the malevolent Viet Cong respected their Buddhist faith. Bravo Six also knew that Sgt. Lee would have been upset with such disrespect to his cherished faith. Rahskle checked it anyway.

Even SP4 Tony Paine, the very proficient but usually reserved First Platoon RTO, had doubled over another guerrilla about to wriggle loose from his captors with a surprise punch to the stomach that not only paralyzed his will to escape but also precluded the digestion of his evening rice.

During the skirmish, Bravo Six had tried to keep his command group at hand to help watch for any sign of an outside countermove. PFC Lobo Wolfe would have enjoyed that donnybrook, but he happened to be with Third Platoon. After all had quieted, Bravo Six felt satisfied with his expedient defensive position and radioed a report to his doubtlessly anxious Badger Six.

"Badger Six, this Bravo Six. Over."

"This is Badger Six. What the hell is going on?"

"The objective is secured. A unit was here. We have body count, prisoners, and weapons. No friendly KIA (Killed in Action) or serious WIA (Wounded in Action). Over.

"Roger. I'll be there at daylight. Out." That last transmission sounded as if he had turned his head to somebody else as he spoke.

Did he detect a slight tone of disappointment instead of joy? He knew that he did and exchanged a beaming grin with RTO Forney who felt good for his commander.

After an hour of tense quiet, the dawn was breaking and the medics were already working the bruises of the wounded. Then appeared a new twist to the already bizarre outcome. The always supportive Sgt. Lee reported that one of the prisoners was impressed with his assurances of fair treatment and wished to tell some others who would surrender under the Chieu Hoi repatriation program. Bravo Six decided to take a chance on the intuitive counsel of Sgt. Lee. The prisoner was instructed and freed. All the Bravo soldiers were briefed that any "Chieu Hoi" prisoner would be coming only by boat.

At 0630 hours Badger Six arrived with Col. Langham in his command helicopter. Badger Six was very formal as usual and appeared to be only "officially" impressed with the display of victory. Col. Langham really was beside himself with excitement and wanted more than just a debriefing. He even called for a photographer.

The propitious luck of Bravo Six continued in the same design. With the Col. Langham still present, the surrender began of those Viet Cong disillusioned and tired of their arduous guerrilla roles and superfluous goals. Two white-shirted swarthy Vietnamese with their rifles held over their heads glided downriver in a small study wooden sampan to waiting American soldiers.

Knowing that apprehensive eyes were probably watching from somewhere in the bushes, Bravo Six called for his men to treat them well and not tie them. The Chieu Hoi program of repatriating VC without reprisals had been advertised by leaflet drops and these two were presenting one. With Badger Six present but surreptitiously silent, Bravo Six spoke directly to Col. Langham about that prisoner release. He requested to spend the rest of the day there and then flabbergasted Badger Six by crediting him for putting together the mission (Major Domsavich could kiss his ass!). He could not have asked for more. Bravo Six was permitted to leave at dusk, and Badger Six was leaving with Col. Langham.

Badger Six was already thinking of the impressive report that he would be delivering at the morning staff briefing. Of course, he still had to worry about that written operation order that Bravo Six had demanded.

Without a further word, Badger Six left with Col. Langham. However, he knew that the side-line battle with Bravo Six was not over and could suddenly and dangerously emerge in several negative ways.

At the onset, Bravo Six had given the written operation order to the pilot of the utility helicopter with instructions to deliver it to headquarters. The sealed envelope had a specific boldly printed instruction, "Open only at my death! Otherwise, return." At least somebody would realize the foolhardiness of that operation order.

As the hours passed, more defectors came at irregular intervals. In all, twenty guerrillas in eight sampans were received with good will. Bravo Six again noticed that uneasy oriental smile as they nervously approached their dreaded enemies. A helicopter brought insulated containers of fried chicken meals from the Bam Nam base and even a container of rice and bottles of American brand soy sauce for the "guests" since that's all that they usually preferred. As expected, they told Sgt. Lee that the American style rice was "number ten" (bad), but the soy sauce was "number one" (good).

After 18:30 hours, no more defectors had come in and all the Chieu Hoi defectors and the prisoners had been evacuated. It was now dusk and Bravo Six discussed a concern with Sgt. Lee. The released prisoner had certainly kept his word and had done his job, but had not returned himself. They supposed that the wrong VC had heard his message.

Bravo Six weighed all the plusses for his mission aftermath. Col. Langham certainly didn't want any problems with any of his officers. He only wanted successes as a reflection of his own command posture. Bravo Six knew that this difficult mission was a success for himself because of the outstanding performances of his subordinate leaders and the courage and fortitude of his squad soldiers. Without a nasty investigation, the upper brass would have lots of time and consideration for pending commendations and decorations.

Mustang Six would go along with anything to promote favor for himself. If the most successful small unit commander in the brigade wanted to give him praise instead of accusations, Major Domsavich could go to hell! In addition, Bravo Six knew that Badger Six would soon be writing an efficiency report for his term as a company commander. What choice would he have but to declare his top-quality competency?

The next afternoon at Bam Nam base, Bravo Six was called to Col. Langham's office to explain the course of the operation. As this was unusual procedure, did the judicious commander suspect that this mission had been tainted with intrigue?

Bravo Six asked about the letter. Col. Langham laughed as he admitted that he and the staff had a good laugh over a beer while reading it. "We just couldn't help it," he admitted. "Knowing you, we just couldn't wait for you to die." He punctuated his last words with a friendly whack to the shoulder and Bravo Six of course acquiesced.

Bravo Six had personally asked Badger Six to accompany him. He didn't say anything except that his presence would be better for all concerned. Because Badger Six anticipated allegations, he was glad to be hearing Bravo Six report the mission firsthand.

After the fanfare of the formal congratulations for his total victory at the sugar mill guerrilla base camp, Bravo Six voluntarily reported the factors of the attack with a pointer at the big map board on the wall. He was careful to credit Badger Six for masterminding the operation but neglected to mention Major Domsavich in the normal area of his responsibility. Badger Six was an opportunist and would not easily excuse Domsavich for his contravention of military discretion. Bravo Six could sympathize with Badger Six for his wretched desire to promote himself despite his own flaws in tactical acumen. Then Bravo Six further added that his own prior successes were often the result of his commander's willingness to gamble with his own inexperience and then prod him into accepting nothing but victory even at the expense of personal feelings and subsequent resentment.

Badger Six said practically nothing. He had never heard Bravo Six talk so much and so favorably toward him. He was dumbfounded but wasn't arguing. Col. Langham then asked Mustang Six to wait outside the door for a minute.

A short while later, Bravo Six joined him in the hall. He offered a handshake, and Badger Six eagerly complied. Then Bravo Six told him that he had just accepted a job as the Brigade Staff S2 Intelligence officer. With only three months remaining in his tour of duty, Col. Langham wanted to use his experience and knowledge of the command operations area by having him visit friendly outposts and advise the S3 Operations Staff on developments in and around the brigade's area of responsibility.

Badger Six spoke to Bravo Six with a new tone and demeanor. "Captain Smithe, despite our differences, I'm glad to have served with you. We have the best battalion in all the Wolfhounds and somehow, you had my best company. Oh, and by the way. I commended Major Domsavich for his outstanding operations and service. I hope you don't mind. "

After a few seconds Bravo Six answered, "Oh what the hell." He laughed and now that whole thing was over.

That "somehow" was said through a smile. Then he wished him luck with, "I know you'll do well on staff, and I know that this really isn't goodbye. Give 'em hell, Smithe." That made Bravo Six officially Capt. Hasel Smithe again.

Col. Langham knew that he had missed much of the gist of this matter, but he also knew that it was probably better that he didn't know more. Everybody and everything was looking complementary and shiny.

For the next two months, Captain Smithe had almost complete freedom to travel the tactical region by an OH13 observation helicopter and conduct long range reconnaissance via the Air Force fixed-wing Cessna O1 "Bird dog" piloted by a forward air controller (FAC). Captain Smith, of course, enjoyed it and felt that he had strategically influenced at least a couple successful brigade operations. At the staff briefings, he could surmise that his reports were taken seriously, which gave him a good feeling of satisfaction.

He still enjoyed a beer in the "club" but the revelry was gone. Everything has to change, and "Bravo Six' had gone with the flow.

Two weeks later tragedy struck. The indomitable Reggie Trainor didn't finish his command time. An incident in the Tay Ninh Jungle caused him to be relieved of duty (fired). Roger's Delta Company had been quickly airlifted to secure a downed Chinook helicopter loaded with munitions. A subsequent development caused the G3 Staff to send explosives for Roger to destroy the Chinook and its cargo. The scenario didn't develop in his favor. The pick-up task force was approaching early and Roger had already ignited the fuse cord.

The squadron commander radioed for permission to land, and Badger Six also immediately interrupted to ask Delta Six if the demolition charge was clear. The timed fuse should have allowed Delta Company to load and be clear, but of course even hand grenades explode in "plus or minus" four seconds. Even knowing the danger of the unpredictable fuse, Reggie allowed his jagged gaming nature to overpower his sense of responsible reasoning. "Roger on the demolition. Bring 'em in!"

With his usual buffer of liability, Badger Six issued a warning. "You'd better be right."

It could have been worse but not much.. The Huey formation cleared the tree line at the only open spot allowing a field expedient landing. The Delta troops awaited in a loading pattern. They reflexively dropped to the ground as a monstrous explosion lifted the giant Chinook into the air along with its tons of volatile munitions. In a millisecond, all was reduced to fragmented wreckage, fiery shrapnel, and secondary explosions.

The helicopters were far enough away to escape the brunt of the blast, but were close enough to sustain three damaged windshields and numerous punctures but miraculously no injuries.

Of course the pilots were barking exclamations on the radio and Badger Six interrupted with the caustic tone that unmistakably meant that a blistering verbal salvo was coming. He ordered the Hueys back to base and released all his fury on the company commander that historically had embarrassed him both in the field and at the base. In the past Reggie was able to survive repercussions simply because the shortage of replacements would have complicated the configuration of the overall command structure. That no longer being the case and this being such a flagrant incident, the radio transmission carried such a poignant message that all who monitored were aghast with empathy for the well-liked and admired but impossibly incorrigible Reggie Trainor.

"Delta Six, you're finished! Damn you, you're fired!

Fired! You'll be picked up immediately and I don't want to hear anything from you! Out."

Those words slashed painfully through Capt. Smithe. The memories of this extraordinary friend flashed before him and chilled his composure. The redoubtable Captain Reggie Trainor had been cast into ignominy. To further the discredit, he was not even assigned another position to complete his last three weeks of duty with the battalion. Of course, he spent most of that time in the officers club at the bar, with most other officers reluctant to be anymore than civil with him other than Capt. Smithe, of course. The bond with them was indissoluble. A week later they had a chance to talk.

"It was a mistake and all my fault. Even so, you know me. I just couldn't help it. I have to be the clown."

"I know, and I'll stand by you if you're going to do anything."

"No. It's finished. I was to leave in two weeks, but they said I can go tomorrow. My German wife and kids and my American wife will all be meeting me at Travis Air Force base. Won't that be an ass kicker?" He was even smiling!

That statement would have been staggering to anyone who didn't understand Reggie as well as this fellow commander who had been through so much with him. "Good luck. You're a survivor. God bless you, Reggie Trainor. "Someday I'll see you again.

"I know that." In a rare show of emotion, Roger hugged his best friend and let out a hollow groan. They parted with a knowing glance and it was over.

CHAPTER THIRTEEN

OPERATION PARTY CRASHER

This was the freaky one. Commanding a heliborne infantry company was a fantastic experience, but what was now offered was right from the annals of gutsy commando missions. Maybe his battle experience, riddled with close calls, blessed with lucky escapes, and fraught with mystical assistance, hadn't allowed the expected combat fatigue and short-timer fears and queasiness. Maybe he hadn't quite reached the next level of personal battle. Successfully commanding a Badger heliborne infantry company should have been an ultimate satisfaction. And, of course, maybe his successes, his jaundiced ego, and his lack of intellectual sophistication had befuddled his brain into imagining that no mission was too much for his ability or even his own safety. With only a month remaining in his year of duty, he jumped into a mission of personal peril.

About six months previously, he had been cleared for a Top Secret status. At the time he had accepted it, he had no idea why he needed it and really wasn't told anything that he didn't already know. Of course, he knew that secrets were shared on a "need to know" basis. This clearance and his combat experience, along with the accompanying reputation, caused him to be nominated as a candidate for the wartime "surgical" task that "wasn't going to happen" and "never would be known to have happened." He had been vetted one of the chosen and the one most likely to accept.

Capt. Smithe had been visiting the MACV outpost at Trang Bang not far from Bam Nam when four military policemen (MP's) in jeeps pulled up to the building. They knocked at the door while entering and immediately looked to Capt. Smithe. One spoke in that hollow, tone that needed no response. "Sir, by the order of the division commander, you are to accompany us to headquarters. We will send your helicopter back." No one would ever bother to ask these guys what it was about.

The trip was fast with no conversation. Smithe had no idea what was going on, but he knew that it had to be interesting. He didn't worry about anything negative because that would have happened long before now. Whatever the reason, he could certainly use something exciting or at least out of the ordinary. "By order of the division general" didn't have to mean that the general himself wanted him, but it could. "Wow!"

Upon their arrival, two of the MPs actually walked

with him to the adjutant's office and saluted him as they departed. Such decorum was surprising to a roughneck company officer. Especially since he had never thought that he would ever see the inside of the General Hought's office, Capt. Smithe was starting to feel the splendor of this bizarre happening. He knocked and was immediately escorted inside by a decorous aide. He offered his best salute to this general who acknowledged it with his usual hurried half-salute. "Good afternoon, Smithe. We've already met in a rather fleeting manner a couple times. How have you been?"

"Very well, sir, and I'm quite honored to be in your presence."

"Okay, let's forget all the formal crap. We have some serious talking to do. I want all the rest of you to leave the room." Two aides and the adjutant saluted and quickly left.

One aide gave Smithe a brief side glance as he passed him. Intrigue was heavy in the air. The headquarter's staff usually knew all that they weren't supposed to know.

General Crooks (nametag) poured himself two fingers of Jack Daniels and offered the same. Although Smithe imbibed only occasionally, he did enjoy a drink of quality whiskey. This exceptionally judicious general probably already knew that and much more. It wasn't hard to admire this great man's military bearing along with his keen sense of human perception and acumen.

"Drink up, Smithe. It will relax your receptors."

"Sir, I learned in Lynchburg, that one should warm this whisky to body temperature to fully enjoy the flavor and then sip it out of respect."

"That's impressive, Smithe. You've been around, and you remember what you should. I'll follow your advice."

This General Crooks was not the division commander, but with all the introductory fanfare and in this venue, nothing needed to be questioned. Capt. Smithe knew that this preliminary chatter was preparing him for something big and he was getting anxious. "What's going on, sir?

The old general took a hearty swallow and changed to a resolute expression. "I want to know if you are interested in a strategic assignment that will probably get you killed. We know that General Ranh will be at a family gathering tomorrow afternoon. He controls liaison between the Viet Cong and the NVA for supplies and information. This guy is good but has micromanaged for so long that, without him, his supervisory network will be in disarray. This Wolverines have been given the task of killing him. I think it will take a Badger officer to do it."

Capt. Smithe knew that he was being unfairly inveigled, but he felt proud that it was happening. "Should I volunteer now or wait to hear more?"

"Wait awhile. Don't be too anxious to be yourself. I need someone like you to co-command a small task force to be helicopter lifted from Bang Chao, Laos, into North Vietnam. At General Ranh's home hamlet of Bam Tham, you will attack his father's funeral event to kill Ranh and bring evidence of his death. No need to worry about collateral damage. What are your questions?"

"What is that co-command stuff?"

"It's in case we lose one of you."

Capt. Smithe changed to a bossy tone. "I want to have the power of veto on this co-commander and anybody else on the task force. I also want to help plan the operation and have line item veto on the logistics. You picked me for a reason to make it come true."

General Crooks really was not very surprised to hear this impertinence from such an crudely uncharacteristic ground commander who would take this assignment and probably pull it off. However, he recalled that he was a three star general for a reason that left no room for compromising his authority. "You'll make 'requests' to me and I'll do any vetoing."

"Yes, sir. I'd like to have PFC Rahskle on the task force, if possible."

"I can say okay to that right now, pending a personal scan."

"Thank you, sir."

"Be here in the operations room tomorrow at 0900. We'll get started. And Smithe, not one word to anyone. This is top secret! You hear me?"

"Yes, sir. Thank you for considering me. I won't let you down."

"Get out of here and do some thinking over a couple beers. You can still back out."

Capt. Smithe saluted and walked proudly out of the building. This would be the highlight of his combat experience, but a voice in the back of his mind was shouting "What the hell are you doing?"

However crazy, at least two-thirds of his mind was full of confidence and a desire for more of the same excitement that had stirred his masculinity, and he wasn't paying much attention to any sensible voice of sane counsel.

The next morning the planning went well. To his pleasure, Capt. Smithe would have no co-commander because both the other candidate captains declined to accept. A notable Special Forces Master Sergeant accepted the responsibility of next-in-command. Within his reputation of character, this guy would be proficient and easy to work with in executing a mission. The other members of the task force were multi-tasked and just as impressive. Two M-60 machine gunners, each with an ammunition bearer, who doubled as a substitute M-60 gunner and spare radio operator, appeared to mesh well with six riflemen armed with AR-15 Commando submachine guns (the same as what Capt. Smithe and the co-commander carried)

The task force weaponry would have common ammunition for mutual support. In addition, four of the rifleman carried an M72 LAW (Light Antitank Weapon). The LAW was a fiberglass, self-contained, one shot "bazooka" that was lethal against a plethora of vehicles and structures. The other two riflemen were equipped with a

M67 recoilless rifle and four rounds of ammunition that were anti-vehicle and anti-personnel. Capt. Smithe was especially glad that Rahskle accepted the mission and was approved.

The target area was in a rural suburb area of Ky Son, a mid-size urban district just inside the North Vietnamese border with Laos. This area, that was almost exclusively agricultural, contained nothing of military significance or even political interest. It did happen to be the family home of General Ranh. The event of attention was the funeral of his aged father. The S2 Division Intelligence staff had a credible report that Gen. Ranh would be present for the funeral. The task force was to attack the funeral gathering to kill Ranh. Final planning would be done at the scene. Any collateral killing would be tolerated. He also had to bring proof of Ranh's death. Capt. Smithe wondered what that would be, other than the body or the head. A name tag, if he wore one, probably wouldn't be sufficient. An aerial map of the target area showed an isolated upscale residential compound of four buildings with a small pond. The orange ceramic tile roof shingles were a given on that.

About five hundred meters to the west after dense trees and brush was a very narrow clearing about three hundred meters long and fifty meters wide. This would be the LZ (landing zone). A Long Range Reconnaissance Patrol (LRRP) five man unit from the 101st Airborne would secure the site and act as guides. With detailed planning, seriously aggressive action and some luck, it could work!

Capt. Smithe took the advice of mulling over this with a couple beers at the brigade makeshift saloon. He knew the answer before he even started to think about it. Reggie Trainor would have cuffed him on the head and exclaimed "What the hell's the problem?"

Too bad Reggie wasn't here to go along. What a bash that would have been! Yet, Reggie's specter would be with him and help him win the day. Capt. Smithe would take this challenge and get it done. No other option was in the offing. Even though he sensed that Gen. Crooks wasn't telling him everything, he was going.

The 0900 meeting added to the overt intrigue. General Crooks was glaringly absent with an imposing gentleman in his place as the operation commanding officer-in-chief. He wore no rank or even a name tag.; His personal manifestation caused instant respect and cued everyone to call him "Sir."

The plan was so simple that no one in the task force was uncertain. They would "jump off" from the U.S. Air Force base near Bang Chao, Laos, at 0400 hours in two HU1B helicopters and fly directly to the LZ, shadowed by an F105 Fighter Bomber. When in position, they would observe the residence to determine the plan of attack. They would get only one crack at General Ranh. It would have to be a fast hit. The "pick up" choppers would be accompanied by two UH1G Cobra gunships and the F105 if needed. The task force was not too big for all to evacuate in one chopper if necessary.

Somebody knew what he was doing. Two diversionary forays were planned in the adjoining province near a suspected POW camp to implicate a possible attack there. It would be far enough away to avoid suspicion about the real target.

Capt. Smithe was surprised that the mission was leaving the next morning to the ready position in Laos. But, why not, he considered. Let's get on it on! This was how he liked to do things. The task force landed at 1000 hours at a small supply airstrip and was immediately whisked to a small building with a classroom atmosphere. The room was equipped with several cots, food items, and munition supplies along with personal items that any of them might need. That mysterious officer-in-chief was present to offer a final briefing, to verify any part of the mission, and to resolve any problems. All present appeared to be content with the conduct of the planning. Hardly anything had been changed. They would still land at 0400 hours and would be recovered "on call". Of course, Capt. Smithe was thinking that "it seemed too good to be true, and probably wasn't."

They landed at exactly 0400 hours without incident. One of the three LRRPs on the ground had signaled with a strobe light that the LZ was secure. One of them then escorted Capt. Smithe's task force through the dense foliage to the observation position where the other two LRRPs were waiting to signal with an owl hoot that it was also clear. All positioned themselves so well that Capt. Smithe saw no reason to make any adjustment. The LRRPs would remain to guide them back to the LZ. Without question, these guys were good. Then the whole team would leave with them in the evacuation.

About one hundred meters downhill across the open field that had obviously been reserved for grazing, Capt. Smithe could see the compound buildings. Only the upscale residence building showed a dim light. With the light of a three-quarter moon and a fortunate downhill view, Capt. Smithe could distinguish one large military tent along with several small expedient shelters. His Starlite Scope revealed three guards providing local security. The shelters indicated a probable light platoon-sized unit. He thought that this was either an escort unit, with Gen. Ranh sleeping in the house with his family or an advance force to greet him later that day when the funeral procession would commence.

Using another scope, Rahskle nudged his captain to inform him of one the sentries was now moving along the tree line. A quick check found that another guard was pacing the tree line on the opposite side. Captain Smithe reckoned that they had been patrolling around the edge of the open area to discover anything amiss that would compromise their unit security. That, of course, was this diabolic American task force. Something definite would have to be done when they arrived at the task force location.

Capt. Smithe decided that they would have to be killed. Capturing them would be too risky and they couldn't take a chance on being noticed. Since the two LRRPs had silencers on their rifles, they could shoot them silently and simultaneously when they arrived at point blank range. If their bodies were then dragged into the bushes, nobody at the compound would immediately notice.

As each guard arrived twenty meters from the task force position, they were shot several times and pulled into the bushes in practically one well-executed motion. Not only did that action preclude the imminent danger, but the task force was now psychologically primed for the subsequent aggressive violence and killing that was imminent.

Capt. Smithe preferred to think that General Ranh was at the house now. He would have wanted to spend the night with his family at this heartrending time. With such a sizeable escort, there was a good chance of a couple high ranking accompanying officers to provide a bonus for the mission. If Gen. Ranh was not there, destroying that advance guard unit and some of the family members would not be worth endangering his task force and really would make little difference in the war effort. However, Capt. Smithe couldn't accept a scenario of returning to the LZ without an attack and then finding out later that Gen. Ranh really was there for easy taking. He called the small task force together to issue the operation order. This hand-picked task force was anxious to hear the order delivered with the expertise of the experienced commander as they hoped he was.

A hundred meters at "quick step" and downhill would not tire them significantly. They would also easily move as a unit and execute their firepower as a team for maximum efficiency. At about fifty meters, Capt. Smithe would command a halt. Three of them would fire a LAW at the house and one would fire a LAW at the large tent. Also, the 90mm recoilless rifle team would fire a falcate round at the tent area. Surely no more than two of them would miss the house. Then everybody would charge the compound area at full speed. All military personnel and any civilians presenting a threat would be killed. These specially selected men only had to be told what was expected of them.

At 0500 hours, they advanced silently to get as close as possible before the enemy became aware. As they moved on line Capt. Smithe could sense the fervor of this exclusive task force. Even in the dim light of early dawn, they advanced purposefully without any sensation of fear. The quick step that he had ordered was more like two-third jog. Within fifty meters, Capt. Smithe signaled the halt to launch the LAW missiles. To his surprise, not one missile missed its mark. The three LAW rockets that hit the thick concrete-walled residence brought down the whole facing side of the house. The unexpected blast of flying debris inside savagely wounded anyone standing or even sleeping.

The blast of the rocket that hit the large tent caused the structure to immediately collapse and superficially wounded any soldier inside. The M67 90mm recoilless rifle also effectively showered the target area with all 2400 of the steel fin-stabilized nails that "pin-cushioned" some of the more unfortunate soldiers. Very few of the enemy soldiers were still able to return fire when the task forces brutally attacked.

The American attackers unceremoniously made certain that all the enemy soldiers found were lifeless. Two were observed fleeing the scene, but were not followed. Capt. Smithe joined those who entered the residence. Rahskle ignited two M49 trip flares to illuminate the scene. About fifteen persons there were either dead or severely wounded. Captain Smithe noticed one middle-aged man standing in a crouched posture with military clothing lying at his cot. With his hands raised to surrender, he whined piteously in hopes of not being shot. Before Capt. Smithe could make any decision about the disposition of this most likely person of interest, Rahskle shot him down with a blast from his 12 gauge Remington 870 shotgun (his weapon of choice). All the others in the residence were left as found. Was this General Ranh? His military clothing was decorated with badges that surely indicated high rank.

Because a response force might already be on the way, Capt. Smithe blew the pre-planned three blasts on his U.S. Army Thunderer Whistle to signal the rapid retreat back to the LRRP guides at the assault position. None of his task force suffered any wounds. He only had to decide on the body of General Ranh, if that's who it was. He instructed two of the men to grab the ankles of the body and drag it on its back. This procedure is how the Viet Cong often evacuated their dead as a field- expedient way of recovering the body for a later Buddhist burial. Two strapping Americans could perform this battlefield task even better than the wiry VC. Other task force members could spell them, thus keeping up with the others. In this manner, the body would have minor damage and the withdrawing American soldiers only slightly endangered. The identified body could be later returned as a humane gesture.

With no one lagging behind, the task force met a LRRP guide at his red signal light. He hastily moved the group back to the LZ where the remaining LRRP team members were waiting. They had already called for the recovery helicopters, which were enroute. The task force along with the LRRP team divided themselves into two loading groups and positioned local security listening posts. These LRRP guys were good!

Six very long minutes later, at 0535 hours, a gunship was spotted flying high in the distance. A prearranged green smoke grenade brought that Cobra and another to "buzz" the LZ. Now the two recovery UH1Ds landed beside the waving task force groups with the door gunners yelling for them to hurry. Capt. Smithe and Rahskle tossed the corpse onto the deck of their chopper. The co-pilot first assumed it to be an American casualty and then changed his caring expression to surprise and anger that a dead Vietnamese was being transported. He bellowed in disgust, "Get that piece of shit out of here!" He also looked to the pilot for support.

Capt. Smithe responded true to his nature. "Turn around and shut up!"

"You can't talk to me like that."

That brought an impatient response along with a

brusque change of tone. "You want me to kick your ass right here?"

The pilot then told his co-pilot to knock it off. Besides, he was familiar with this infantry captain who was one of the few allowed at their exclusive "flyboy watering hole." Any one of those pilots would rather have a beer with Smithe than fight him.

Both recovery helicopters were quickly airborne without interruption. They circled the operation area as they rose to 2000 feet and headed west. At the residence compound, the task force could see enemy soldiers jumping from three trucks that had just arrived at the large tent location. A few muzzle flashes from the small groups of response soldiers aimed at the departing task force accomplished nothing. The American Cobra gun-ships feigned a strafing run at them. The sight of those in-coming killing machines unnerved those inexperienced North Vietnamese soldiers and caused them to scatter as quickly as cockroaches. However, the mission was over and no further engagement was necessary. Also, Capt. Smithe was glad that those wounded civilians would now get medical attention.

Enroute, the pilot radioed forward his ETA (expect-ed time of arrival) along with a request for a body bag. At the Xiangkhoang base, the operation commander-in-chief greeted them with obvious joyfulness and relief. Somehow, he already knew that they had annihilated the enemy guard unit and brought a body that was possibly General Ranh. With his hand on Capt. Smithe's shoul-der, he guided him to a debriefing room at the terminal.

The description of the complete victory, along with a report of no casualties, brought the dignified commander to his feet with a show of delight. He poured two drinks of about two fingers each of Black Velvet whiskey and toasted Capt. Smithe. In return, he thanked this anonymous commander for his professionalism and toasted the task force for their combat expertise. In only two hours, they had pulled off a tactical "tour de force."

Black Velvet would now replace Jack Daniels as Smithe's favorite. It would always have a special flavor.

Capt. Smithe excused himself to return to the tarmac. He wanted to thank all the task force and be sure that they were guided to the EM (enlisted man's) Club where a buffet and drinks were waiting. He would have joined them himself if the pilots hadn't forced him to the base officers club. That co-pilot had obviously been cued about his faux pas because he also walked along as if nothing had happened. All was over now.

After a few beers and some very satisfying camaraderie, Capt. Smithe walked to the EM Club to pay proper homage to the soldiers of the task force. All during his stint in this war, he knew that his successes were largely a result of those young men who were willing to follow his audaciously impudent leadership.

Rahskle was discovered on a bar stool alone and was quickly invited to a table. This loyal macho American soldier was with him throughout his Vietnam War experience. With no sign of superciliousness or any condescension, Capt. Smithe conversed with this favorite warrior about the conclusion of their fighting and how they planned to approach the next chapter in their lives. Capt. Smithe was amused when Rahskle stated that he suspected his homecoming would cause an ass-kicking of his girlfriend along with his best friend that he trusted to "watch" her. In the universal language of fellow combatants, they both expressed their virtual familial affection for each other. Their parting involved a mutual embrace that all who witnessed understood. Of course, they also punched each other on the arm to satisfy the masculine syndrome.

That night he was surprised at his composure as he mused about that bizarre mission. What a donnybrook! A myriad of disasters could have happened, but the war gods spared him again. Okay, he was not going to stretch his luck any farther. It's finished! Now it was time to turn to another facet of his life, however challenging or satisfying.

At breakfast, again he was called to the commander's office for a final briefing.

The corpse was not General Ranh, but was his brother-in-law. Obviously, nepotism also contaminated the North Vietnamese Army as anywhere else. The identification was Col. Nguyan Xian. He had been the "domestic resource officer" for the southern tier and had been commissioned a colonel without ever holding any other rank. In other words, he did practically nothing but hold a title and collect compensation under the good graces of the influential General Ranh. In addition, with the return of his body, he would probably be decorated posthumously and be honored with a stately funeral. What a crock! Maybe Rahskle did the right thing after all!

General Crooks also instructed Capt. Smithe that the mission as he had originally described it had been scrapped. The identity of the anonymous operation commander would never be known and the mission actually never happened. Under the regulations of his top secret clearance, if he ever mentioned anything about that maneuver, he would be prosecuted with a court martial. Capt. Smithe understood. This was war, and he would take nothing from this experience but the pleasure of the excitement. No medals, certificates, or otherwise to be savored. He and all the task force simply had the pleasure of belonging to the exclusive brotherhood of extraordinary warriors known only to the ancient gods of war.

Outside the office, a conversation with the adjutant cued Capt. Smithe about the intrigue of this whole affair. During their casual discourse, the adjutant glared at Capt. Smithe and said that there was no General Crooks! Actually, he loved this intrigue! He would never know the true nature of Operation Party Crasher. Was it only a diversion for a more important maneuver? What the hell was it? In the great scheme of the Vietnam War, Operation Party Crasher would probably rate no more than a postscript, but it was his postscript and that was good enough. And, Reggie Trainor was right when he said, "This war is a big circus, and we're the clowns."

EPILOGUE

For the rest of his life, the author was glad for his Vietnam experience, happy that he had served his country, but disappointed that things didn't turn out better for the Vietnamese peasants. However inconsequential, as Bravo Six, he had crested his name in the annals of the Vietnam era. He never forgot any of his battles.

The Viet Cong eventually did win their war of attrition against the hated Americans who had come to help preserve the maligned freedom of those South Vietnamese who savored it. Also, those who hadn't understood, as well as those who hadn't cared, had lost the visage of their dignity.

The American soldiers who had willingly done their duty to their God and country had actually fought a greater number of protesting Americans at home than communist enemies in South Vietnam. These marching masqueraders were shouting moralistic protests more riddled with prevarication than truths and moral values. Because not everybody across the American countryside was of the same opinion about the war, the citizenry of the USA was seen by the world as a clown of many faces. The vilified American flag was hardly recognized.

You can believe that we lost a war to a heathen regime because enough of the American public were chanting lies about their cowardice, were stupid enough to believe that we had no business defending freedom so far from home, or were actually enemy sympathizers. The "Hippy" type youth not only stooped to disrupting public activities and organizations along with commercial businesses, but they also engaged in collusion with the North Vietnamese government against our troops.

Even upon arrival in the USA, individual soldiers were ostracized in public by shameless groups of decadent demonstrators. At several major airports, returning soldiers were attacked both verbally and physically as they disembarked airplanes and later walked on public streets. The public "silent majority" spurned those who actively sought to demoralize the patriots of the Vietnam War Era but feared retribution from those activists who had even targeted servicemen's families. However, the author was gratified that he never knew of any similar incidents in his home territory of Bedford County or any other counties in South Central Pennsylvania.

In retrospect, it was the cleanest and most efficient war ever fought by Americans. You would have to know about that aspect of American history to understand.

It was also the least appreciated sacrifice of those who served. Too many Americans were unwilling to help others in resisting communism-especially so far away. God willing, this will never happen again.

9 781478 779445